FAE MAGIC

THE KENZIE CHRONICLES

GENAVIE CASTLE

ISBN: 978-1-962047-06-7 eBook

ISBN: 978-1-962047-02-9 Print

Cover Design by: Crey-ative Designs

ABOUT THIS BOOK

Everything about this book is completely fictional. This is a why choose romance novel containing graphic sexual content, some violence and explicit language suitable for mature audiences only. Proceed with caution.

CHAPTER 1
KENZIE

For the third night in a row, I watched my mark across the way as he began his nightly ritual. The city buzzed with activity below me. Music blared, people laughed and shouted, horns honked. Somewhere out there, vampires walked the night and rubbed shoulders with other supes and with humans. The typical downtown Vegas scene.

My mark set his briefcase on the table by the door and shrugged off his tie while walking to the next room, going straight to the bar. He poured himself cognac from a crystal bottle. Then, he retrieved a cigar from the humidor behind the bar, clipped the end, and lit it. He took his drink and cigar and walked wearily out onto the balcony. After sitting in a plush lounge chair, he gazed at the city before him, sipped his drink, and puffed on his cigar.

Patiently, I waited while he puffed away. When he tilted his head to throw back his drink, I sat up in rapt attention and began counting down . . . Five, four, three, two, one. His body slumped over, appearing as if he'd passed out. But I knew better. A mixture of herbs, minerals, and chemicals laced his cup, causing a massive heart attack. An autopsy would reveal nothing untoward, and the coroner would rule his death as natural causes.

A mix of emotions washed through me. I felt sadness for the loss of life. He may have been a sinister individual, but I wouldn't know; I never knew why a person was on my list. Regardless of any misdeeds, his life ended by my hands. I never liked this work, but a girl had bills and a certain lifestyle to maintain. This was my last job. My contract was over. A pleased smile tugged at my lips.

I took one more look at the slumped man across the way, packed my binoculars, and then moved from one rooftop to the next. I made my way down to mix in with the crowd on the streets, feeling like a burden had been lifted from my shoulders. Now I awaited my wire transfer.

The next morning, I rose before the sun, anxious for the wire to come through. To ease my anxiousness, I got in my car and made a short drive to the dojo.

THE DOJO WAS a place of refuge for mercs and soldiers here in the desert. It was not only a place to train in many forms of combat, but it was also a place of reflection and meditation. My father always said, "A good warrior needs both physical and mental training."

I took my time following the path that led to the Japanese structures that housed the training center. The pathway was designed to send one on a tranquil journey to clear the mind. A sense of calm washed through me as I leisurely meandered down the pathway surrounded by verdant laurel and hawthorn hedges. The tranquil sounds of water trickled into the stream filled with koi that swam gracefully. Seating areas were tucked into the gardens and provided a space of solitude for meditation. I sought out my favorite meditation spot hidden amongst bamboo trees and bonsai just off to the side of the waterfall behind the dojo.

Today my favorite spot was occupied, so I went straight into the dojo to begin my training. Upon entering through the shoji doors, a gust of cool air rushed in, earning me a few dirty looks from the few students that were training on the tatami mats. I turned my phone to silent mode and left it in one of the cubbies next to the door along with my keys.

I bowed to Sensei Hiro who was with a student, then stretched and went through fighting stances on my own, waiting for my turn in the sparring circle. Finally, the young fighter motioned me forward.

My opponent's punches were swift and relentless. He was a student, not a seasoned fighter, but he was effectively kicking my ass. I could've used my magic. It wouldn't be fair though. He was human and not a threat. I swerved my body and dodged each swing. He threw a right jab at my nose. *Oww.* I moved backwards, and my eyes watered, my lashes fluttering.

"Fight back, Mackenzie!" my sensei called out to me. Sensei Hiro was such a hard ass sometimes.

The distraction earned me a kick to the side of the head. *Owww, fuck me.* That kick rang my bell. I refocused my energies and blocked another hit aimed for my gut, then sidestepped to dodge another shot aimed for my face again. I swept out with my leg and dropped him. After landing on top of him, I hurled a barrage of punches at his head, but my opponent threw me off. He swiftly moved behind me, and caught me in an arm bar. Luckily for me, the bell rung.

"Where is your focus today?" Sensei asked me, as I stumbled back to my corner, panting.

"I almost won that round. What are you talking about?" I replied, stretching my overworked muscles.

"You should have knocked him out a while ago. Not like you, Mackenzie." He shook his head.

"Have a lot on my mind, I guess." I shrugged.

"Go home. You've been training for almost three hours," he said with a dismissive hand wave.

Three hours. I scrambled over to the cubbies and pulled out my phone. Wire received.I sighed in relief. My merc life was officially done and over with.

I wanted a normal life, a job I didn't have to lie about, and maybe, just maybe, a family. But first, it was time to celebrate.

"You need to spend more time practicing your magic, Mackenzie. Why are you avoiding your tutor?" Sensei said to me, interrupting my train of thought.

"I'm not avoiding anyone." It was a lie, and he knew it, so I quickly amended my statement. "I will, Sensei." I bowed respectfully and took my leave.

In all honesty, this was probably another reason I was so antsy. Magic was difficult for me. I have two main types: combat magic and Fae magic. I excelled at combat magic, thanks to my lineage on my father's side. Dad had trained me since I was a child. It made me faster and stronger than any human twice my size which is saying something when you're a size zero at a hundred and ten pounds soaking wet. I can put more force into my hits, more speed into my movements, and I can shield my body from injury. I can and have gotten hurt, but the injuries were never lethal.

Despite these talents, I wasn't meant to be a merc for life. Although the pay was great and I was good at it, a merc's life was dark and lonely. I wasn't cut out for that lifestyle. My father, on the other hand, felt differently. He was a lifer.

I inherited Fae magic from my mother. She is Fae and that was all I knew about her. She left me, or rather us, shortly after I was born, and she had never mentioned any family. Thus, my Fae magic was a complete mystery. I do have a touch of elemental magic. Small magics, nothing extraordinary. I can harness the elements to a minimal extent. It isn't all that impressive, but it did come in handy every now and again.

Dad made sure I had magical tutors of all sorts throughout my childhood, even now. In all of our travels, we had never encountered another Fae or a mage that had any understanding of Fae magic.

Supposedly he found a tutor that could help. I made an appointment, but I rescheduled . . . a few times. I was procrastinating.

Expanding my gifts was on my to do list, but I kept postponing because it was hard. Every time I pushed further with my Fae magic, it didn't amount to much and it drained the ever-living life out of me. Recently, I tried teleportation, something I was supposed to be able to do. It took me nine hours of sheer determination, unwavering focus, and lots of sweat to get me from one room to the next, a good ten feet. An accomplishment, sure, but it had come at a cost. I was down and out with the worst hangover for thirty-six hours. Let's just say I am not planning to do that again anytime soon.

Most of magic practice was like that for me. I spent hours for small gain and ended up physically drained. So not worth the effort. If it weren't for this constant churning in my gut, I wouldn't bother at all. Life was good amongst the humans for the most part. I had money, my magic kept me healthy and youthful, and so far, I haven't needed my Fae magic. Grandmother had told me to keep my elemental magic a secret, that there would be those who would want me dead or worse, imprisoned if they knew. I respected her too much to disregard the warning, and thus far after all these years, I haven't run into any issues. But that could be because I kept my magical signature locked up tight. I was tested at twelve, as all children were. But the mage from the Registrar's Office that had tested me was a personal friend of my father's. Dad had called in a favor. The mage determined I had access to all elements, plus combat magic. However, aside from reporting that I had a small scale of combat magic, he didn't record anything else. He recorded my combat magic level at Tier Two, the bottom tier. This meant I didn't receive a brand that would allow the world to know what kind of magic I possessed. This worked to my benefit. I was able to fly under the magic radar. Being unknown had come in handy as a merc.

CHAPTER 2
KENZIE

"Damn, girl, you're looking good." Tristan sat behind the large oak desk that was in front of the massive floor-to-ceiling window.

He stood to greet me, and I took in his ethereal beauty. Dark, thick, wavy hair framed an angular jawline and sharp nose. His emerald eyes shone brightly against his dark skin. Tall and slim, he could've easily been a model. Runway, print, you name it. Women swooned in his presence, and he knew it, and moreover, he didn't care.

"Twirl for me, honey!" He twirled his finger in the air.

I spun for him a couple of times, my cowgirl boots scraping the hard floor, and my lavender floral dress flared out around me, revealing the dagger I always wore strapped to my thigh and my white, lacy boy shorts. Tris had seen me completely naked a ton of times and he'd never been weird about it. The first time had been a humbling experience, and I'll never forget it. We were out of town, sharing a hotel room. This was when we were both broke. I was in the shower and he joined me. Back then, my young mind was open to having sex with the handsome man before me, consequences be damned. But he'd remained limp even while he'd soaped me up. I had been disappointed for sure but glad in the end. Our relationship would've changed had we gone that route.

"Where are you headed all decked out?" he asked.

"Nowhere in particular, but you never know who you'll meet at the office. Besides, isn't it Friday?" I replied. I was honestly ready to celebrate the end of my mercenary work now that the funds had arrived from my final job.

"True, you never know. There's a hot UPS delivery guy that comes in. I could use a little of that. And No! No, it is not Friday, and you know that. But whatever, boss bitch, your talents pay the bills," he said with a wink.

Laughing, I replied, "I know everything is good because if it wasn't, you'd tell me. But I'll ask anyway, so that you know how much I do care and how much I love you. Tristan, best friend in the world, is everything okay? Is there anything that I can do for you? Or am I all clear to bugger off and enjoy a fine day of debauchery," I said in a sing-song voice, a sickly sweet smile plastered to my face.

Tris smacked my ass before I could get away. "You're such a brat. And yes, everything is fine, my Queen," he said with a flourishing wave of his hand and a bow.

"Now, look who's being the brat." I rolled my eyes. We both laughed.

"Seriously though, is everything good?" I asked, pretending to be all business-like.

"All good, a couple offers came in on the Florida properties. Not sure if you knew that," he stated while sitting back down at his desk.

"I did. I'm making them wait till the end of the week for my answer." I smiled at him. Some offers were insulting, which is why I was taking my time.

"Of course you are. A couple emails came in about some properties in Texas. Didn't look familiar." He faced his computer screen to me.

I quickly glanced at it, noting the commercial building and acreage: interesting, not urgent. "Send it to my personal email."

"Expanding, are we?" He typed away on his keyboard.

"You know it. There are a couple little towns that are up for sale. I'm sure they are dust and tumbleweeds, but can you imagine, having an entire town to yourself?"

"Me? No. But you, yes. Let's see . . . what else?" He rubbed his chin. "Spring products continue to fly off the shelves, production is running smoothly. And the samples for the summer body care line promo is expected next week. You'll need to approve those, so do try and be here for that. Oh, and don't forget you have mage training in the morning."

"You're the absolute best, Tristan! I could kiss you, but you know, sexual harassment laws and all that." I winked at him.

He laughed and said, "That's why you pay me the big bucks, honey!" His office phone beeped, and he answered via speaker phone.

Tristan has been at my side from the beginning. He assisted me with just about everything, and I trusted him implicitly.

"Tristan? Is Ms. Kenzie in your office?" our receptionist asked.

"I'm here."

"Ms. Kenzie, there's a man here asking for you. I told him he needed an appointment, but he refuses to leave. He said it's important. Should I call security?"

My brows knitted together. "Did he give you a name?"

"Yes, Mr. Avery Knox."

"Not familiar. Send him to the conference room and have security on standby." I hated it when people showed up without an appointment and expected to be seen. I hated it more when people harassed my employees. This Avery person needed to learn a lesson.

"Join me in the conference room?" I asked Tris.

"You know it," he said.

We ran a quick web search of Avery Knox and found nothing.

Using our security cameras in the conference room, I got a few close ups on his face and saved the file.

Avery Knox was an unassuming, older gentlemen, mid-sixties, hair on the sides of his head, bald on the top. I never understood why men wore their hair like that, and I wanted to shave those sides off. It wasn't doing him any favors.

He wore an expensive suit, Rolex watch, and Italian loafers. He was sporting wealth but he looked uncomfortable in it, as though he only dressed up on special occasions.

"Mr. Knox, I presume."

"Yes," he replied.

No polite greeting, no introduction. Not even a smile. Huh, so, that's how it's gonna be.

"Water?" I asked.

"Sure," he said.

Our receptionist brought in a tray holding glasses and a pitcher of water. She set the tray near me, poured water into the glasses, and then left. Seated across from him, I handed him a glass, which he emptied in one gulp. Tris waited by the door.

Knox opened his briefcase, pulled out an envelope and slid it over to me. It was a legal-sized envelope sealed with wax, the crest unfamiliar. Hmm . . . old school. I was relieved there for a moment, and had thought this guy was here to serve me papers. Still, I didn't touch it.

"Open it."

"No." I gave him a flat stare.

"It's a job offer."

"I'm not looking for work," I replied, wearing my best resting bitch face.

"That's okay. This one doesn't pay," he added smugly.

"This meeting is over. Out you go."

"Take the job, or we go to the Super Natural Registrar's Office and report you for hiding your gifts."

I burst out laughing so hard I doubled over in my chair. Tris was laughing with me.

After a few minutes of the much-needed comedy reprieve, I looked over at Knox. "Thank you for the laugh. Whew, I needed that. You've wasted your time. And mine. I'm not taking your job, and you are welcome to call the Registrar's Office, right now in fact. Hell, I'll help you dial the number."

I picked up the phone. "What's the number?"

He just stared at me with a blank look.

Tris tapped on his tablet, and then handed it to me.

The screen showed the contact info for the Super Natural Registrar's Office. I showed it to Knox and said, "These people, right?" I started dialing the number but he reached over and hung up the phone.

"Rude." I placed the receiver back in the cradle.

"If you care about the people you love, you will take this seriously." Sweat beaded on his forehead.

With a subtle burst of movement, I struck out and pinned his head on the table, my dagger at his neck. Blood trickled on the blade.

Knox turned pale white, and his body trembled.

"I am done with your threats. Get the fuck out." My voice was a calm whisper.

I grabbed him by his suit lapels and threw him out of the office into the hands of security who escorted him out of the building.

"Well, that was interesting," Tris muttered.

I headed to my office and took a pic of the wax seal, and then left the envelope locked in my safe. It seemed innocuous, but I'd rather it be locked away and safe. I had zero plans on opening it. My gut warned me, I didn't want anything to do with it.

The entire exchange bothered me. No one knew about my side work. Tris knew I had combat mage skills and that I made large sums of money. He just didn't know all the details. The less he knew, the better.

And my merc contract was over as of that morning. Besides, I had a handler. I was never approached in public like this. Sighing, I texted the pic of the seal to Dad and Uncle Brian. Dad had connections in the merc world. And Uncle Brian was my handler. He wasn't my uncle by blood, but he was a family friend. Between the two, one of them would know something.

Security was taking care of tracking the guy and, most importantly, tracing his employers. Until I heard back from someone, there was nothing I could do. I could've opened the darn envelope, but my gut was telling me I needed plausible deniability, so that was out . . . for now. Tension tightened my shoulders. The experience with Knox made me uneasy.

CHAPTER 3
KENZIE

By mid-day, most of my priorities were addressed. Everything else could be handled remotely. After dealing with Knox, I needed to get out of the office. I waved goodbye to Tris who was on the phone, and I told the receptionist to cancel all my appointments for the day and to have the security team contact me on my cell as soon as they were done with their analysis.

I was craving a Green Goddess drink from my favorite juice bar, so I hopped in my Range Rover and drove to Raw.

My favorite juice bar was located about two miles from my office. The juices were fresh, organic, and ridiculously overpriced. Plus, the guy that owned Raw was a total hottie. I liked supporting the local hotties, I meant local businesses, as often as I could.

As I walked in, juice hottie was on his way out. Jake picked me up off my feet in a bear hug.

"Mackenzie!" he said excitedly.

"Hey! You leaving me?"

"Yeah, unfortunately. Business issues at the other location but I'd rather be here with you," he replied with a flirtatious wink.

Pushing him away, I laughed "Go, big man, do that business thang."

He pulled me in for another hug. "See you next week?"

"Like you could keep me away." I entered his store as he got in his car.

I found myself in a short line. The woman in front of me held her toddler. The little one was fussing, and the mom was searching in her purse for something. The little whiny girl reached out to me grabbing hold of my hair, not pulling, so I smiled at her and raised my hand to extract my hair from her tiny fingers. She let go of my hair and grabbed on to my finger.

Her mom turned to me, "Oh, she really likes you. She's been fussing until you walked in." She bounced and cooed at her child.

The mom was next in line. She placed her order and searched her purse again, while trying to balance the little girl with one arm. Her daughter started to cry. Not having success with her purse, the mom turned to me and said, "Do you mind?"

She practically shoved her child in my arms. The little girl reached out toward me, leaning away from her mother's body, so I put my hands out and grabbed hold of the baby.

Who lets a stranger hold their child? Thankfully, the little one stopped crying. The baby who must be a few months, or maybe a year, was now speaking to me in that heart-melting baby talk language. I could not comprehend a single thing, but darn it, it was so freaking adorable.

"You are absolutely adorable." Awe in my voice was evident. "What's your name?" I asked, even though the baby couldn't possibly understand me, let alone answer me.

"Sophia. She loves you. She's usually not friendly with strangers." Mom's eyes lit up.

I would think your child being wary of strangers was a good thing. But I guess not.

The mother turned to talk to the staff behind the counter, apologizing for taking too long. I held her kid and felt a sense of peace, of rightness. I leaned in and inhaled the child's heavenly smell. Why do babies smell so good? Like innocence and unconditional love. If this were bottled as a fragrance it would be a billion-dollar business, no doubt. I leaned in again, taking a deep breath. Uh-oh, my maternal strings were pulling at me.

"Hi Kenzie! Here's your usual," the gal behind the counter said to me, thankfully breaking me out of my baby haze. "I started on it when I saw you talking to Jake."

"Oh, thank you!" I pulled out a hundred-dollar bill from my purse that was resting on my hip. I placed the bill on the counter. "I'll cover whatever Sophia and her mom want as well."

Sophia's mom gave me a surprised look. "You don't have to do that. Sorry I'm taking so long. My wallet is here somewhere."

"No, please, I insist. Your daughter is precious," I said as Sophia curled her tiny body against mine, her head in the crook of my neck.

"You are so good with her. Do you have children?"

I shook my head, unwilling to answer that question out loud.

"Well, you're going to be a great mom. My kids are the best thing that's ever happened to me."

I didn't respond, because I didn't know what to say to this stranger. Instead, I handed Sophia to her mom. Back in her mom's arms, Sophia looked back at me as though she wondered where I was going. My insides were topsy turvy, and I felt the waterworks pooling in my eyes.

After grabbing my drink, I told the staff to keep the change and wished Sophia and her mom a good day. Mom and the gal behind the counter thanked me profusely.

"You're welcome," I shouted behind me as I all but ran out of the juice shop and vowed to never return.

I rushed to my car as though my ass were on fire. I closed the door with shaky hands and wet cheeks and paused a moment to take a breath. My heart hurt. I knew I needed to get moving, needed to be somewhere, anywhere but here. On autopilot, I put the car in drive, not really knowing where to go, but I kept driving as the unwanted memories flooded back.

CHAPTER 4
KENZIE

I recalled how the doctor had peered at me, his brow furrowed. "I'm sorry, but having children the natural way is not an option. Your ovaries are producing eggs, perhaps you could consider a surrogate, but . . . your uterus is . . . inhospitable. You won't be able to have children on your own. I wish there was better news."

Inhospitable!? Who says that? I should've kicked that doctor in the balls.

Overwhelmed by thoughts of the past, I blinked my eyes to focus on the road. Then I shook my head and swiped my face dry with the back of my hand. After fifteen minutes of driving, I was on the freeway, and took the next exit, knowing exactly where I was headed.

There was always something to do here in Vegas. Old Vegas started out as casinos owned by the mob to continue their shenanigans in the middle of the desert. Then corporations took over, growing the city and commercializing everything. When the magical community came out, Las Vegas became Vegas where the things that go bump in the night took over. It was always a nocturnal city. Now even more so.

Every casino was practically owned and run by vamps, shifters, and mages of every sort. And it was run by the Guild, a group of powerful magical types that policed the city. It was considered neutral territory. Disputes between clans and species were to be handled peacefully. If problems arose, the Guild handled supernatural affairs and worked alongside the human police if humans were involved. As far as I could tell, those rules were adhered to. But I was a nobody and did my best to keep my head down.

My home and business were off the Strip, only a twenty-minute drive. But I wasn't headed home; I needed a distraction. I have a condo, my lady lair as Tris dubbed it, in one of the hotels called The Majestic. The building was indeed majestic and magical. When I learned of this condo/hotel going up, I made sure to meet with the owners, the Gaspari's, and I persuaded them to sell me a couple units. I got Tower I units at phase one prices. In return, I brought them buyers who'd paid premium prices. The units sold out, and the Gaspari's were able to build another tower shortly after announcing Tower I. Before the second tower went up for sale, I locked in a Penthouse unit, paying it off in full when my other units in tower one had sold. The Penthouse was my refuge, a place where my alter ego could come out to play. Spring was always busy in Vegas. I was sure I'd find someone to play with. And that was exactly what I needed at the moment, a safe place to hide out and bury my sorrows in hopefully a lot of dick.

Yes, yes, I know that sounded crude. But it was true and I wasn't sorry. I was not ashamed of my sexuality. I loved cock, I loved sex, and had no problem owning it. I had my boundaries. My rules were no married men, no men with girlfriends, and no expectations. I wasn't the type to lead men astray or intentionally hurt anyone. I was always clear on my expectations. I'd only spend one night or one weekend with my hookups, depending on how the one night went. Besides, I wasn't susceptible to human diseases nor was I able to get pregnant, so it was all fun for me. And as far as relationships, for a merc, that was a pipe dream. Everyone wanted to love and be loved, me included. Another reason merc life was not for me. Merc life meant secrecy, and secrecy didn't make for healthy relationships. But as of this morning, that life was over. Maybe love was a possibility for me after all. One night stands probably wouldn't yield that type of result but it didn't hurt to try, or at least that's what I kept telling myself.

Maybe I was jaded after the shit show of a marriage I had. Still, I couldn't close myself off to the possibility of love and marriage, despite my past.

I remembered the day our marriage started to unravel.

"I'm sorry this didn't work, Mackenzie. Since this is your third round of IVF, have you considered adoption?" The reproductive specialist was talking, but the words were just as foggy as they had been when he'd said them, two feet in front of me.

I recalled turning to my husband, my knees trembling.

"No Mac, if it's not of our blood, not our genetics, then I don't want children. I don't want to adopt. We'll be fine, just us. We'll be enough," Ray, my ex-husband, said to me.

I replayed this conversation over and over in my head with my ex-husband because in the end, it wasn't enough.

As I drove my car into my designated parking spot, I took a quick look in the mirror. Puffy green eyes tinged with red blotchy skin, looked back at me. I was an ugly crier, most people were. It's a fact, or at least I liked to think that because it made me feel better. Sighing, I leaned my head on the steering wheel. The reality was one thing. I was well aware of my biological deficiencies, but having it thrown in my face in public was not something I was prepared to deal with.

My heart was still breaking for losing something I never had and never would. I wanted to sit in my car and cry forever. But I couldn't. I'd been crying over this for years, and if I really wanted to be a mom, I could always look into adopting. My ex didn't want it but he was history. I needed to rethink all this.

The day was turning to shit. First, I had to deal with the asshole at my office and then I had to meet the precious little baby that wasn't mine. Fuck my life. Time to put my big girl panties on and enjoy life the best way I knew how.

I took a deep breath stepped out of my car and headed into the lobby to check in with the lead concierge. She had all the latest news and gossip going on in town, plus she had access to exclusive restaurants, bars, clubs, you name it. The magical community was a lot more creative when it came to extra-curricular activities. We enjoyed alcohol, specially brewed alcohol of course, since human alcohol didn't work on magical folk. We enjoyed dancing and music and gambling, like humans. The supes, what humans called us, did things a little more extreme. Sex and violence were widely acceptable, which worked just fine for me.

The lobby was completely open like a cavern. Magic served to hold up the structure in places where normal pillars and studs would be used. The walls and every counter space were smooth alabaster stone. Pearlescent veins running through it emitted a sparkle and sheen. The marble flooring had an intricate pattern that was rumored to be an inlay of actual gold. The lighting was sensational. Floating lanterns drifted throughout the lobby, illuminating the area. Vines of flowers sprouted from the floors and extended upward toward the ceiling, adding a splash of vibrant color. White silk draperies flowed and framed surrounding windows that overlooked the well-manicured lawn and water gardens. The dreamlike space was both sedate and seductive.

There was a gaming floor. An area below, literally called the Dungeon, was for fighting. And of course, there were the usual restaurants, clubs, etc.

Most hotels here now primarily catered to the supernatural community. The Majestic was no different. Here on the main floor all supes were in their human forms. Vamps were easy to recognize. They had a weird way about them. It was almost as though they were moving statues, barely breathing, no facial expression. It was strange. Since it was still daylight, none were out at the moment.

Shifters were harder for me to spot unless they were close. It seemed there were more shifters in this world than other supes. Not sure why, but I'm guessing it was because their ability to procreate was more successful than other supes. Because of the larger shifter community, this property was adjacent to a wooded area for them to shift, hunt, and just run. Mages, on the other hand, were humans with special magic, and they were easier to spot. Testing happened when magic manifested, usually around twelve years old. Once tested, you were registered and marked if you had any magical abilities. Registered mages were marked on their cheeks, necks, or forearms depending on their level and type of magic. The Registrar's Office called it a tattoo except it was more of a brand, one that mages were proud to show. Whatever they called it, the mark signified their rank and specialty. I was happy I wasn't branded. Fae magic was rare, and rare types of magic wielders were often sequestered away from their families at a young age and then utilized according to how the Registrar's Office decided.

It was just about midafternoon, still early for night life, but supes partied twenty-four-seven without a break. It didn't matter what day of the week it was or what time of the day. You could always count on magical beings to be indulging, especially here at The Majestic.

Rules were no killing. Everything else was open season.

Bunny Lee, the lead concierge, was at her station talking to a few people. She looked up and smiled as she saw me approaching. She was dressed in a business-savvy suit. Her sleek bob accentuated her pixie-like features, and large glasses perched on her delicate nose. She was an info Mage. Kind of like a walking encyclopedia. She knew everything, was always a busy body, and was always high energy. Everyone called her the Energizer Bunny. She was tiny at four and a half feet tall, but she made up for her size with a vibrant personality.

As I got closer to the concierge station, I could hear her barking out orders from several feet away, while directing guests to where they needed to be with a smile. The woman was a machine. She was one of those multi-taskers, and would probably get on with Tristan really well.

Although Tris wasn't marked, he had some abilities as a tech mage and as an info mage. These abilities made him great in business. The powers that be registered him as a Tier Two, like me. Bunny was a Tier Four, not at the top in terms of power level but pretty darn close.

She came out from behind the desk to greet me with a hug. I had to bend a little because of our height difference. Despite her small stature, she gave the best full-on hugs, not the lame one-arm, shoulder-lean type.

"Ah! Don't snap me in half!" I teased and pulled away from her. She was strong for a wee thing.

She laughed, smoothing down her suit. "Where've you been gorgeous? It's been a while. Here to play?" Bunny wiggled her eyebrows.

"Two months is not a while," I replied.

"Two months?! Honey, you should be here at a minimum every weekend. There's so much going on! But you're here now. Let's get you sorted." She tugged me along guiding me to the side of the concierge station, giving us privacy to speak.

"What's new?" I asked excitedly.

"Well, let me tell you. First and most importantly men, lots and lots of men." She giggled.

"Guess I'm in the right place then." I winked at her.

"Yes, you are! There's a supe conference, a big pow wow with all the North American pack Alphas in attendance and a few master vamps as well. Territory issues, I'm sure."

Wow, that was big. Vamps and shifters had a tenuous relationship at best. And most shifter packs had been in flux for years now. In North America there were two noteworthy dominant Alphas. The Pack Republic of Texas and The Northern Lights Pack of Alaska were dominant because their packs consisted of thousands. Texas was the largest. That Alpha, I forgot his name, had ruled for centuries and was constantly being challenged.

Bunny whispered to me as though reading my thoughts, "The Republic's territory is the biggest and growing quickly, due to their alliance with vamps. The other packs are getting nervous. They have a conference later in the week, but a lot of shifters have already checked in to play before the big meet up." She leaned back and smiled. "And, there's a mage bazaar going on down in the event rooms. It's a huge event. You should check that out if you get a chance. It will be a shopper's heaven."

Once a year, Mages gathered here in Vegas to show off their new inventions. Weapons, spells, clothes, products of every sort, tech gadgets, you name it. It was huge and definitely a shopper's heaven. I had to check that out and support the vendors. I got my start two years ago at a bazaar like this one. My skin care product line was a recognized brand now.

Bunny kept talking, gesturing wildly with her hands. "Of course, pool parties are going on right now, exclusive parties for the shifters, which I can certainly get you access to. VIP of course. And I can get you dinner reservations to any restaurant you want."

"No dinner reservations for now. But yes to the bazaar. And yes to any pool party you recommend," I said, knowing she'd guide me to the best of the best.

There were seven pools on property. All different themed, with different music. Humans and supes usually mingled at pool parties. However, humans weren't allowed at some of the clubs or the bazaar.

"I know just the one." Bunny gave me a devilish smile.

"There's a human bachelor party, military types, so hot. There's like twelve of them. Plus, I just booked a cabana for a shifter and his pack. Ooh girl!" She fanned herself.

I had to laugh. She was just too funny. "I will go wherever you send me, oh wise one."

And just like that, my day was looking up.

CHAPTER 5
KENZIE

My mood improved tremendously after speaking with Bunny. I walked to the Penthouse elevators, fumbling with my purse trying to find my key card. I didn't pay much attention to the two men that walked in the elevator behind me. Once the doors shut, I was bombarded by their magical presence. They were powerful beings, probably shifters. Strength and aggression were coming off them in waves. Dominant males. Just great. Dominant males tended to have ginormous egos. The thing is, if you shied away from these types, they thought of you as prey and expected you to submit. In other words, they'd boss you around. That wasn't going to happen to this girl.

"You in the right elevator, sweetness?" A deep raspy voice came in from my left. Something about the timber of his voice gave me the shivers and not in a bad way.

I swiped the elevator panel with my key, then turned to face him. I had to tilt my head up to look him in the eyes. In shifter packs, there's a hierarchy. Lower rank shifters do not make eye contact with their superiors. I was not a shifter, and I was not afraid. Thus, I didn't give a shit.

He stared back at me with his eyebrows raised. The guy almost looked amused.

"My bad," he said with a smirk.

I could just kiss that smirk right off his face. I meant slap, not kiss. Oh boy, there goes my lady parts trying to take control.

The guy was mesmerizing, and I couldn't take my eyes off him. He was at least six and a half feet tall, all muscle. His blond neatly trimmed hair, piercing pale blue eyes, wide set of shoulders, and trim waist had me swallowing hard. He was impeccably dressed, in a dark suit, white buttoned-down shirt that was opened a bit and revealed a smooth muscled chest. His muscular arms and legs strained against the fabric. Don't drool, don't drool, don't drool, I kept telling myself.

"Don't mind my brother, he loses his manners whenever a beautiful lady is nearby," a male with a smooth voice said behind me.

The other person was too darn close. It was unnerving, but I refused to show it.

My gaze remained locked on the first shifter, while I responded to the second shifter. "I see, so is standing in a stranger's personal space your idea of having manners? Or should I just assume both of you ignored your parents when they were teaching proper etiquette?"

The blond shifter threw back his head and let out a loud, booming laugh. It was infectious, and I had to turn my head to hide my smile, my insides feeling all warm and fuzzy.

"Aww, don't be like that, gorgeous. You're just too enticing. I had to get close to you," personal space invader said.

"Laying it on a little thick, aren't you?" I pursed my lips.

"If you want thick, that can certainly be arranged," raspy voice said.

"I think she'd like that very much, wouldn't you, gorgeous?" the second shifter said, so close to me I could feel his breath on my shoulder.

Seriously! The warm and fuzzy feeling dissipated, annoyance taking its place.

"Please. Both of you together couldn't keep up with me." I scoffed.

They both laughed and stepped in closer to me.

"I bet we could prove you wrong," the one behind me replied.

I rolled my eyes and motioned with my keycard for him to step back. He refused to budge though, so I turned to look at him, exasperated. I was almost speechless when I faced him. "Brother" he had called the other guy, but he was definitely not a shifter. Could he be a vamp? A day walker? Well shit, that wasn't possible. Day walkers were so rare, they were almost mystical.

While his brother had pale tones of moonlight skin, blond hair and ice blue eyes, the other shifter was bronze. He had a golden tan that indicated long days in the sun. His dark brown hair, had the perfect highlights, and his gray eyes were rimmed with blue, which I could see clearly since he was so close. He was equally as tall as his brother but slimmer. Unlike his brother though, he was casually dressed in faded blue jeans, and a gray T-shirt that said "Absofuckinglutely" written across his muscled chest. Ahh, he was the playful one. Judging by the mischievous gleam in his eyes, that assessment was spot on.

I motioned with my key card, telling him to back up, which caused him to take a half step back.

When I turned to face forward, Blond Haired Brother now stood directly in front of me. Much too close, and he was sniffing me . . . his nose grazed my hair. He leaned in even further and sniffed at my neck.

"Are you smelling me? What is with you two and personal space?" I pushed against his chest, he doesn't budge.

"You smell nice. What are you?" Blondie asked me.

The elevator bell rang. Finally. It had felt like I was trapped with these two dominant males forever.

"I am not for you, puppy dog," I said, stepping around him.

They followed me out. The penthouse floor in both towers of The Majestic consisted of two units. One facing south, the other north. Both shared the same corridor for the elevator.

I turned to my door in the south wing, figuring the guys rented the other unit and would go in the opposite direction. Nope. They were right behind me.

I took a couple steps then stopped to face them with a hand on my hip and my best don't-mess-with-me expression. "No puppies, you may not follow me home."

The dark-haired male pointed to his brother and said, "He's the wolf, not me so I guess that means I can follow you home, seeing as I'm nothing close to being a puppy."

"Well, whatever you are, both of you, be on your way." I motioned with my finger to turn around.

"We're just being gentlemen, walking you to your door," Blond guy said.

"Yeah, you know, manners and all that," said the dark-haired brother.

"Oh, so now you have manners?" I was beyond exasperated at that point.

They both grinned and nodded their heads. They looked like mischievous schoolboys. Their smiles lit up their faces, so unlike the arrogance they'd displayed earlier.

"I'm perfectly capable of walking a few feet alone in an empty hallway."

"It's just a few feet, sweetness," shifter said while grabbing my hand and placing it at the crook of his arm. His brother did the same on my other side. I rolled my eyes.

"Don't call me that! I'm not your sweetness. And I'm not inviting either of you in."

"That would be neighborly for you to do so, seeing as we're minding our manners and all," Dark-Haired Brother said deviously.

"Nice try . . . but nope, not today demon, or whatever you are." I retort back, even though I was tempted.

Both brothers burst out laughing, and I couldn't help myself and smiled back even though I was trying to be serious.

At my door, I stepped away from them and yanked my hands out of their grasp. They deftly maneuvered my body and had my back toward the door. If it weren't for their boy-like grins I might have felt intimidated.

They each held one of my hands, one male on my right and the other on my left, and they kissed the top and inside of my wrists. The contact of their lips to my skin, sent tingles through my veins. My blood was singing, and my lady muscles clenched hard. I could already see how this was going to end up.

"Come play with us," Shifter whispered to me, his eyes pleading with mine.

"Yeah, come play." The dark-haired one still held onto my hand.

"Perhaps." I retracted my hands and reached behind me to open my door.

"At least tell us where we might find you," shifter asked.

"I'm going to the pool," I said closing the door behind me.

CHAPTER 6

KENZIE

Exhaling a breath I didn't realize I was holding, I relaxed against the closed door.

Those two were intense, intimidating, and alluring. Two of them! Wow, just wow. I've had my share of men, but two at the same time would be fun. Yep, I'd definitely be into a threesome with those two. They seemed to be open to sharing, which was good for me.

For some reason, I could sense the shifter just on the other side of the door. Curious to see if my senses were correct, I peered out the peephole. Sure enough he was staring at my door with the same intensity he had in the elevator. He stared directly at the peephole, as though he knew I was there. Startled, I immediately ducked down and slowly took a couple steps back, my eyes glued to the door. What the fuck? Why was he just standing there? Did he know I was standing there also?

To answer my question, I heard him say, "See you at the pool, sweetness."

Without thinking, I blurted, "Don't call me that!" He chuckled. So, he did hear me. Shit. Damn shifter hearing.

I moved further into my condo and stopped for a moment to admire my posh penthouse. It was a two-story unit and I did not spare any expense when decking it out. The entryway led to a sunken living room. Floor-to-ceiling windows covered the entire wall opposite the entryway, showcasing an unobstructed view of the East Valley. To the left of the front door was a grand spiral staircase leading up to the bedrooms, and the formal dining room and kitchen were to the right.

"Life is good," I said to no one in particular. Some people were blessed with love, some were blessed with a healthy uterus to have babies, but I was blessed with money. It could be a lot worse. From here on out, I vowed to focus on my blessings.

My phone beeped a text from Uncle Brian.

Uncle B: Not familiar Kid, but I'll look into it. Talk soon.

Me: Thx!

No text messages from Dad yet. Hmm . . . not unusual. I called my office security.

"Tom here."

"It's me. Anything on Knox?"

"So far, just the basics. Avery Knox from Northern California. Divorced, two kids, estranged. He's an attorney currently working for himself. He used to work for a big firm in S.F. called Devine and Patterson. HR department said he walked out a year ago. No criminal record, but his lists of clients are all shady, which is probably where he's getting his money. For a solo attorney with no family money, he has millions in an offshore account. We're researching that to see if there's a connection. He flew on a commercial airline and is staying at the Desert Oasis. He returned to his room after he left here and has been there since. We have eyes on him. No info has been found on the crest, though. We're still working on it."

"Good work." I paused for a second, thinking. "I appreciate all you've done thus far, but I'm hiring a third party to get involved. We need to get into his room. He must have a tablet or laptop or even his phone. I don't want anyone on our team getting too close. Keep me posted on the offshore account. And get me a list of his clients. And once I have a private investigator hired, I'll put you in touch."

"Ok, we'll take care of what we can. Ms. Kenzie, if I may?"

"Speak freely, Tom." I walked into the kitchen and set my laptop and tablet on the counter.

"The contents of that envelope might be helpful."

"No, not yet. I think I know what it is. I don't want the details. I want plausible deniability should something happen to someone important." I shook my head even though Tom couldn't see me.

"Copy that."

"Stay in touch, Tom. And thank you, for everything."

"Thank you, Ms. Kenzie, I appreciate the work."

"Of course. Talk soon." I ended the call.

Tom ran the security department at my office building. He was a low-level combat mage and retired vet. Although he was well past his prime as a soldier, he was incredibly adept at running my security team. He had many daily duties, and he helped run background checks on new hires. Plus, he was great backup to have. Tom, Dad, and Uncle Brian were military buddies from way back.

He was right, though. That was just the basics on Avery. Still, it was something. I really hoped we could get into his room. Fuck. I didn't want this in my brain right now.

Next up, I dialed Tristan.

"You walked out on me. I thought you were leaving me for good," he answered.

"Never, sweet cheeks. I'm calling to see if you wanted to join me for a little shopping. There's a bazaar at The Majestic."

He sucked in an excited breath and said, "You know it! Let's buy shit! Wait, you're at The Majestic? What brought that on?"

"Oh, you know, I figure I'll just work from here. Plus, I really need to make use of the place since I haven't been here in a couple months."

"Liar. You only go to your lady lair when you need a distraction."

He knew me so well. I told him about the little scene at the juice bar, knowing he'd understand.

"Aww, sweet girl! I wish there was something I could do to make things better for you. Things happen for a reason. Your ex was a total shit. It may not seem like it now, but not having kids with that asshole was a blessing. You deserve better, and I am sure your true love is out there. The right man is gonna sweep you off your feet! For now, enjoy yourself. You're hot as hell. Any guy would be lucky to have you. I'll handle everything here."

My bestie always knew what to say. "I'm fine, Tris. Or I will be. I just need a distraction." I truly believed that the way my marriage ended was for the best. And not having children with him was a blessing. He probably would have cheated on me and left anyway, even if we had a child. The maternal drive was still there for me, though. Perhaps adoption would be something to reconsider. I was done being a merc, and I had the financial resources to raise a horde of children if I wanted to.

"If you could do me just one favor and cancel my magic training for the week again, I'd really appreciate it. With everything else going on, the last thing I want is to deal with a mage," I said to my bestie, trying to forget about the incident at the juice bar.

"Of course."

Realizing I was ready to change the subject, Tris peppered me with questions about my plans. I wished he could join me. He was the best wing man, but he was spoken for. His boyfriend was a sweetheart and it was refreshing to see him happy and settled. I was not going to be that girl, the single one who ruined her friends' love lives so she didn't have to be single by herself. Tris deserved a good man, and Robert, his current love, was great.

I gave Tris the rundown I got from Bunny.

"If I was single, I'd be the biggest whore," he said emphatically.

"What are you talking about? You were a total whore before Robert!"

He laughed. "True, true, the good ole days. Well, I get to live my whorish life through you, so do my inner slut proud."

I let out a wholehearted laugh.

Knowing he'd die to meet my elevator companions, I told him about that encounter.

He screeched into the phone, "Girl! Do you know who that was?"

I didn't know. In fact, I didn't even get their names.

"Those were probably the sons of the Texas Alpha. Joseph Reese is his name. He has two sons. One a wolf, the other a day walker!"

A wolf with a day walker son. I was sure there was a colorful story there. Vamps were made, not born, but day walkers came from the original line of vampires. The originals were ancient and there weren't many left. In fact, I didn't think there were any in the US.

"How do you know these things?" I asked while peering into a barren refrigerator. Tris had the inside scoop on everything magical. He could give Bunny a run for her money as far as info on the magical community.

"How do you not know?! They're the most eligible bachelors in the country, magical and non-magical alike. The current Alpha is trying to combine both vamps and shifters under one power. Everyone is up in arms about it because that territory is huge already and it keeps growing. The shifters and vamps have hated each other since forever, but so far it's working in Texas."

"Sounds like a lot of work and a lot of drama and something I don't want any part of."

"Chill, Kenz, you don't have to marry them. Just have raunchy sex with both of them for as long as they're in town and tell me all about it."

"You're a bad influence, you know that?" I replied, smiling.

"Damn straight and proud of it, too. Go put on a sexy, skimpy bikini. Oh, and send pics of the hotties at the pool. Pulleassee!"

He had me laughing so hard I could hardly get the words out to say goodbye. Hmm. Maybe he had a point about the hot brothers.

After my phone call with Tris, I stripped out of my dress and perused my wardrobe for pool wear. I didn't have to look too hard. Thanks to Tris, I had tons of stuff in here. He always made sure I had the latest everything, and he had a knack for dressing me. Everything he chose for me always looked great.

I decided on a tiny bikini. It shimmered with pink sequins and a hologram material underneath. The triangle top was covered in the sequins, and gold-colored straps tied around my neck and back. The front part of the micro bottom was covered with the sequins while the back and straps matched the top's gold. Perfect Vegas pool party attire. I let my hair down from the messy bun it had been in since training that morning. My long locks touched my lower back, and were now wavy from being curled up all day. I finger-fluffed my dark hair and applied a little lip gloss. After throwing a white crochet cover-up over my suit, I grabbed my heels and was ready for partying at the pool.

The thought of possibly seeing the wolf shifter and the day walker put a lift in my step.

CHAPTER 7

KENZIE

The elevator ride down to the pool was uneventful. Admittedly, I was disappointed. No hot anything to accompany me. The disappointment was short-lived as I made my way to Seventh Heaven, the pool Bunny had recommended.

It was crowded, but I found an empty lounge chair poolside. Before I could get there though, someone grabbed my arm.

"Excuse me," a deep baritone voice said.

I looked at the hand placed on my arm and followed it up to the handsome face it was attached to. *Well, aren't you a pretty one?* He smiled warmly at me, displaying the cutest dimples on each cheek. I got lost staring up into his warm chocolate brown eyes, and I waited for him to say more.

He hesitated at first and nervously released my arm "Hi," he said finally.

"Hi." I smiled back at him. Aww, he was kinda shy. It was sweet.

"I, um, I'm usually not this nervous." He glanced down at his feet, and then returned his gaze back to me. "Let me start over. I'm Brody." He held out a hand to shake mine.

And he's a gentleman.

I shook his outstretched hand. "Kenzie, nice to meet you."

"Kenzie," he said, tasting my name on his lips. "I like it. Is it short for something?"

"Mackenzie."

He flashed a bright smile. "Well, Mackenzie, my friends and I have a cabana right there. Would you care to join me? There's a lounge chair and a cocktail with your name on it if you're interested."

I hesitated a moment, thinking about my elevator companions.

"Just one cocktail, please. Then you can continue with your day," he said sweetly.

"One cocktail, then I'll gracefully take my leave and let you boys do whatever it is you came here to do." I smiled up at him.

He was definitely a looker, but not in the obvious "I'm a super model" way like Tristan or my elevator companions. Brody was built like an athlete, his body tall and muscular. He was wholesome, complete with boyish charm and those panty-melting dimples.

When we arrived at his cabana, Brody introduced me to his buddies, who were friendly and welcoming. They weren't creepy and they appeared to respect him as though he was an authority of sorts, which I found interesting. He seemed to be their Alpha even though they were all human.

He handed me a cocktail. Mmm, it was sweet and refreshing like Kool-Aid. You couldn't taste the alcohol until you'd had one too many. We sat on two of the lounge chairs farthest away from his friends, giving us some semblance of privacy.

"So, what brings you here, Brody? Boys trip?" I motioned to his friends.

He smiled and flashed those dimples again. "That's why they're here. I'm here working and they all decided to come out. We were in the Army together."

"Ah, I see, it looks like you're working really hard." I pointed at his glass.

He chuckled. "Guess it's one of the perks to being the boss."

"Cheers to that." I raised my glass and he clinked his glass against mine. "What kind of business?" I asked him.

"Personal bodyguard services and private investigation work," he said.

"Are you any good at the private investigation work?" I asked, thinking about the Knox situation. What were the odds of meeting a private investigator just when I needed to hire one?

"The best." He smiled. "Why, you looking for someone?"

"Something like that."

"Are you alright?" He sounded genuinely concerned.

"Yes, of course. It's nothing," I said, apprehensive about telling him more. My years of merc training made me guarded.

"Hey," he said in an almost protective tone, "I know we just met, but I would be happy to help." He paused and held my gaze. "You can look me up, and I can provide references, too. And I won't even charge you."

He pulled out his wallet and handed me a card. Knight & Associates. Bodyguard and Investigative Services.

"You don't even know what the job is," I said to him.

"I don't care, as long as it keeps you safe and I get to spend more time with you," he said with such sincerity, I decided I was going to hire him.

Before I could say anything further, I heard my name.

"Kenzie! There you are." My dark-haired elevator companion strode up to Brody and me.

Shocked and speechless, I just sat there as he introduced himself to Brody.

"Hey! I'm Caid. Good to meet you."

Brody stood to shake his hand.

"Thanks for keeping our neighbor here company," Caid said to Brody, and then turned to face me. "We've been looking all over for you! When you said meet at the pool, we thought it would be easy enough. But did you know there are seven pools here?!"

Either he didn't realize how awkward the situation was or he just didn't care. I stood, still speechless.

"Anyway. Shall we, Kenz?" he said, sticking his elbow out for me to grab on to. "Thanks again, dude. Join us for a drink when you get a chance. We're in the cabana at the top of the pool." He gestured in the general direction of a VIP area.

Stunned, I looked at him then at Brody and back again. How did he know my name?

Brody grabbed my attention by slipping his arms around my waist and pulling me into his body. "See you later?"

"Yeah, um, yes I'd like that," I stammered.

Brody leaned down and whispered in my ear, "Are you okay?" He sounded concerned. I didn't want him to think Caid was the reason I needed a private investigator.

I hugged him to me. "I'm fine. That job has nothing to do with this guy. But maybe we can talk about it tomorrow."

"Okay, as long as you're good. I'm glad I got a few minutes with you. Talk later, please?"

"Bunny at the concierge desk will know how to reach me," I told him and pulled away.

He didn't release me though. Instead, he brushed his lips against mine. The kiss started out light and sweet. Then it grew more urgent, both of us wanting more. He darted his tongue into my mouth swiftly, exploring. I was swept up in the way he felt against me, and eager to take things further.

Caid cleared his throat, breaking us apart. I reached up to touch Brody's face, my finger tracing the dimple on his left cheek.

"Thanks for the drink," I said over my shoulder as I followed Caid.

CHAPTER 8

KENZIE

"Wow, that guy has balls of steel. Boyfriend?" Caid asked with a shake of his head.

"No, if he was, I wouldn't have left. We just met."

"Just met, huh? Interesting. He has huge balls to claim you right in front of me. Impressive, especially from a human. Is he just a human? He smells kind of funny, but it's hard to tell with all the chlorine and the amount of people." Caid led me to a VIP area on a raised platform overlooking Seventh Heaven pool. It was located at the very end of the pool with its own private swim up bar. From this vantage point, I could see Brody down below where he was with his friends. I glanced down for a second, hoping he saw me.

"Well, look who it is! Thank you for gracing us with your presence, sweetness," that deep raspy voice barked at me.

I glowered at my other elevator companion. "Stop calling me that."

He just laughed and stared at me.

Caid picked up a couple of drinks from a nearby table and handed me a glass. I hesitated knowing that this glass probably contained the good stuff, made specifically for magical folk. He noticed my trepidation and laughed.

"I wouldn't drug you, Kenz. See?" He took a swig and then handed it to me.

"How do you know my name, Caid?" I asked.

"Bunny Rabbit. That concierge knows everything and everybody. That over there is Stellan, my moody brother."

"Good to meet you both." I raised my glass.

A few pack members surrounded us, and I guessed they were all shifters. They were drinking merrily, and some danced to the music. This group was much more intense than the humans below. Although they all seemed to be merry and having a grand time, there was an underlying tension to their body language. Like a taut string ready to snap.

"Don't worry, sweetness, you're in safe company. Unless of course you'd rather be with the humans instead of your own kind." Stellan smirked at me.

I hadn't heard him slip behind me again, which was a testament to his predatory skills or maybe a testament to my lack of situational awareness. Maybe both.

I turned to him and replied, "I am human."

He let out his booming laugh again. "Aren't you cute. You don't have to pretend with me. You may not like who you are or claim your heritage, but you are one of us, a supe, whether you like it or not."

That hit a nerve and I bristled. I wasn't ashamed of my magic. I was just taught to hide it and shield myself. I've never been singled out as a supe. I kept a tight leash on my magic, making sure I was keeping things hidden under the surface on purpose. This guy just threw it in my face as though I was ashamed of myself. Fuck him.

"Bitch, you don't know my life!" I snapped.

"Ah, there it is. You do have fight in you." He eyed me appraisingly.

Staring him down again, I was ready to spew venom from my lips, but Caid interrupted us.

He stood next to me and put an arm around my shoulders. "Now, now, kids. We're here to have fun, yes? Drink!" He raised his glass.

I clinked glasses with him and took a swig.

Stellan was annoying and goading me on purpose. Why? Who the fuck knew? I just wanted to leave. I could be having a good time with Brody, who was sweet to me. This was bullshit. I glanced toward the other end of the pool and spotted Brody laughing with his friends. I set my glass down on the table and got ready to leave.

"Whoa! Gorgeous, don't leave. Stel is usually not that uptight. Well, no not true, he is uptight; usually he's worse. You actually caught him on a good day. Apologize, Stel!" Caid scowled at him.

"He's right. I'm usually worse. But I will tone it down, for you. I really don't want you to go." Stellan held my hand, and my blood zinged in my veins again with the contact.

"You can do that? Tone down assholeness?" I arched an eyebrow.

"Stick around and I'll prove it to you," he said with a sly smile.

Caid motioned for me to sit next to him.

I looked over at Brody again. Hmmm. He was nice. This one is an asshole. I bit my lower lip, unsure what to do.

"Stay, sweetness. I'll behave," Stel blocked my view of Brody and his friends.

"Umm, sure," I said and sat next to Caid. At least he was nice. "So, do tell, what are we celebrating?" I asked, trying to keep the conversation light. Stellan had his eye on Caid's arm that was draped around my shoulder, so I leaned further into his brother's body. He smirked at me, and I winked back.

"Lots of changes are coming, sweetheart," Caid said.

"No talk of politics. Not tonight anyway." Stellan's eyes bored into mine. "How about you, sweetness? What brings you to Vegas?"

I scowled at him. "What will it take for you to stop calling me that? My name is Mackenzie."

"Oh, I don't know. I kind of like it. But I'm willing to negotiate. What are you willing to give me?"

"Ooh, I like this game." Caid leaned away from me, anxiously waiting for a response.

Nervously, I replied, "Well shit, I feel like the stakes are high." My cheeks flushed because my first thought was to exchange a kiss or maybe more. But that was too easy. Relaxing into the lounge chair, I sipped my drink, which was a tropical mixture of magic booze and pineapple. *Mmm, delicious.*

I stole looks at the brothers from above my glass. Oh my gods, they were hot. Stellan caught me staring at him and decided to tease me by removing his shirt, revealing his muscular torso. His broad shoulders framed his wide chest that narrowed down to a trim waistline. A treasure trove patch of pale hair peeked out from the waistband of his shorts. My mouth watered. I licked my lips, and he focused on my mouth. It took everything in me to tear my gaze away from him, but I did and I found Caid staring at me with the same intensity. His shirt was off now, as well. Cheeky bastards. They were doing this on purpose. Caid rubbed tanning oil over his smooth bronze skin. His arm muscles bulged as he moved them up and down his muscular frame. He wiggled his eyebrows at me as though saying, "you know you want this."

"Your face is flushed, sweetness. What are you thinking about?" Stellan leaned into my personal space. I squirmed a little in my seat.

"It's the alcohol," I lied.

"You've barely had two sips," Caid said.

"I had a drink before this. You two have some catching up to do." I sat my drink down on the table.

"Trying to get us drunk so that you can have your way with us?" Stellan chuckled.

Feeling bold, I got up, removed my cover up and sauntered into the water, making sure to put an extra sway to my hips. I turned back to them and said, "I don't think I need to get either of you drunk to have my way with you."

Stellan followed me into the pool. His gaze was intense, and butterflies swarmed my belly. Caid waded into the pool holding our drinks. He handed me mine. I almost slipped on the pool tiles, but Stellan was right there to hold me steady.

He drew me against his body. Ooh, he was solid muscle. I got closer, holding on to him with one arm, my drink in the other hand, as he drifted into deeper waters. Caid floated alongside us, staying close.

"So, beautiful," Caid said behind me. "Tell us something about yourself."

"What would you like to know?" I sipped my drink.

"Let's start with today, sweetness. How has your day been so far?" Stellan asked me, and his warm breath brushed my cheek. I wrapped my legs around his torso.

"Today has been an excellent day. I finished um . . . my last assignment. And I went to the office, and then came here," I said. I was being evasive on purpose. It was too soon to divulge too much.

They both laughed. "Well, that was vague as fuck," Caid blurted. I laughed.

"To be fair, we just met." I took another sip of my drink.

"I tell you what, we answer your questions, you answer ours. And if you don't want to answer, you take a drink," Caid said. My, my, he was inquisitive.

"You're an interrogator, aren't you?" I asked. Stellan tipped his head back and let out his booming laugh. I stretched my arm to the side so he wouldn't knock his noggin on my drink.

"She's got you pegged," Stellan said with a big smile on his face.

Caid had a mischievous smile. "Okay, point to you."

I sipped my drink, and then placed the glass against Stellan's lips to give him a sip. He arched an eyebrow at my offering, but sipped, keeping his eyes on me the whole time. "Thank you," he said.

"You're welcome. You're carrying me, so the least I can do is ply you with alcohol," I said like it was a big deal, even though it wasn't.

"Ready to play our question-and-answer game?" Caid spoke right behind me. I was so focused on Stellan I hadn't notice his brother getting so close . . . again. Not that I minded. I clenched my legs around Stellan, and he groaned.

"Is that a yes or no, sweetness?" Stellan's nose bumped my cheek.

"Um . . . sorry, what was the question?" Endorphins flooded my sex and threatened to take over my brain.

They both laughed and proceeded to tell me more about themselves. They were much more forthcoming about their lives, which drew me in. Life as a merc was keeping one secret after the other. Lie upon lie. They confirmed the info I got from Bunny and Tris. Still, I sensed this was what it was like to be normal and not guarded all the time. I needed to get with the program. Now that I wasn't a merc, I didn't need to be so defensive.

We floated around for a while, casually getting to know one another. The conversation was light and they had me laughing. They had a special bond that went beyond being just brothers. Sometimes they said the same thing at the same time. It was kind of cute.

Stellan handed me over to his brother, and then he got out of the pool to refill our empty glasses. I was reluctant to leave him for some reason, but that reluctance went away as soon as I wrapped my arms around Caid's back. I perched my chin on his shoulder while he held onto my legs and floated us in the water.

He floated deeper into the pool, and I got a glimpse of Brody down at the other end. His shirt was off, revealing a well-defined torso. Yummy. Was there a thing as too many hot men? Nope. Absolutely not.

"There's your human boyfriend," Caid said as though he read my mind. "Do you want me to take you over there to say hello?"

He floated in Brody's direction. Brody saw us and waved, and then disappeared into the water.

"You're a little troublemaker, aren't you?" I said to Caid.

He laughed. "I know you like him, which is fine as long as you like me more."

I shook my head and smiled.

"Hi!" Brody said from behind us.

Caid spun us around so we both faced him. "You again." He still held me up with his hands around my thighs, my legs stretched out in front of him.

"Yep, me again." Brody focused solely on me. "I just wanted to tell Kenzie that I'm looking forward to our date tomorrow."

"You held your breath for a really long time." As soon as the words came out of my mouth, I realized what a lame response that was.

Brody chuckled. "I'm good at a few things." He came closer to Caid and me.

"Aww, isn't that sweet," Caid said. "Dude, don't be upset if she cancels. Because she'll probably cancel."

I felt Caid's body tense. I leaned my face closer to his and nudged his cheek with my nose, and then traced his collar bone and the top of his chest lazily with my fingers. His body relaxed.

I was speechless. Brody was awfully brave to approach us like this. I admired his assertiveness. Gotta love a man who knows what he wants.

Brody grabbed my foot under the water and ran his hand up my calf. Oh my. I wriggled against Caid's back.

"It's okay, I'm a patient man." Brody slid his hand slightly above my knee. Any closer and he'd run into Caid's hand. Something about this man pushing boundaries like that made me hot. I rocked my hips and tightened my hold on Caid.

Brody winked at me, and then he disappeared into the water and swam away.

"He is in love with you. I should be pissed," Caid said, "but fuck, I felt you get all hot, and my dick got hard."

I stared at the water and waited for Brody to resurface, but Caid turned us around and floated in the other direction.

"What was that all about?" Stellan asked when he got back into the pool. He handed me a drink and floated behind me. His chest was pressed against my back. I squeezed my legs around Caid.

"Kenzie's human is obsessed with her," Caid said. "He thinks they have a date tomorrow."

"Is that right?" Stellan's breath fanned my neck. "Hmm . . . I'm pretty sure you'll be occupied tomorrow." He brushed his lips against my shoulder and my entire body shivered.

"Occupied doing what?" My voice was low and breathy.

Caid turned his body to face us while keeping my legs wrapped around his waist. Oh my, the seduction game was driving me fucking crazy.

"I'll give you two guesses." Caid stared at my mouth. I lifted the glass to his lips, he drank. I leaned my head back against Stel's shoulder. Stel pressed his glass to my lips and I took a sip but dribbled. I was about to wipe away the drops of stray alcohol, but Caid beat me to it. He gently swiped the corner of my mouth with his tongue.

I was creaming in my bikini. Between Brody's assertiveness and being so close to the brothers, my sensory nervous system was on overload.

Caid didn't kiss me. Stellan didn't kiss me, either. But Caid's hardness was in a perfect position against my crotch, and Stellan's hard length dug into my ass. Yeah, they were into this. Okay, we were into this.

"And perhaps, if your human doesn't annoy me, I'll let him watch," Stel whispered in my ear.

Hell yes. I made a slow exaggerated thrust of my hips. Caid closed his eyes and sucked in a breath. Stellan groaned and pushed harder into my back.

I was very familiar with lust and seduction, but this was so much more. My brain was short-circuiting. It was just too much.

Splash!

Someone jumped into the pool a few feet away from us, jostling me away from the brothers and splashing pool water into our drinks. Stel and Caid scowled at the intruder. I used that moment to float a little further away. If I didn't create some space from the brothers, I would, without a doubt, be having sex in the pool.

Caid and Stel stalked me in the water. I floated further away, and they kept coming until I was up against the side of the pool with nowhere to go.

"I have to pee," I blurted as I set my glass down on the edge, and they chuckled.

Stel also set his glass down on the edge and hoisted me up. He placed a kiss on my knee. I may have moaned a little.

"We'll be right here, love," Caid said from behind his brother.

When I got back from the ladies' room, I sat at the edge of the pool, and waited for a waitress to bring us fresh drinks. The guys were still in the pool on the opposite side from where I sat with my legs dangling in the water. They were joking around about something, laughing. I envied their bond and couldn't help fantasizing about having a tight-knit family of my own someday. That last thought caused the dull pain in my heart to flare for the second time. I quickly shoved the thought of having a family of my own away, along with the aching loss of it. I was determined to stay in the present, and not allow the ghosts of the past or phantoms of the future to plague me.

Over my left shoulder, I felt the presence of someone. "You don't belong here. You should leave," said the sultry female voice.

I looked over my shoulder. The woman who I sensed was a shifter. She crouched behind me, slightly to my left. Despite the menacing scowl on her face, she was stunning. Her honey-colored hair fanned out behind her and she had a perfect hourglass figure. I couldn't help but envy those curves even though I wasn't exactly flat chested.

"Are you speaking to me?" I raised my eyes to meet hers.

"You know I am, bitch. You should take your scrawny human ass out of here. The Alpha's sons deserve better than a human," she snarled.

Of course, she would call me scrawny. Next to her huge boobs and apple bottom ass, I practically looked like a strung-out crack whore. On a normal day, I was satisfied with my appearance, but this girl was really pressing my insecurity buttons.

"If they didn't want me here, they wouldn't have invited me. They can ask me to leave themselves."

"I'm speaking for them, that's what I do. If you don't leave on your own, I'll make you." She showed me rows of her sharp canine teeth.

Bloody fucking hell. I hated girls like this, and I was pissed that the guys were spoken for and had put me in this position. But it wasn't like me to back down, ever. Call it bravado, call it stupidity. Whatever it was, it prompted me to antagonize she-bitch further.

I gathered my magic, letting it build up in my fingers and up my arms and back. I turned my body to face her, smiled sweetly and said, "I'd like to see you try."

In a split second, she lunged toward me, snapping her canine teeth.

My magic gave me the power boost I needed to swiftly dodge her lunging body. Her teeth connected with my forearm but were unable to break my skin. *Ha!* I slipped an arm underneath her chest for leverage. My other arm slipped out of her jaw to the top of her neck I was able to grab hold of her hair, and I tossed her into the pool.

She-bitch hit the water with a splash. Wolves weren't known to be good swimmers. When I had asked Stellan about why he could swim, his response had been "I'm special."

This wolf didn't seem all that special to me, so I was not betting on the fact she could also swim. Since I dunked her in eight feet of pool water, I reacted quickly with my magic and pulled her out of the water, landing her safely on the side of the pool about a foot away from me. Once on dry land, I used more of my magic, water magic this time, and called to the water that filled her lungs and pulled. I didn't have to pull too hard, since she had only been under for a short time. I was being extra cautious because now I had an audience of upset, snarling shifters. Of course, she was coughing dramatically and making it look way worse than what it was. I did, however, make a move to harm one of their own, which would not go unnoticed. The tension made my skin crawl. Could this get any worse?

She looked like a drowned rat, and she was glaring daggers at me. With zero intention of apologizing, I stared her dead in the eyes.

"We understand each other, honey?" I said with conviction, making it clear that this was over.

She nodded, shuffled to her feet and stalked away.

The entire scene was done in under two minutes. The spike of adrenaline left my body, and the strain from using magic depleted my energy. I was about to pass out. Trying to play it cool, I steadied my breath and leaned back on my elbows as casually as possible.

Wet hands glided up my legs, startling me, but I was too tired to react. I lay there and watched Stellan pull my legs apart. That tingly feeling struck me again as our skin connected, and I felt a warmth starting at my core.

Between my legs, he hauled himself up halfway out of the pool. He paused when his face was directly in front of mine. "You okay?"

"Sure," I said, since that was the best thing I could come up with.

His body was completely over mine, but not touching. I was acutely aware of the proximity between us. Heat rolled off him, and droplets of water trickled off his body onto mine. I fought the urge to press my body to his, the need to feel the strength of his large muscular frame against my much smaller one was so strong.

He leaned down, placed a kiss gently on my lips, and then looked over at the crowd gathered around us. The crowd I forgot was there.

"Go," he said, power lacing his words.

As the crowd dispersed, he slid back into the water, taking me with him.

I was wiped out from expending magical energy. I slumped against him, clinging, not sure I could save myself from drowning if he let go. He gently turned my jaw and angled my face to his, so that our eyes met. He placed his lips against mine ever-so-gently, not as a kiss, but as though he was breathing into me. I pressed my mouth against his, harder, wanting a kiss, and I darted my tongue, licking his lower lip. He gasped and that's when I felt a sudden rush of magical energy wash through me. Shocked by this odd exchange, I pushed away from him a bit.

He shook his head and said, "It's fine, Kenzie. Take what you need."

Honestly, I had no idea what he meant. Before I could question him further, he had a hand on the back of my head, keeping me still while he pressed his lips to mine. The transfer of energy flooded through me once again and it was both heavy and light.

After a quick moment of the magical exchange, I felt energized and whole, as though he'd put me back together. I leaned against him with a sigh, and turned my head. He kissed my shoulder, his lips lingering on my skin. We drifted in the water, my arms around his neck, my legs wrapped around his waist.

"Feel better?" he asked.

"Yes, um . . . that was different. What was that?" My energy level was up. I couldn't run marathons at the moment, but at least I wouldn't pass out.

"A pack thing. I'm able to share power when one of mine is in need," he said almost reassuringly.

"One of yours?" I looked up at him.

He didn't say anything, but his smug smile told me the answer was yes.

"Really? When did that happen? I don't remember authorizing that," I said.

"Would it be so bad to let someone care about you, Kenzie?"

His question took me by surprise. I didn't know how to answer him at first. "I suppose not." It was lame but it was the only answer I could give him.

The sun was setting behind the mountains to the far west, casting the sky in brilliant hues of pinks and oranges. Twilight was my favorite time of day. I rested my face against his shoulder and sighed. A few people were still at the far end of the pool, and the cabana area we were in was empty.

"You cleared out the place," I said.

"I needed them to get busy elsewhere. Give them something else to do."

"Where did they go?" I skimmed my lips across his neck and goosebumps prickled on his flesh. I was proud to have such an effect on him.

"They'll go for a run and find some food. I'm not worried about them." He paused, then drew away to look at me. "That was quite the display of power there, beautiful."

"Combat mage," I said absently.

Concerned I might have painted a target on my back, I asked him nervously, "Is everything gonna be okay?"

"Of course! You did nothing wrong, sweetness. Caid and I were about to step in, but you threw her in the pool before we could blink. Obviously, you didn't need saving." He smiled. "Still, I apologize for Sandy's behavior. She gets territorial over us even though neither of us belong to her. We had a thing in the past, but she thinks there's still something there."

"Huh," I respond, resting my head on his shoulder, deep in thought.

Sandy was still in love with him or Caid or both of them. That sucked. I knew what that was like, pining over a guy that was over you. I felt like shit, even though I had no reason to. What they had was in the past. Then it dawned on me.

"Does she know that it's over?" I asked.

Some guys were unclear about how they felt and strung girls along. They gave them false hope and continued the sexual part of the relationship. It was a shitty situation, one I wasn't okay with.

"Hey, look at me," he said, drawing away from me again.

"You have nothing to worry yourself about. Sandy and I broke up over twenty years ago, possibly more. I have not slept with her since and have been with lots of other girls that she is fully aware of. It's a pack thing. We know everything about everybody. But there's nothing between Sandy and me, or between her and Caid."

"Talk to me. What are you thinking?" He ran a hand up and down my back.

"I umm . . . I probably should have asked this before . . . but is there someone, a significant other, waiting for you at home?"

"No, sweetness. Wolves mate once. A mated wolf couldn't have sex with anyone but his mate. It just wouldn't work."

"What about vamps?" I asked

"Vamps are similar. Mating happens for vamps but it is rare, and it's a blood thing. Shifters, wolves, we imprint and mark."

"Interesting." I relaxed, feeling better about the situation.

He held me in his arms as he climbed the stairs to get out of the pool.

"I can walk, you know," I told him, even though I loved being in his arms.

He was huge, and cradled me as though I weighed nothing. It was comforting and felt safe.

Stel paused on the pool deck, still holding me in his arms. I tilted my head to look at him and our lips met. His lips sucked on mine, then his tongue slowly swept through my mouth. I grasped the back of his head, my tongue caressed his, and I moaned against his mouth. My body tingled all over, while heat rose up in my core. He tried to break our kiss but I wasn't done yet. I sucked on his lower lip, and gently tugged it with my teeth. He groaned and I swooned in his arms. Now *that* was a kiss.

Reluctantly, he set me down on my feet. My knees wobbled a bit so I clung to him for a moment, my cheek against his chest.

When I stepped back, he asked, "Have dinner with me? Us?"

"Us?" I asked.

"Yeah, me and Caid. He went up to make sure the pack was doing as they were told."

"That was nice of him. But I . . ." I wanted to say yes. Food sounded amazing, but I was beat.

The power he'd loaned me helped tremendously. After using that much magic, I would normally be passed out by now. But going out to dinner was pushing it. He gave me a slight nod, appearing to notice my hesitation.

"We don't have to go anywhere. Maybe order in? Do something fancy tomorrow?" he asked, his eyes hopeful.

I stretched up on my tip toes and kissed his lower lip because that was as far as I could reach. "Thank you, yes, ordering in would be great."

He smiled, grabbed my hand, and led me upstairs.

CHAPTER 9

KENZIE

Alone in my condo, I literally lugged my tired ass up to the bathroom to get cleaned up. Being with them both was one of the most pleasant days I'd ever had. In all my life, I never felt like I belonged with two people more. It was like finding the missing pieces to a puzzle. I loved the mix of being friendly and flirtatious.

There had been intense heat between all three of us, and yet, I'd found myself glancing toward Brody. Sometimes I had caught him gazing my way, which made me smile. For some reason, I had felt like he'd fit right in with the three of us, or that could just be me fantasizing about having all three of them to myself. Greedy, perhaps, but I wasn't sorry. Why have one, when you can have three, am I right?

Still wrapped in my towel, I got my phone out of my purse and scrolled through to see that I'd missed one call from an unknown number. I listened to the message.

Hey Kenzie baby, it's Brody. The concierge transferred me to your voicemail, so hey, just wanted to say hi and leave my number. Just in case you can break away from your Alpha friends. 3107884966, call, text, whenever, no matter what time, Kenzie baby. Yeah, I have a new nickname for you. Can't wait to hear your voice.

I lay back on my bed, grinning up at the ceiling. He was a sweet guy and a private investigator. I dialed his number.

"Hello?" he answered. I could barely hear him over the background noise.

"Hi, I just got your message."

"Kenzie baby! I'm glad you called. Wanna hangout?"

"I'm good. And, um . . . sorry, but I have plans. I just wanted to call you back. Where are you?"

"We're in the casino, blackjack. I know this may sound a bit weird, but I miss you. Wish we had more time. Tomorrow, right? We'll talk about that thing if you're comfortable. If not, we can just hang out." Crowd cheering erupted from the background. "Sorry beautiful, it's crazy loud in here."

"Yes, tomorrow, works," I replied.

"Sweet. I'll text you in the morning." He sounded excited. "Hey, you looked stunning in that bikini. It was hard not to stare. What are you wearing tonight?"

"I haven't decided," I responded.

"You're naked right now? Aww babe, you're killing me."

I laughed, "I should get ready, Brody baby."

"No wait, baby, give me a minute. I need a moment to fully appreciate that visual. Are you completely naked?" He sounded hopeful. Men.

"No, not completely naked, and that's all you're gonna get. Go wild with your imagination." Suddenly feeling antsy, I turned over on my bed.

An amused chuckle rumbled through the phone. "That's cold, babe! But, okay, I'll let you go. The guys are getting restless. Thanks for calling back."

"Have fun and win lots of money."

"Will do, Kenzie baby. Have fun also. See you tomorrow."

A wistful smile splayed across my face as I ended the call.

Yeah, I was definitely onboard with seeing him again tomorrow. Something about that man had me hooked. Glancing at the time on my phone, I calculated I had ten minutes before the brothers arrived. On most occasions when men were involved, I liked putting in an effort to look nice. Tonight, I was too tired to care so I decided on a pink shorts onesie that had hearts on it. Freaking magic drain totally sucked. To finish up my prepping, I applied moisturizer, lip gloss, and combed out my still wet hair. I tried to use my magic to dry it, but the small amount of wind I could muster made me lightheaded, and I had to lie down for a moment.

I must've dozed off for a minute because the doorbell startled me awake. It was Stellan. I sensed him downstairs, or perhaps my mind knew to expect him so my body anticipated his presence. It wasn't a bad feeling, just odd.

"Coming," I called from my bedroom doorway and made my way down. Not sure why I yelled because I was sure they could hear me if I used my normal voice.

As soon as I opened the door, Caid scooped me up in his arms and spun us around, making me giggle. He kissed me full on the mouth before setting me down on my feet. "Did you miss me, Caid?"

"Yes, but I thought of you every second since I last saw you."

He was still holding me in his arms when Stel walked in. Someone with a cart piled with food walked in right behind him.

"We ordered from one of the restaurants downstairs, love. Hope you don't mind," Caid said, releasing me.

"Hi, sweetness." Stellan wrapped me in his arms as soon as Caid moved away. He kissed me passionately while Caid sorted out the food delivery.

Stel released me, leaving me breathless. He tilted my head up to meet his gaze and he assessed me. Without warning, he scooped me up in his arms.

"Are we eating in bed or down here?" he asked me.

I hesitated at first to answer because I'd rather be in bed, but I'd fall asleep if I got too comfortable. "Here is good."

Stel carried me and set me on the couch, then grabbed the nearest blanket and tucked it around my body. He was spoiling me rotten and I loved it. I should be calling him sweetness.

He and Caid brought the food over and started laying things out on the coffee table like we were having a picnic in my living room. Everything smelled delicious and my mouth watered. Ravenous, I moved to help them along, only to be pushed back on the couch by Caid.

"Relax, love, we got this. What would you like to drink?"

"Just water to start." I noticed the bottles of booze they brought with them.

"I'll get it," Stellan called over his shoulder as he made his way to my kitchen. He'd never been here before but he looked right at home.

"You look adorable in that little onesie," Caid said to me, a playful smile on his pouty lips.

"Thank you." I untucked my feet out from under me and placed them on his lap, my toes brushing against his arm.

"Yikes!" He flinched away from my icy feet.

"Fuck, love, your toes are freezing!" He cupped them in his hands and warmed them up.

"Oops, sorry," I said, giggling.

Stellan returned and dropped off a couple bottles of water and three wine glasses. He looked over at his brother, and then walked up the stairs. Yep, he was right at home for sure.

I watched Stel, and Caid was watching me. When I looked back at Caid, he flashed that megawatt smile of his.

"What are you thinking?" I asked.

"Oh nothing, just admiring. Your skin is silky smooth." He ran his hands up the length of my leg, one on the outside and one on the inside. When he reached my inner thigh, I could barely keep a moan from escaping my lips. I was suddenly hot and tingly all over.

I didn't hear Stellan return to the living room, but I sensed him behind me. He handed over a pair of socks to his brother. He must've gotten them out of my drawers. How he found them so quickly was beyond me, and I honestly didn't care. I didn't even care that he'd gone through my underwear drawer.

Caid slid the socks on my feet while Stel moved the pillows away and took their place. He propped me up against him so the brothers were on either side of me. I leaned back and stretched out my legs toward Caid. I was doing it again, that thing where all rational thought left me and all I could think about was sex and more sex. Stel kissed my neck, and Caid placed kisses on the inside of my knees.

"Food's getting cold, sweetness. And I know you're hungry. We can continue this later," Stel said.

I answered him with a moan, spreading my legs wider.

"He's right, love, we can continue this later." Caid closed my legs together.

I groaned in protest at the same time my tummy let out the loudest, most un-lady-like growl.

We all laughed, then sat around the coffee table and dug into the food.

They ordered from Papa Georgio's — the best Italian restaurant in The Majestic. I devoured everything. The last time I'd eaten was after training early this morning. After drinking at the pool all afternoon and using magic, my body was in sore need of some sustenance.

I was on my third plate of food. First, I'd had a little lasagna, then grilled swordfish and veggies topped with a lemon white wine sauce, and now, I was enjoying the last bit of chicken marsala and moving on to an Italian salad. I glanced up and they were staring at me.

"Damn, you can put away some food," Caid said in admiration.

"I love to watch you eat, sweetness, but are you sure you're not part shifter?" Stellan asked me between bites of food.

"What? I was hungry."

"No judgment, love, it's perfectly fine. It's just surprising is all," Caid said.

"And here I thought that's all you'd eat." Stellan pointed at my salad.

"We have dessert, right?" I smiled.

"Of course we do. I ordered everything, 'cause he told me to." Caid nodded toward his brother.

"Good call." I winked at Stellan.

Caid narrowed his eyes. "Hey, I was the one that did the ordering. You know? The heavy lifting."

"You sure did. Your ordering skills are exemplary," I told Caid, my lips curled into a mocking grin.

After dessert, we moved into the kitchen to clean up. I was more than happy to help, but they ushered me onto the barstool that allowed me to watch. There was something hot about seeing two muscular men doing the dishes. I was enjoying the view.

I tried to hide a yawn behind my hand, because I really didn't want the night to end.

They noticed my yawn, of course, and insisted on calling it a night after the kitchen was cleaned.

"Time for bed, sweetness." Stel pecked me on the cheek.

"What did you do earlier, at the pool, that pack magic thing?" I asked him. "There must be more to it. I felt energized. Usually when I use my magic like I did, it wipes me out for a good twenty-four hours."

Stel shrugged his shoulders, "I sensed you were weak, so I transferred a little pack magic to help you."

"Um . . . okay, thank you. But, is that allowed?" I looked to both of them for answers.

"We don't know, love. Stedman, one of the guys staying with us," Caid cocked his head, motioning to next door, "said it's an Alpha gift. Stellan here must be deeply connected to you, which is why he could do that."

"Have you done this before?" I asked Stellan.

"No."

"What about you?" I turned to Caid.

"Vamps are different. Masters have some connection to their seethe but not like shifters. Our way of bonding is through blood."

"Bonding? Did you bind me to you? You called me one of yours," I asked, suddenly fully alert.

"Well, maybe. Yes." Stellan scrubbed his hair through his blond locks.

"You can't just bind a person. That's a decision that two people should make, and I was not involved in that process." Honestly, I wasn't sure what to make of this. But I was awfully annoyed.

"Relax, sweetness." Stel rubbed my shoulder.

"Love, you are overreacting, we chose you as our mate," Caid said earnestly.

I gaped at them. "Wait both of you? What? How?"

"Try not to panic, love. We haven't marked you or anything, not really anyway; it wasn't anything formal. We both know without a doubt that we've met our mate." Caid pointed at me.

It was absurd, so I laughed. They had to be joking. "You must be joking. Right?"

Their faces were serious.

"Do you guys do this often? Meet girls you want to share and give them a story about making them your mate."

"No, never," Stel said with an adamant set to his jaw. "Well, not no, I mean, we've shared before but have never found our mate. There's only one mate for our species, Kenzie. We just happen to have the same one."

"Shared what?" I immediately regretted asking.

"Women," Stel said, not appearing willing to offer up more.

"Love, we're one hundred and twenty-two years old. There's been tons of women in our lives. The last time we shared was the woman in . . ." Caid started to say, but I rushed over to him, clasped a hand over his mouth and shut him up.

"No, hell no. Not another word." Thinking about them sharing another woman had me pissed as all get out. Anger mixed with a nasty side of jealousy had me huffing. Needing a little space, I drew my hand from his mouth and walked into the living area.

"Love, I'm sorry." Caid wrapped his arms around me.

"You really don't need to apologize. I'm being unreasonable. But please, no details. I just might shoot a bitch in the face." I knew I was being ridiculously unreasonable, but I couldn't seem to help myself. I blamed my newfound jealousy on being tired, and yawned audibly.

Before I knew it, Caid was carrying me, following Stellan upstairs.

He deposited me in the middle of the mattress and Stel pulled the covers over me. They both placed kisses on my head and wished me goodnight. It registered that they were leaving me, so I sat straight up.

"Don't go. Stay, please."

They glanced at each other, silently communicating, then climbed in bed with me, keeping me in the middle.

My head was resting comfortably on Stellan's shoulders, and he spoke softly to me, "Kenzie, there never was or ever will be anyone but you for us. I know it's a lot so soon, but we know we've found our mate. Wolves, for one, imprint quickly. Vamps sense blood that is a match to their own. We're not rushing you into anything and we'll gladly answer any question you have."

"This seems very sudden. I don't know where to begin," I said honestly, then sat up to face them. "I don't mean any disrespect to your shifter and vamp customs or traditions, but mating for life with a person you don't even know seems absolutely ridiculous."

"Love, it's not so bad having the both of us as mates," Caid said. "We're predators, yes, but it's not like we're out there killing random people."

I paused, thinking about his statement and my merc life. "What if . . . what if I was out killing people?" I asked them.

"That just made my dick hard," they both said at the same time, and then they pulled me back down to mattress.

"You two are impossible," I giggled, even though it was a serious question.

But they weren't lying. I could feel how hard they were with their bodies pressed against mine. Stupid magic burn had the worst timing. I really hated to waste a good hard on, or two, in this case, but my body wasn't having it. I thought about making them do all the work, and then decided against it. I didn't want them to think I was a shitty lay.

Stel snuggled into my side and said, "Seriously, sweetness, for us, it's not sudden. It's undeniable. We couldn't have resisted this bond even if we tried. I don't regret it."

"Claiming you means we are yours, that's all, love. And we're not shy about it. We want everyone to know. And that part means our species will scent that you've been claimed and shifters and vampires will stay away from you," Caid added, cuddling my other side.

"That doesn't sound so bad," I said in a sleep-tinged voice.

There was probably a lot more to it, but I was lying on my bed safe and comfortable between two insanely hot men. I was not going to kick them out of bed. Not tonight anyway. I didn't have the energy.

Stellan placed a kiss on my head and Caid nuzzled into my breasts. Sandwiched between them, completely content, I fell asleep.

It was still dark outside when I woke up. My legs were numb due to Stellan's much larger, much heavier leg resting on top of mine. The top of my onesie was askew, buttons undone. Stellan's lips were pressed against my bare shoulder. I was on my back with my head leaning on Caid's shoulder, our arms entwined. We looked like we were doing a sleeping version of Twister.

My body was hot and sweaty from all the body heat in my bed. Stel and Caid were snoring, sleeping soundly.

I needed to stretch a bit, so as gently as I could, I slid my legs out from under Stellan, and he rolled over. I stretched my legs overhead and brought my knees close to my chest without waking Caid.

When I lowered my legs back on the mattress, Caid rolled over. His head moved to the crook of my neck and one of his arms snaked between my legs. Holding my breath, I tried to remain as still as possible in this precarious position. His forearm rested across my stomach along my pubic area, and his hand was almost cupping my pussy. The slightest movement caused a bit of friction, and I had the urge to grind on his hand harder.

Stel turned again, lying flat on his back. His hand landed on my knee spreading my legs further apart and opening my shorts. Caid's hand was scant millimeters from my exposed pussy. Uh-oh.

I was wide awake now, and my heart rate quickened. The heat from Caid's hand warmed my core and drove me crazy. Juices flowed between my folds, and I wanted so much for him to touch me. I took a silent but deep breath, and the movement of my chest shifted his arm away in the opposite direction of where I wanted it.

They looked peaceful. I really should have left them alone, closed my eyes and went back to sleep. But I couldn't. My greedy cunt wanted attention. I tilted my hips up slightly, and Caid's hand was now directly over my pussy. The fabric of my onesie was between us but he was directly where I needed him to be. I pulled both knees higher up, bringing Stellan's hand to my inner thigh and the heel of Caid's palm directly over my clit.

Yes! This I could work with. I pushed my hips up ever so gently, slowly grinding and delivering pleasurable tingles throughout my body. The pressure was so light, it was maddening. I closed my eyes and did my best to keep my moans to a minimum. The fabric covering my pussy was completely wet. The slow, gentle build-up and having to hide my pleasure sent my pulse into overdrive. Slowly, and gently, I continued rubbing my pelvis against Caid's hand.

I wanted more though. I needed them in me. The thought of being filled by both of them had my hips practically bucking.

Without warning, Caid plunged in his finger. I barely stifled a loud moan. Trying my best not to wake Stellan, I shoved the thin fabric of my onesie to the side, and pushed Caid's finger in further, chasing my orgasm. Caid was fully awake, and he rolled his thumb in gentle circles around my clit, pumping his finger in and out. My pleasure was building. My pussy was so wet, every thrust produced a loud sucking sound.

Caid pulled down my onesie and pulled out my breast to suck on my hard nipple. I wiggled and tried to undress, wanting to be completely naked for him.

Once the onesie was off, he rolled me to my side, facing me toward Stellan. He withdrew his finger and quickly replaced them with his hard, throbbing cock. He held me tight against his torso as he slid in slowly from behind. Inch by glorious inch, he took his time, allowing my body to adjust to his massive girth. Once he was completely sheathed into my cunt, I gasped louder than I'd intended.

Stellan woke up and stared directly into my eyes. Desire flickered in his gaze. I wanted him, too. I wanted to feel them both. He must have noticed what I wanted because he leaned in and pressed his lips to mine while his brother continued to fuck me. Caid's thrusts weren't gentle. His body was slamming into mine. He reached around and flicked my clit. I immediately came undone, and bit down on Stel's lip.

I was still riding my orgasmic waves when Caid said, "Suck my brother's cock while I fuck you, love."

He flipped me over so my ass was in the air and my mouth was at the perfect angle to suck on Stellan's enormous cock. I swiped my tongue over his velvety, smooth skin, licking up every drop of precum seeping out the head. Caid plowed into my pussy, gripping my ass cheeks, which I was sure would be nice and bruised later.

My head bobbed up and down on Stellan's cock as I stroked and sucked at the same time. I took as much of him in my mouth as I could. My eyes watered as he hit the back of my throat. I moaned around his cock as Caid pumped into me relentlessly. With one final thrust, he groaned and his hot seed exploded inside of me.

Stellan withdrew his cock from my mouth and pulled me away from his brother. He flipped me on my back and dragged me to the foot of the bed where he covered my body with his. Stel kissed me, then turned my head so I had to look at Caid who was sitting on his heels, cock still hard and slick with my juices and his. I licked my lips.

"You want to suck all those juices off his cock, sweetness?"

I nodded eagerly. Caid moved closer, bringing the tip of his thick cock to my lips. The taste of his cum and mine mixed together made me want to explode all over again. I released his cock with a pop and looked over at Stellan.

"Fuck me, Stel."

He happily complied, throwing my ankles over his shoulders, and lined up with my core. He sank into me slowly and watched me take his brother into my mouth. I came again as soon as he was buried deep inside me. My body trembled from the aftershocks of my second orgasm. With Caid in my mouth, I moaned and gasped. The angle I was in made it hard to deep throat Caid, so I ran my tongue up and down his shaft and sucked greedily on his head, massaging his balls. Stellan pumped his hips, moving his large cock in and out of me. My legs were straight up in the air and held up against his chest.

I caressed Caid's balls while I sucked and stroked him, matching Stel's thrusts in and out of my pussy.

My body was overwhelmed with pleasure and need. I wanted this to last forever. I wanted to be fucked like this always. They spoiled me. No other lover could ever compare.

Caid's balls tightened up at the same time my pussy squeezes Stellan's cock.

Stellan let out a groan, "I fucking love your tight little cunt."

Caid came in my mouth, his cum dripping all over my lips. I swallowed every drop, rolling his dripping seed around my tongue.

"That's so fucking hot," Stellan cried, pumping faster.

My body spasmed as I climaxed once again while he shot his load. I arched my back and groaned.

He collapsed on top of me and rolled over, keeping me between him and Caid who was now pressed against my back and kissing my shoulders. I reached an arm behind me to hook around Caid's neck, my other hand stroking Stel's hair. I was a sweaty mess. We all were. But I didn't care. The pleasure thrumming through every part of my body was well worth it. Relaxed, I closed my eyes.

The room was silent, other than the sounds of our heavy breathing. I was aware of a warm cloth brushing against my tender pussy. It wasn't erotic. It was gentle and nurturing. One of the guys was cleaning me. When two sets of arms enveloped me, I drifted off into a deep sleep, completely sated.

Voices drifted up to my room from downstairs. Panicked, I sat up in bed, rolled over to the side and reached behind the nightstand to find my .22 pistol. My onesie was wrapped around my ankle, and my sex was nice and tender. Maybe Caid and Stellan were still here. Excitement tickled my stomach. With a sigh, I reached down to pull up my onesie and headed downstairs, the .22 still in my hand . . . just in case.

From the landing I could see Stellan on the phone and Caid typing on a tablet. Relieved it was them and not an intruder inside my house, I relaxed and watched them. They were both so handsome. They had that fresh out-of-bed look. Caid's hair was sticking up all over the place, a frown marring his beautiful face, his gray eyes focused. Whatever he was working on was puzzling. Stellan was shirtless, staring out the window, one arm propped against the glass, his muscular back on full display. From the anger in his voice, it sounded like whoever was on the other line was receiving the riot act. Often times, people were completely themselves when no one was looking. Stel and Caid were relaxed yet confident. They were doing different tasks yet working together. Their combined synergy was evident and awe-inspiring.

Instead of bothering them, I went back to my bathroom and began my usual morning routine. I almost skipped showering because their scent still lingered on my skin, and I found it comforting, but my lady parts needed a wash so I hopped in the shower.

The hot water glided over my skin, washing away the remnants of my activities last night. I sighed as the memories came flooding back. What a surreal night. I wasn't a prude when it came to sex and I had my share of experiences, but hooking up with two at the same time was a first. And those two were next level shit. Definitely an experience I'd like to repeat. I smiled to myself as I dried off, got dressed, and then took my happy ass downstairs to greet them.

Stel abruptly ended the conversation he was having and stalked toward me. He stopped a few inches in front of me, sweeping his gaze over my body. I was both nervous and aroused. He placed his large hands gently on each side of my face, and kissed me. I melted into him, swooning from his reverent caresses.

"Good morning, my mate," he said between kisses.

I soaked in everything he was giving me. My mate. That was different but in a good way.

Caid stepped up behind me, his body pressed against mine. He kissed my neck and down to my shoulders, and shivers ran from my head to my toes. I felt like I was floating and my two guys were floating with me. Their kisses, and this moment changed everything.

CHAPTER 10

KENZIE

Over the next few days, the three of us were together as much as possible. I was still not entirely on board with the whole bonding idea, but the more time I spent with them, the more I accepted it. They stayed at my place, working remotely alongside me. I was getting really comfortable having them around.

Caid was right when he'd said I'd cancel my date with Brody. I was busy doing . . . the brothers. The sex was addicting.

One day, Tom called and asked, "Any luck finding a private investigator?" I had forgotten all about Knox and couldn't put that off any longer. I texted Brody to meet for lunch.

Caid and Stel assured me that life as I knew it wasn't going to change much. Well, mate or not, I had a life to live, a business to run, and an appointment with a very hot private investigator.

The brothers' weren't happy to hear about my lunch date.

Doubt flashed over Caid's eyes.

"Hey, I like you more." I caressed his cheek and he relaxed.

Stel was sitting on the sofa in my living room, calm and silent. He extended his hand to me, and I held it and perched on his lap.

"Kenzie." He crushed me to his body. "I want to say no. But I know if I do, you'll run away and then I'd have to chase you down and bring you back to me caveman-style."

I chuckled. "Stel, it's just lunch and business. If I promise not to have sex with him, will that make you feel better?"

"Somewhat." He paused, thinking, and rubbed his lips together.

He was going to add other conditions to my meeting. What did I get myself into?

"No sex. Caid and I get to stay here. And . . . you let us take you out tonight," he said with seriousness.

I agreed to his terms, got dressed and was ready to leave when Caid stopped me at the front door. "No, hell no." He swept his discerning gaze over my body from head to toe, and shook his head.

"What now?" I glanced at Stel who was also shaking his head.

"You look beautiful, sweetness." Stel crushed me to him.

I was wearing a white skirt that sat low on my hips and a cropped light blue scarf-print halter that showed off my belly.

"Do you have to dress up, love?" Caid pressed his body to my back.

I sighed, and then pulled away from them. "I love being with both of you, but this isn't going to work. I have friends, male friends. And I like Brody. You know this. You've read his texts. I'm not saying that I will run off and marry the guy. I just want to be with him for a little while." I didn't want to end it with Caid and Stel, but I didn't want them to start telling me what to do. If this is what it was going to be like after a few days, the rest of our lives together would be hell. Nope. Not having it.

Both men decided they would rather work through this than walk away. With reluctance, they escorted me to the elevators and gave me a kiss. They were trying to prove I still had my independence.

I left the brothers and met Brody at Triton, a seafood restaurant. He waited for me at a table that overlooked the water gardens below. He stood when he saw me approaching, a big smile on his face.

I smiled back, looking him over from head to toe. He was wearing jeans and an untucked light blue button-down shirt. I remembered getting a glimpse of him shirtless at the pool and felt sad that he was dressed. He had the same muscular physique as Caid but was maybe an inch or two shorter.

I expected a quick peck on the cheek, but Brody was certainly not shy as I had originally thought. He went all out with the kisses. His full lips were soft against mine, and I parted my lips for his tongue. He left me breathless, and I moaned into his mouth.

"Hello, beautiful," he said breaking our kiss.

"Hi, handsome."

He put a hand on the small of my back and pulled out my chair. Then he sat next to me instead of on the opposite side of the table.

We ordered right away and as soon as the waiter left, he leaned over. "I love kissing you."

Kissing wasn't sex. I did feel guilty, truly I did, but his touch felt so good. Fuck me. I had issues.

Our food arrived, but we hardly touched it. We were more focused on one another. The restaurant was shutting down to make the transition from lunch to dinner, so before they threw us out, Brody wanted to find more out about the investigative services I needed.

"Talk to me, Kenzie baby. How can I help?" Brody held my hand and gave me his full attention.

I told him about Avery Knox showing up in my office and what Tom had discovered so far.

"You seem awfully calm for someone that received a threat." He made small circles on my hand with his thumb.

"He wasn't all that threatening," I said and offered no more.

Brody looked into my eyes as though I was a puzzle he was determined to figure out. That was fine. He could guess all he wanted.

"Avery Knox, easy enough. And all you need is his laptop and phone?" He tapped on his phone.

"Yes, and I'll text you Tom McGinnis's info. He's my head of security at my building. He can give you all the latest." I sent him a quick text, so I wouldn't forget later.

"Got it." He put his phone away.

"And of course, I will pay you. Please send me an invoice," I said.

"No, consider it a favor for a friend." He kissed my cheek. At some point, we repositioned our chairs to face one another, and my legs were caught between his. His hands rested on my knee.

"But you can have dinner with me." He kissed my neck.

"Dinner?" I tilted my head so he could continue kissing my neck. "Okay." I kissed him back.

"I'll have answers for you by morning," he said to me.

"No you won't," I said, wondering how anyone could work that fast.

He chuckled. "Are you doubting my ability to perform, beautiful?"

I laughed. "Perhaps I am." I uncrossed my legs and my skirt rode up and exposed more flesh.

"Good," he said with an eager tone. "I'm dying to impress you." His hands slid up just above my knee. I groaned.

Out of the blue, he asked, "Are you serious with the vamp and the wolf?"

That was a very personal and very direct question. I wasn't sure how to answer him. I paused to think about it. "I like them a lot. And I feel guilty being here with you," I finally said.

"You feel guilty because you like me, too. Good, I like you a lot." He kissed my neck again.

"You can't possibly." I rolled my eyes.

"Why not?" He let out an amused laugh.

"Because. I just told you I like two guys."

"So?" He drew away from me to look directly into my eyes.

"So?" I arched an eyebrow at him.

"I know I'm human, but the human stereotypes of how relationships should be defined is not something I agree with. Plus, I find myself lucky to be able to spend any amount of time with you. You're mesmerizing. Tremendously."

I had no idea how to respond to that. Thankfully he didn't pressure me for an answer. Instead, he gave me a long, slow, sensual kiss. It was exhilarating. I kissed him back, running my fingers through his hair. Brody moaned against my lips, and he moved his hands down to my knees again, and slid them over my thighs.

Being with Caid and Stel was incredible, but I could not get Brody out of my head. Kissing him like this made it nearly impossible.

He drew back and nibbled on my ear. "What did they say about me?"

"If you're not annoying, you can watch," I blurted and he sat back and let out a hearty laugh.

"Wow. That was not the answer I was expecting. I am going to do my absolute best not to be annoying." He cupped my face and kissed me on the mouth.

"Excuse me," someone said beside our table.

Brody and I broke apart and laughed. The restaurant manager waited patiently for us to leave.

We left the restaurant and said a sensual goodbye at the elevators. Our kisses were full of promises of what was to come later. He knew about my feelings for Caid and Stel and about my plans with them for the evening. Brody didn't make a fuss about it at all. He was gentlemanly about the situation and ushered me into the elevator, promising to keep me updated with the Knox situation.

As soon as I exited the elevators on my floor, Stel opened my front door as though he'd known I was in the corridor.

"We kissed, but we didn't have sex." I said, feeling a little guilty.

"We know." He pulled me into my place and whisked me up to my room where Caid was waiting, and then tore my clothes off.

CHAPTER 11

KENZIE

I was thoroughly sated and late for dinner. The nice thing about rushing to get ready was I didn't have time to be too picky about outfits.

I chose a red, flowy satin dress. The halter style accentuated my breasts and cinched my waist with an A-line skirt that flowed around my hips. It was short but long enough to hide my sheath for my dagger. I couldn't be too careful considering I had no idea where we were going. I chose red peep-toe Louboutin heels and a small purse. I accessorized with diamond stud earrings, a diamond-encased anklet, and left my neck bare. With a final swipe of lip gloss, I was ready to go.

"Right on time, beautiful. I'm impressed." Stel placed a kiss on my cheek.

"You look ravishing," Caid said, drinking in my appearance. Then he rushed to me, and enveloped me in his arms, kissing my lips.

"Thank you, Caid; you clean up nice. Both of you." I eyed them up and down.

Caid wore a pinstripe gray suit, sans tie. His hair was combed back neatly, his face freshly shaven. Stellan wore a black suit, and the dark color brightened his blond hair and enhanced the paleness of his eyes.

Their suits were expensive and tailored to their muscular physiques. How did I get so lucky? I kissed Caid's cheek. Then I held Stellan's outstretched hand and placed a kiss on the corner of his mouth. With my men on either side of me, we headed to the restaurant which was conveniently located in The Majestic.

As we walked into Stetsons Steakhouse, Caid on one arm, Stellan on the other, the hostess sized me up. Yep, I was a lucky bitch, and I was planning to enjoy every moment of it. Both men were completely stunning in their own right. They commanded attention from everyone. It was arousing to see both men and women lust after them from afar. All the ladies wanted to be me and gave me skunk eye as we walked by and that reaction made me giddy.

The hostess led us to the back of the restaurant to a large half-circle booth on a raised platform. We could see the restaurant in its entirety yet we were seated far back enough that it was almost private and intimate. I slid into the middle of the booth, the plush velvet seating soft against my skin. I rubbed my arms, warding off the chill from the air conditioning, until both men slid their big bodies into the booth, warming me. Caid draped an arm around me, and Stel glided his hand down my leg.

The server introduced himself and showed us two bottles of wine. "From our private collection. Would you like red or white wine, Mrs. Reese, or can I get you something from the bar?"

"Red, please." Wait. What? I did a mental double take.

"Of course." He poured the wine. "Your first course will be out momentarily." The server bowed, and then left.

The guys started laughing.

"Why did he call me Mrs.?" I asked the two squirrelly brothers. "You told him to say that." I rolled my eyes.

"No, no, we didn't, I swear, but your face, love, that was priceless," Caid said, still laughing.

"It's not that funny," I huffed.

"The best part is you answered him." Stel scooted closer so that he could kiss me.

"I was shocked." I allowed him to kiss my cheek.

"Sweetness, would it be so bad for you to be ours?" Stel said with a serious expression.

Oh no, here we go again.

"Do you have something against marriage, love?" Caid sat closer to me as well.

"No, I loved being married. It just didn't work out," I said. They were silent, and I couldn't stop talking. "He wanted to have children and I can't." I blurted my most private secret, which was unusual for me, so I grabbed my wine glass and took a huge sip.

"He's an idiot, love." Caid kissed my shoulder.

"I'm glad he's an idiot because now you're ours. His loss." Stel hooked my chin to kiss me. His tongue parted my lips and did a playful swirl through my mouth. "Mmm, that's good red wine," he said.

I was grateful for the change of subject even though admitting my deepest insecurity to them didn't make me want to fall apart in tears.

"What about you two?" I asked.

"No marriages for either of us." Stel pointed at himself and his brother.

"Lots and lots of umm . . . relationships, but nothing serious," Caid said.

"You were going to say sex." The thought of them having lots of sex with other women irritated me.

They both laughed. "I like it when you get jealous, sweetness." Stel grasped my hand and kissed the inside of my wrist.

I didn't like it. Jealousy was not a good look on me. I took another swig of wine.

The waiter placed a salad in front of me and about five different appetizers in the middle of the table.

"We took the liberty of ordering, sweetness," Stel said.

"I trust you," I said. "So tell me, how was your meeting today?"

The smaller packs that were in town for the conference all wanted an audience with the Republic. Stel was often stressed about meetings, and I was hoping he would open up to me at some point. I wasn't trying to be nosey, but I wanted him to know that he could confide in me.

He compressed his lips. Caid wasn't that tight-lipped about things. "Strange shit is going on, love. Tell her, Stel."

Caid was so good at knowing what I wanted and even better at prompting Stel to respond to me.

"Pack members have gone missing in California. They all think these shifters or vamps have come to us. We cross-referenced their lists with our records and nothing is matching up. It's like those shifters disappeared into thin air." Stel rubbed his chin.

Shifters always had to register with the new pack when they moved. It was odd that shifters moved suddenly and hadn't reappeared . . . somewhere.

"What are the Alphas in California saying? If members have moved territories, there must be a reason. That seems like a good place to start," I offered.

"The Alphas and Betas haven't showed up yet. We're getting these reports from concerned families," Caid replied.

"Well, that doesn't sound good. Hmm . . ." I thought through the situation trying to figure out if there was anyone in California that would have some insight.

"Okay, so you may not want to hear this, but it's just a thought. Brody owns a security firm that was doing a lot of business in California. Perhaps he could help," I said with a small voice. I was just trying to help. Neither of the guys said a word. I sat there, nervous tension squeezing my shoulders.

"That's a great idea, sweetness," Stel said. "I was trying to figure out a way to do some investigating without alerting the packs. A human firm would do the trick. Plus, I'd love to meet him . . . your human."

I climbed onto Stel's lap, straddled his legs, and then kissed him with passion. He was trying to involve me in small ways, which meant a lot, and he was also making an effort to meet a friend of mine.

The server stepped up to the table and cleared his throat. I stopped kissing Stel and slowly sat back in my seat.

I was very pleased with everything the guys ordered. We had a delicious five course meal that could feed an army. And I didn't hesitate. I always had a big appetite. I wasn't a shifter, but I could eat like one, which the brothers thought was adorable. I was lucky to have a fast metabolism. It must be a Fae thing. Besides, all I had for lunch earlier was Brody's lips. *Mmm . . .*

"What does this human of yours say about us?" Caid asked, using his fork to point at himself, then me, then Stel.

"Umm . . . well, he said he would do his best not to annoy you. I'm guessing so he could watch." My voice got softer at the end.

Both brothers set their forks down and looked at me, then glanced at each other, and then started laughing their asses off. They were bowled over in their seats with laughter, tears coming out of their eyes.

It wasn't that funny. The idea of it was hot, though; the corners of my lips turned up in a smile.

Our dessert arrived with flare. Bananas Foster was made at the table, and they had ordered chocolate lava cake and seven-layer ice cream cake, supposedly all for my benefit because they weren't sure what I preferred. I was amazed at how attentive they were to my preferences and how they went out of their way to make me happy. It wasn't that difficult when it came to dessert since I was a sugar freak anyway, and I had every intention of having at least one bite of everything.

As we were enjoying our sugary delights, a shifter approached our table. He kept his head lowered. "Excuse me, sir, I have an important message for you."

"We're in the middle of dinner. It can wait," Stellan said in a quiet yet deadly voice.

Apparently, he'd made it clear he would not be interrupted during dinner.

"I'm sorry sir, this cannot wait, I'm afraid," the shifter said, eyes still focused on the floor.

I could feel the tension radiating off of Stellan. He was in charge of the shifters here until his father arrived. This, whatever it was, must be important. I leaned over to him, pressing my upper body into his massive arm, and when our bodies connected, the tension slid off him. I turned his face to meet mine and kissed him on the lips, and then whispered, "Go, it's important. I'll be here waiting with Caid."

He kissed me. "I'll be right back." After standing, he looked at Caid. "Don't let her eat all of my dessert," he said with a smile.

I glanced at Caid and said, "I'm so gonna, just because he said that." I took a swipe of the chocolate lava cake.

"I heard that," Stellan said while walking away.

Caid laughed and said, "You handled that quite well. Any other time he would've ripped Mark's head off for interrupting him."

"Really? He's a hot head, huh?"

"He's been groomed to take over the pack and has done a great job of it. It's stressful though. I'm glad I'm not him."

"So, what is your role in all of this, the pack and all that? You're brothers. Don't you have to share the burden?"

"No and yes. We are brothers. His parents are my parents, and we are a family in every way that matters. I'm a vamp, a day walker though, and I've got troubles of my own. My role is keeping peace with the seethe in Texas. The masters of the seethes there are old. They don't like me much because of what I am, but Dad is Alpha for a reason. He is more powerful in every sense, and he keeps them in line."

Caid continued talking, and I continued eating and listening.

"We've been dealing with all the Alphas and Masters across the nation. They're worried about the vamp and shifter alliance in Texas and how quickly our pack has grown. Plus, the whole California puzzle is a problem. Thanks for recommending your friend, by the way. That will be helpful."

"It bothers me that you both are under so much pressure. It makes me want to help."

He patted my hand. "You are, love, more than you realize. You are."

"So, obviously there's something happening on the West Coast and you two are here to figure out what that is?"

"Yep." Caid nodded.

"Does that mean you and Stel are targets?" I frowned.

"Yes, there are always Alphas and Betas from other packs that think taking us out, especially Stel, will derail our Alpha. They think that Dad's following has a lot to do with the fact that he has an heir a powerful one. With Stellan out of the picture, Dad's empire comes tumbling. That's what they think, but it'll never happen." He shrugged.

"Why is that? Not everyone is indestructible." I cocked my head to the side.

"Dad groomed us both for this life. We've spent all of our lives studying and training to become warrior leaders. We're ready for the unexpected," Caid said casually.

"It's a lot to bear. Yet, you seem incredibly chill about everything." I moved around the seven-layer ice cream cake around on my plate.

"I spent some time with my sire and his seethe. My sire and his second, actually almost every member of that seethe, are fucking psychos. His second thought he could break me and turn me against my brother and my dad. That was a complete shit show. It was the worst time of my life. Stellan saved me from the madness. And Dad, well, he made sure those fuckers would never touch me again. After that hell, I just appreciated everything I have – my brother, my parents, my life amongst the pack. Not everything smooth sailing but everything, even this shit show we're dealing with, is a million times better than dealing with my sire. If I never see that asshole again it will be too soon." He had a faraway look in his eyes.

He seemed vulnerable after revealing so much. I admired his outlook on life and his appreciation for his family. Wanting to comfort him, I hugged him, and then kissed him on the lips.

I pulled away, cupped his face and said, "Your sire sounds like an asshole, I'm glad you're nothing like him."

He leaned into my hand. "Yeah, he is. Day walkers are apex predators, and we kill because it's our nature. It's like we were created to be killing machines. That's what he is, just a killing machine. Me? I can kill just as easily but choose not to. I choose to be different."

My poor vamp. I knew exactly how he felt as I considered my own combat mage lineage. I climbed onto his lap and kissed him as though our lives depended on it.

"What did I miss?" Stellan settled back into the booth. He was light on his feet for a big man.

Both men were capable of taking care of themselves, yet suddenly I was nervous about their safety. I did not like hearing some assholes were targeting their lives.

I settled back into my seat and reached for Caid's hand, and then pulled Stellan in for a kiss.

"Everything okay?" I asked Stel.

"Yeah. Fine. Just some concerns about Dad's arrival. We got it handled." He glanced at Caid. "You? You seem anxious."

"I gave her some background about what we're dealing with here. I think our girl is worried about our safety," he said with a small smile.

"Is that right?" Stellan put an arm around me. "We got this, sweetness."

I was not assured though. Something warned me this whole situation was dangerous and they were in the middle of it. My mind was spinning. I tried to puzzle this out, but I didn't have enough information. It was frustrating me.

Caid must have noticed that I was lost in thought. He massaged my bare leg, and asked "Tell us what you're thinking, love?"

"I'm just processing. And yes, I am concerned. I know it's not my business, but I wish I could help somehow."

"Aww, love, you care," he said in a sweet sing-song voice.

I smacked his arm.

"Excuse me, sirs, Mrs., is there anything else we can get you?" the server said, getting our attention.

"No, we're good." Caid sat straight up.

"Thank you, everything was exceptional," I said to the server.

"You're very welcome, Mrs. Reese," he said with a bow.

I didn't have the heart to correct the poor dude. Both brothers snickered.

Stellan took another bite of his dessert. "Thanks for leaving me a bite," he said to me with a smirk.

"Come on, love, the night is young." Caid extended his hand to help me out of the booth.

KENZIE

From the restaurant, we made our way down to the hotel's lowest floors. Most hotels and nightclubs humans frequented were located either on rooftop lounges or inside clubs; many boasted city views. For supes, we went down, down, down, down.

When The Majestic was built, they had dug deep. Magical folk were comfortable underground. That was where most liked to play. Play for supes could be violence, or sex, or both. One of the key attractions of The Majestic was The Dungeon. Humans thought their MMA cage fighting matches were the shit. The Dungeon made that look like kids playing in a sand box. It was brutal, and deadly. The Dungeon was the only area of The Majestic that allowed violence, killing included. Everywhere else in the hotel was considered neutral territory.

We weren't heading to The Dungeon tonight. Instead, we went farther down, to The Catacombs.

The Catacombs was the largest and hottest club on the Strip specifically catering to supes. Each floor was dedicated to a different genre of music and different levels of kink. The lower you went, the more deviant the kink. Humans were not allowed, unless they were guests of a registered supe. I had been here before, once or twice, but only on the first two levels. I was curious to see what else The Catacombs had to offer.

We bypassed a long line of people and walked right into the club. Caid took the lead with me in the middle and Stellan behind me.

The first floor played hip hop and rap music. At first glance, it seemed like a basic human club. People danced to the music's pulsating bass, and there was VIP seating around the dance floor. On the back wall was the bar, at least six people deep. One of the main differences were the go-go dancers. At a human club, the dancers were scantily clothed, but here male and female dancers were completely nude, and they danced on small stages surrounded by patrons. Guess you could say it was a strip club and a dance club all in one. However, if you wanted more than just naked bodies dancing, you needed to go down a floor.

The second floor played house music, and had a live DJ. Like the first floor of the club, there was a dance floor, and a packed bar. Instead of naked dancers, like on the first floor, this floor had a voyeur room located behind the bar. There was one main stage where performers were engaging in various sexual acts. Private rooms lined the back wall, and patrons could watch private performances by their favorite performers.

We continued down the stairs, bypassing the first two levels. I looked around as we passed by and scanned the crowd. I thought I saw one of the guys that had been with Brody down by the pool, so I hesitated and strained my neck a bit.

"Oh no you don't, gorgeous. You're with us," Caid said to me.

I was so busted! I smiled, embarrassed heat creeping up my cheeks and allowed him to guide me.

"Where are we headed?" I shouted over the music.

"One more level, love," Caid shouted back.

The third floor was larger, twice the size as the other floors. It had the same layout as the first two, but the dance floor and bar were larger. And there were a lot more people, too.

The bar here carried only magically brewed alcohol. And unlike any bar in the entire town, this was the only one to offer human blood, straight from the vein. Willing humans were displayed like mannequins on one wall, and they held placards that indicated their blood type. Some scantily clad donors walked the floor like waitresses, offering a drink from their vein. Now that I thought about it, I had never seen Caid drink blood. Maybe day walkers didn't need it as much.

The kink section here was one big orgy. The brothers checked us in with the hostess, who allowed us to take a tour. There were locker rooms set up, where patrons could undress and purchase masks, for anonymity. From the locker rooms was the entrance to what they called the "Play Room."

Everyone here was naked and fucking. Men and women, women and women, men and men, they were all going at it.

Everything about this room was titillating. There was something about naked flesh, and watching people have sex that got me all riled up. A naked foursome caught my attention. The woman was on top of one man, while another took her from behind and another had his cock deep in her throat. I imagined being in the same position with the brothers and Brody, and my pussy gushed.

By the time we finished the tour of the third floor, I was hot and more than willing to fuck both men in front of all these people. To my disappointment, we didn't stay in the Play Room, but went to the bar.

We were standing at the bar, sipping our drinks, and a shifter approached us and asked us to join their table. Stellan got that tense look on his face again that told me he didn't want to but saying no would be a diplomatic no-no.

"Tell you what. We go say hi, then I'll start pouting about wanting to dance," I said to them both.

The brothers looked at each other and shrugged. "Sounds like a plan," Stellan said.

We went to the table but the shifter who'd approached us insisted on speaking with Stel. Caid took me to the crowded dance floor, and I followed but I was reluctant to leave Stellan behind.

Once on the dance floor, Caid captured my attention. The man sure could move his hips. We were dancing to the beat and before too long, I was a sweaty mess. Caid didn't seem to mind as he turned me around with my back against his chest, my ass rubbed against his cock. His hands kneaded my breasts, and I continued to sway my hips. I leaned farther back, and wrapped my arms around Caid's neck. I allowed him to roam his hands all over my body, and we swayed to the music. I was restless and wanted more of him, so I turned and crashed my lips to his.

Our kisses were feverish, our tongues doing a dance of their own. My skin was on fire, and the soft feel of my silky dress felt unbearably stifling. I desperately wanted to be naked, and I wanted Caid's nakedness fused with mine.

He touched the hem of my dress, hesitant at first. Urging him on, I hooked a leg around his hips and grabbed hold of his hand, guiding him to my dripping pussy. He moaned into my mouth and slid his hands under my dress, pushing my drenched panties to the side.

"You're soaked, love," he said against my ear. "Do you want me to finger fuck you right here?"

"Yes, please!" The need to feel his fingers inside me was overwhelming.

He pushed a finger in me, I gasped and moaned, arching back a bit. People surrounded us. I was sure they could see what he was doing to me, but I really didn't give a fuck. There were others probably doing the same or more in this orgy-fest. His fingers felt so fucking good slipping in and out of me while he maintained pressure with his palm against my swollen clit.

Thinking it couldn't get any hotter, Stellan appeared behind me and leaned against my back. He tugged gently on my hair, just enough to pull me away from kissing Caid, and he kissed me on the mouth.

"Having fun, sweetness?" Stel asked.

I reached one arm behind me to drape over his neck, moaning my response.

"All good?" Caid asked him while removing his fingers.

I protested by guiding his hands back to where they'd been.

"It's fine. Nothing to worry about," Stel said.

"I'd say we could go, but our mate has my fingers in her tight little pussy right now," Caid told him.

"Is that so? That's so fucking sexy." Stel slid his tongue down my neck, and I arched against him.

"You think you can handle another finger, sweetness? I think you can." Stel slipped his hands under my dress and cupped my ass. Then he slid a finger between my cheeks down to my cunt where Caid's finger was already gliding in and out of me.

"Fuck, I love how wet you get." He squeezed his finger in alongside Caid's.

My moans grew louder, and my hips were gyrating back and forth riding their fingers. Fuck me, I had two hot men fingering me on the dance floor. I absolutely loved it and wanted more.

"You fucking love this, don't you?" Caid growled.

"Let's take this upstairs, sweetness. We both want our dicks in this tight cunt," Stellan said. They both pulled out of me at the same time.

I felt bereft, empty, and unsatisfied. And a little pissed. I was so close to my first orgasm. I grabbed both of their arms and said, "Don't you dare stop." They paused for a second, eyes widening.

"Make me come first," I lifted my chin in defiance.

"Yes, ma'am." Caid sucked my neck while pushing his finger back in.

Stellan kissed the other side of my neck and slid his finger back in. They both found a rhythm and worked together to create the perfect amount of friction. Stel pushed my halter down, cupping my exposed breasts. Caid latched on to my hard nipple, swirling his tongue over the tip.

My hips gyrated to the music, and electric shocks rode over my skin. I was loving every pleasurable sensation my guys were giving me in front of everyone here on the dance floor. Before too long, my body tightened, and squeezed the two fingers inside me. I came hard, squirting all over their fingers and down their hands. It was absolutely liberating to come in front of all these strangers. I was onboard for so much more.

Panting, I beamed; my men were kissing my lips, cheeks, neck, and shoulders. My breathing and heart rate slowed to a normal pace.

Caid pulled out, showing me his finger that was covered in my pussy juices. "Look how beautifully wet you are. I love it."

I leaned in to lick his finger and tasted myself. He watched me with intensity, and then bent down to devour my mouth going after the juices I'd just licked off his fingers.

Stellan was still inside me, his finger slowly sliding in and out. He noticed me licking Caid's finger, I heard him mutter "Fuck! You're going to make me come in my pants, sweetness."

His slow strokes started speeding up and excited me further once more. But he pulled out, the big tease, and I glared at him over my shoulder. He was well aware he was teasing me, and he knew I wanted more, but he wasn't sorry, the little shit. Instead, he shoved his finger in my mouth allowing me to lick my juices off his fingers. Oh hell, I might come again.

The guys were eager to get me back to the penthouse, I insisted on stopping at the ladies room on our way out of The Catacombs. I needed to tidy up. My thighs were coated with my juices, but the mess was so worth it. My lips were swollen, my hair a mess, and my dress was wrinkled. I looked thoroughly fucked.

I did my best to straighten up and left the bathroom to meet up with Stel and Caid. They waited in the corridor leading to the restrooms. Their body language was tense and I became edgy. Obviously, something happened. Each held one of my hands, and they escorted me to the elevators.

In the penthouse elevators, I asked, "What happened while I was peeing?"

Caid pushed me against the elevator wall and kissed me till I was breathless.

When the elevator door opened, he handed me over to his brother, who picked me up and carried me the few steps to my place.

Caid opened the door, and Stel waltzed in. He went straight to the stairway and gently sat me down on the steps. He knelt in front of me, and then kissed me all over my neck and my face. I'd lost my panties somewhere on the dance floor, so Stel had easy access to my throbbing cunt. He went in face-first and devoured me whole. He licked, sucked, and nibbled. I grew desperate for his cock. I writhed under him. As soon as he slipped a finger in my pussy, I came undone and squirted lady come all over his face.

"Kenzie, I'm sorry, we have to go," he said in his raspy voice. My juices glistened on his chin.

"What happened?" I asked.

He kept kissing me. Caid had disappeared to who knows where.

"Stel!" I said, and then gave him a shove with my magic. It wasn't a forceful shove, it was just enough to make him stop.

His eyes widened at my force of magic.

"Talk to me, Stel, please."

He nodded. "We have a couple of vamps here gunning for us. We have their location. We're catching up with them before they can come after us."

I was pissed, but not at the brothers. Those vamps ruined my sexy time. And to top that off, they were threatening my guys. Nope, that was not going to happen.

"How can I help, Stel?" I cupped his face with both hands. "I am a combat mage, you know. Perhaps I can be useful." I offered because right then, I wanted to shoot somebody. All that pent-up sexual energy and finger orgasms were great but I wanted the brothers' cocks inside me.

"Thank you, Kenzie, but it will make me feel better knowing that you're out of harm's way. I want you to stay here where you are safe." He kissed my nose.

We both stood. I walked out with him to the elevator. Caid was waiting there with a few other pack members I hadn't met. Stel kissed me one last time, and then left me to speak with the pack members.

Caid took Stel's place in front of me. "We'll come back after we're done, okay?"

"Okay." I gave him a kiss. "Keep each other safe," I said, as they got into the elevators.

CHAPTER 13

KENZIE

The guys snuck back in bed with me shortly after midnight. We exchanged kisses, and then I went right back to sleep.

I awoke the next day and the brothers were already gone from bed. Eager to see them, I rushed through my morning routine. I wanted to know what had happened with the vamps last night.

Caid was in the kitchen washing dishes, his back toward me. He wore his usual attire of jeans and a t-shirt. Stel sat at one of the barstools at the kitchen counter, his body faced toward me. He seemed to be reading something on the tablet in front of him. I stared openly as though my guys were delicious treats. Having orgasms on the dance floor had been hot, but I wanted more.

I stood in the kitchen doorway. I loved watching them like this. In public or even around their pack, their body language was rigid, as though they were ready and waiting for trouble, ever vigilant. When it was just us, they were relaxed.

"Take a picture, sweetness, it'll last longer," Stellan addressed me without even looking my way, a sly smile on his face.

I blushed. Caid turned his head toward me. He had me in his arms within moments and lifted me off the ground.

"Good morning beautiful. Sleep well?" He placed me gently on my feet, pecking my forehead.

I kissed him back. "Good morning, Caid, and yes, I did. You?"

"Never better. Now come have breakfast."

I walked over to the kitchen counter and held Stellan's outstretched hand. I greeted him with a kiss as well, and he hauled me onto his lap.

"If I had my phone, I would've definitely taken a pic. How long have you two been up?" I repositioned myself on Stellan's lap so his one leg was between mine. His thigh was so thick and wide, I could feel the strong muscles beneath me, and I squirmed a bit.

"We grew up on a ranch, sweetness. We wake up before sunrise most days." Stel nuzzled my neck. He pulled my robe down just enough to expose my shoulder and rested his head there. His breath against my skin made me wiggle a little more. The thin fabric did nothing to conceal the wetness pooling at my core as my hips subtly grinded against his well-muscled leg.

"Why didn't you wake me?"

"Oh no, you were sleeping like a babe. Besides we had pack stuff to do." Caid placed cooked bacon on a platter. "We went hunting, and then did a ten-mile run on top of that. And when we returned, you were still asleep, so we started breakfast."

"We thought the smell of bacon would wake you." Stel lifted a piece of bacon to my lips, and I bit into it.

Caid set a glass of green liquid in front of me that looked like the Green Goddess.

Eyeing him with a raised eyebrow, I opened my mouth to ask him how he knew, but he responded first.

"We may have done some research on you and discovered one of your favorite drinks is the Green Goddess from Raw. Trust me. This one is better."

"You did a background check on me? Of course you did. I'm not sure if I should be flattered or freaked out." I took a sip. *Mmm, goodness me, it is better.*

"Did everything go okay last night?" I asked.

"Not so much." Stel reached around me and piled a lot of food onto a plate.

I guessed all that food was for him, but I helped myself to it anyway. He kissed my cheek and focused again on the tablet in front of him. The screen showed a series of charts and graphs. I ignored it and kept eating.

"The transportation company we used to get here was also supposed to pick up Dad. But the vamps that work there at night were planning to take us out," Caid said.

"The info we got said they were at The Catacombs while we were there. Which was why we had to get you to safety and go back to find them," Stel added.

"But they weren't there. The two pack members that spotted them at The Catacombs let them slip." Caid shook his head.

"So, we went after them, running around the city for hours and found nothing. But we got a lead on their lair. We're having a meeting in a few to go over our next plan." Stel sounded optimistic.

"Well, I'm glad you two are okay. I was worried," I said, which earned me a few kisses.

While I ate my breakfast, I listened to the guys talk about pack business. I did my best to be inconspicuous about grinding against Stel's leg. There would be a wet spot after I got up.

Both brothers took out their phones as though they rang at the same time. I didn't hear a thing.

"Yours again," Caid said, giving me a hard look, and he turned on his vamp speed to get my phone, which was apparently in the living area.

"It's probably your boyfriend from the pool. It's been vibrating all morning long," he called out.

"Enjoying yourself, sweetness?" Stellan whispered into my ear. He shifted the one leg I was dry humping a little higher, giving me more friction against my clit. Since I had been caught in the act, I grinded a little harder, making myself moan. He ran his hand up and down my thigh, and I was hoping he'd move it up higher to my drenched pussy.

Caid returned to the kitchen with my phone in hand, scrolled through.

"How do you know who it is? Have you two been reading my texts?" I reached out and snatched my phone out of his hand.

"Yes!" they both said at the same time.

Un-fucking-believable, although I wasn't surprised. "Quit touching my shit," I said with a smile. What surprised me was, I didn't care that much.

I was certain they wouldn't like what they found on my phone. But oh well, they shouldn't have looked in the first place. I sipped my Green Goddess drink and continued grinding on Stel's leg.

"In case you're wondering, we already deleted all the dick pics," Stel said.

I spat Green Goddess juice out my nose.

The guys laughed.

I wiped my face and said, "Hey, it's not my fault guys like taking pics of their junk. And furthermore, if you're going to delete those pics, you should replace them, with pics of your own."

They continued laughing and I continued moving my hips over Stel's thighs. My phone buzzed again. Brody.

"Is that guy going to be hanging around forever?" Caid asked.

"Well, I suppose so. I do need a replacement, for when you two leave me after this conference of yours," I said absently, scrolling through several texts from Brody that came in last night and this morning.

The room was uncomfortably silent. When I looked up from my phone, both men were glaring at me.

"Last night he was a potential business contact and now he's our replacement?" Caid regarded me with raised eyebrows.

"Get that guy over here. Now, Kenzie," Stel growled.

Caid had a feral glint in his eyes, while Stellan's eyebrows were drawn together and his jaw muscles clenched.

"Relax. I wasn't serious about the replacement part," I said. Or maybe I was. I hadn't thought about it much, but they were going to leave me. That was a fact. Aside from them claiming me as their mate, we hadn't talked much about the future.

"Good, because we're not leaving you," Caid muttered and went back to the kitchen.

Stel hugged me tightly to his chest and whispered in my ear. "Kenzie, you are MINE, forever. You will never replace me. I might be willing to share, but I will never leave you." He wrapped a hand around my throat, keeping my arms bound with his other. "Look at me."

I turned to face him; our foreheads touched.

"Never in a million years will I ever let you go. Understand me." A serious glint hardened his eyes.

He was making a declaration. A part of me swooned. A part of me was nervous.

I nodded in acknowledgment. He kissed me, fiercely bruising my lips. I ground my hips on his leg and rocked back and forth.

He tightened his grip around my neck. His dominating, possessive nature had my pussy wet with want. His hard cock pressed against my ass. My hips gyrated faster. I was at the edge, ready to explode.

He broke our kiss and his released his grip on my throat. "No," he said with a hoarse voice.

My chest was heaving, my mind whirling. *What the fuck?*

I groaned and moved my hips again, but he gripped them and held me still. It felt like someone had thrown cold water on my face.

"Finish your breakfast," he said in a clipped tone.

He was punishing me and I didn't like it. But I didn't hate it either. His dominating nature aroused me.

Caid bent over the counter and kissed me, nipping at my lips. "You deserved that," he said, smirking.

"Does this mean Brody can't watch?" I asked, trying to lighten the mood; they both laughed.

"I want to meet that friend of yours, Kenzie. Soon," Stel said.

"So that he can watch?" I asked again, just to be a pain in the ass.

He grazed my shoulder with his teeth and whispered, "Yes, so he can watch."

I almost lost it, and I rocked my hips over his thigh again. He stood and gently helped me off his lap. Damn him.

Caid glanced at the wet mark on Stel's leg. "You marked him on purpose, didn't you?" I shrugged, grinned, and sat back down to finish my breakfast.

While the guys took care of pack business, I cleared the breakfast dishes and took my Green Goddess drink to the dining room table, and then sat next to Caid. I noticed he was drinking out of a glass filled with red thick liquid. It was blood. He caught me staring and brought the glass to his lips and took a large gulp. He held my gaze as though he was daring me to say something. There were so many questions running through my mind, but I didn't know what to say so I kept silent.

He licked his lips. "AB positive, not the best I've had but it suits me well enough. I didn't kill anyone for this, if that's what you're thinking. The hotel supplied it for me. I took the liberty of stocking up your fridge. Unlike most vamps, I don't need it to survive. For me, it's like taking weekly medication. Does this bother you?"

"No. Not at all."

"You can ask me anything, love." He leaned in closer to me.

I could smell the coppery scent of blood on him. With my finger, I swiped the dab of blood from the corner of his mouth. His licked the drop of blood from my finger, and I swallowed hard.

"You're curious to taste it, aren't you?" He grabbed my hand and placed kisses on my knuckles.

Oddly enough, I was. That should be worrisome, but all I could think about was kissing him and tasting the blood off his lips. But he leaned away from me, clearing those thoughts from my mind.

"Oh no, beautiful, if you're going taste anyone's blood, it will be mine." Possessiveness laced his words.

I slid my tongue over my lips, as longing built inside me. Vamps were never attractive to me, but the thought of tasting Caid's blood stirred my desire.

Stellan finished up a call and joined us at the dining room table. "The pack will be over in thirty minutes." He glanced from Caid to me, narrowed his gaze and sat next to me. "What's going on here?"

A little wet spot was on his thigh. I smiled, satisfied at leaving my mark, no matter how temporary it was. He looked down at his leg, smirked, then lifted me off the chair to sit with me back on his lap. Straddling his leg, I found that perfect position, and kept my eyes on Caid.

"Well, besides our mate marking her territory, she is also very curious about tasting my blood," Caid said to his brother.

"Is that right, sweetness?" Stellan whispered into my ear, and I nodded. He untied my robe and reached into my bralette to pinch my hard nipples. "Will you let him drink your blood? Let both of us bite you? Mark you as ours?" He grazed his lips along my neck.

"Yes, please," I responded, happy Stel was done punishing me. I grabbed his hand and forced it between my legs.

I didn't know much about werewolf or vamp bites, but I was down for both making their mark on me. Both Caid and Stel were adamant about not leaving me. Did I feel the same way? Yes. I wasn't ready to let them go either, and that day may never come. I couldn't imagine life without them.

I was still riding Stel's fingers, and Caid knelt before us. He held my gaze and tore my panties in half. I gasped, turned on by his passionate display.

"It would be my pleasure to mark you, love." Caid ran his tongue along my knee cap.

"Mine too." Stellan said.

He placed me between his legs so my legs were spread open, and draped over the outside of his, giving Caid a full view of my wet, aching cunt.

Lust clouded his eyes. He sat back on his knees and pulled out his hard cock. He gripped it while he watched his brother finger my pussy.

I moaned and arched my back.

"We don't have time to mark you right now, sweetness. I'm sorry to make this quick," Stel said, pumping his fingers into my pussy harder and faster. The pressure of my orgasm was reaching its peak.

"Here, let me give you a hand." Caid slid in a finger next to his brothers, stretching my pussy. I closed my eyes. He removed his finger and grabbed my chin.

"Eyes on me, love. I want to see your eyes while we finger fuck you and make you come," Caid all but commanded me.

I complied and chased his hand with my mouth wanting to suck on something. He switched his hands, placing the finger that was drenched in my juices into my mouth.

"Fuck, you could take another cock, couldn't you?" Caid grinned.

I moaned and nodded sucking his fingers into my mouth while riding Stellan's fingers.

"Oh, fuck," Stellan said behind me, his hard cock pressed against my back.

Caid returned his fingers to my pussy and fisted his cock. "I wanna watch your pretty pussy squirt. Can you do that for me?"

My hips gyrated faster and I used their fingers for my pleasure.

"That's it, sweetness, come for us." Stel's teeth grazed my neck. I let go completely, squirting all over their fingers.

Caid kept his eyes on my squirting pussy and pumped harder on his cock. I continued rocking my hips till his seed spilled all over his fist.

Without warning, Stel picked me up and placed me on the table in front of him. On my knees, ass up Stel pressed his face to my core and licked from my pussy to my ass. He tongue-fucked me relentlessly. My pussy was overly sensitive. I was not far from another orgasm, but he stopped, denying my release.

I looked over my shoulder and gave him a scathing look. He chuckled, my juices glistening on his face.

"This what you want?" He pulled out his massive cock and stroked, smearing precum all over his head.

"Yes!" I pushed my hips back toward Stel's cock.

He lined himself up with my throbbing cunt and slammed in. The pain was excruciating. I cried out for more.

Stel bounced my ass on his cock, setting a demanding pace. He was punishing my cunt in the best of ways. I thrashed under him, screaming his name. My body grew tight, and my second orgasm tore out of me.

Stel let out a savage growl as he released himself, pumping into my pussy as though he was pushing his seed deeper into my body.

We slumped over the dining table, our sated bodies were still fused together. My breathing was ragged.

Caid leaned over gathered my hair from my face and kissed me. "You are incredible. I love watching you get fucked."

"Didn't you say the pack was on their way?" Caid asked as he moved away from me.

"Yes, I did, we need to get cleaned up," Stellan said, his cock still in me.

"I'd rather stay and fuck you all day long, sweetness, but we have important matters to discuss. And I'd like to introduce you to the pack." He pulled his cock out with a suckling pop.

I raised my body, coming up on all fours and looked over at him. "Why now?"

He didn't respond. He just stared at my pussy and gently ran his cock through my swollen pussy lips.

"Take a picture, it'll last longer." I smirked about using the same line he had earlier.

"Don't tempt me," he said breathless. Then dove back down to my pussy, laving at my cum and his, while stuffing me with his fingers. Stel pulled back right away, still fingering me, still staring. He grabbed my phone that was sitting on the table next to me.

"You're fucking beautiful and so fucking delicious."

Caid came back to the dining room with clothes in his hand. "Did she just say what I think she said?"

"You heard her right," Stellan said, and slid the tip of his still hard cock into my pussy. I heard the sound of a camera clicking.

He just took pics of my wet, well-used cunt, and I wanted more. I was fully aroused again. I could not get enough of these men. I moaned.

Stel removed his cock and replaced it with fingers. I writhed my hips back and forth against his fingers, fully expecting another orgasm.

Stel set my phone back on the table and tugged me up to a seated position, his fingers still lodged in my pussy.

"Sweetness, please. I promise more fucking, more pics, more of anything you want later," he said between kisses that he trailed from my neck to my shoulder.

Caid stood beside Stel, and planted kisses on my other shoulder.

I reached back and wrapped an arm around each of them.

"I can't get enough of you two." I whispered. My pussy clenched Stel's fingers. I did not want to let him go.

Caid rested a hand on my hip, holding them still. "Love, more later."

I groaned and squeezed tighter.

"I need my fingers back, sweetness," Stel told me.

"No," I pouted.

They chuckled.

The doorbell rang.

"I'll go let everybody in," Caid said.

"Don't you dare!" I released Stel, and then ran upstairs.

CHAPTER 14

KENZIE

"What's keeping you, love?" Caid entered my huge walk-in closet, which also served as a dressing room.

"I'm ready." I laced up my combat boots and glanced up, admiring his blue t-shirt that read "Adulting is Bullshit." "I like your shirt."

"I like yours better." He helped me stand and placed a kiss on my belly, exposed by my cropped tank.

Caid escorted me downstairs.

Stel was in the living room with two shifters. He held out his hand to me, which I took. He kissed me on my lips, in front of the other wolves, as though he was making a statement. When we broke apart, the men nodded at me and averted their eyes. My assumption seemed to be on point.

Stellan draped his arm around me and made the introductions. Except for she-bitch who had given me trouble at the pool, I hadn't seen nor been introduced to any of the other pack members.

First up was John Thomas or JT. He wasn't as tall as the brothers, but he was brawny with big arms made for working huge machinery or something of that sort. His bald head had a couple tattoos scrawled on top, and he had a thick, bushy beard. His light eyes were kind as though the quick-to-violence tempers shifters were known for stayed hidden down deep under the surface.

The other man was the complete opposite from the brothers and JT. Jason was in my weight class, and he looked like a teenager with red sneakers, ripped jeans, and Henley tee. He could easily pass for a hipster. I'd be surprised if he was even eighteen. But he was in a casino. Hmm, perhaps age limits didn't apply to shifters. He had that same youthful exuberance that reminded me of my next-door neighbor, a kid named Bear.

"Nice to meet you, miss. I liked your red dress last night. You looked really pretty." He shook my hand longer than necessary. He was about to bring my hand up to his lips for a kiss and Stel growled. Jason paused, thought better of it, and slunk behind JT instead.

"This is his first mission outside of Texas. He's sort of young," Caid said.

I smiled sweetly at them both and said, "Nice to meet you both and thank you for the compliment, Jason."

His face and ears turned beet red. It was kind of adorable.

"Sweetness, these two are just dropping off some info on the vamps we are dealing with today. The others will be by shortly," Stel said.

"Sure, you're welcome to stay." I leaned into him.

"Thank you, sweetness," Stel said, then directed the other two shifters to the living area.

Within a couple minutes, Caid introduced me to the rest of the pack as they entered. Along with Jason and JT, there were four other pack members. She-bitch aka Sandy was the wolf I'd dunked in the pool a few days ago. She gave me a curt nod and a wide berth. She still hated me. Warren, a coyote shifter, was an older gent who spoke with a southern drawl. His salt and pepper hair and beard were indicative of his age because shifters didn't age like humans. He was definitely older, but judging by his athletic physique, he was as strong as any of the shifters here. Stedman was a tall, lean black man with a military haircut. His slim build made him appear weaker than the others, but I had seen him at the pool. There was shredded muscle under those clothes and not an ounce of fat on him. Plus, Caid had told me that his second nature was a seven-hundred pound Kodiak bear. Mark was Asian, with a bald head, goatee, and friendly eyes. He was the unassuming one that shifted into a panther. He smiled and joked around with Jason. Those two kept the group dynamics light and less intense.

The entire pack was tasked with tracking the vamps. These pack members had worked together before. They had a special comradery. I understood why Stel chose these six to accompany him. And although Sandy didn't seem to like me much, she, like everyone else here, did everything and anything the brothers requested. No questions asked.

They were making plans on retrieving the vamps, but Stellan stopped what he was doing, looked at my dinging phone again and stalked toward me. "Who the fuck is Tris?"

Caid focused possessive eyes on me, and Stel was barely keeping his anger in check. The pack sat completely still at the dining room table.

Well, shit, drama much?

"We talked about him. He's my best friend, and business partner and we were supposed to go to the bazaar today." I took my phone back. "And he's gay."

The brothers relaxed. Caid smirked and Stel pecked my cheek. "Just making sure, sweetness."

I shook my head. I forgot about our shopping date and was glad Tris remembered. I texted him back, telling him to come over. Shit, after that exchange with Caid and Stel, it would be good for me to have some space from the brothers.

CHAPTER 15

KENZIE

After introducing the brothers to my bestie, Tris and I walked over to the elevators.

"Those two are no doubt sexy as fuck. But they're fucking scary, Kenz," Tris finally said to me when we got into the elevator. "But I bet the sex was hot." He wiggled his brows.

I laughed and pressed the floor for the ballrooms where the bazaar was taking place.

"Just be careful. Don't get attached. And give me some details!" He laughed with me.

"They certainly don't disappoint, that's for sure." My cheeks flushed.

As soon as we got out of the elevators to the ballroom floors, it felt as though we were transported across the world. The Majestic outdid themselves. This section was like any other ballroom area you'd find in large hotels. There were wide-open spaces, connected or separated via retractable doors, depending on the event. For this event, the ballroom had been decorated like a Moroccan street bazaar.

We had to dodge people crowded around the vendor booths. It

would take days to walk through the entire thing. Rows upon rows of different stands filled up the area. Vendors showcased all of their magical wares. Spicy scents filled the air from all the street food vendors like a real Moroccan bazaar.

Tris and I strolled through the aisles, hand in hand. There was a lot to discover and I hoped to find a peculiar rare item. I also loved supporting those little mom-and-pop shops that were just getting started.

We'd come upon a stall that was selling magical wine. There were no patrons lined up at the stall, which was odd to me. Who doesn't want magical wine? Unless, of course, it tasted like ass. We walked in, and the owner of the stall stood, an eager smile brightening his face. He insisted on us taking a seat on two of the folding chairs he had in the stall. Tris and I sat and allowed him to show off his wine.

The signature wine in his collection was called Starfish, but it wasn't a typical red wine. It was purple like grape Gatorade. He told us that his wines were made from a special hybrid of red grapes plus a purple flower called starfish, which was a cross between an orchid and a hibiscus. Starfish apparently only grew on his farmland, and the alcohol content was three percent greater than most magically brewed wine. He gave us a generous sample, which we both found delicious. Judging by the color, I was expecting something awfully sweet, but it wasn't at all. The flavor was reminiscent of a Pinot Noir but light like a Rosé. Both Tris and I gave it a thumbs-up. The gentleman, Pierre, was absolutely charming. I took his card and purchased a bottle, as well as a case, which would be delivered to my place. Tris opened the bottle straight away and refilled our cups.

Wine in hand, we continued our perusal. Tris found a stand that sold charmed jewelry. He tried on practically every necklace, bracelet, and ring. He was so gorgeous, all of the saleswomen were eager to help him. After almost an hour, he decided on a charmed ring for his boyfriend and several items for himself. I picked up a pretty belly ring for me and a gaudy gold ring that had a large teal-colored stone which would heat up if something in my hand was poisonous. I thought the magic ring would be a fun item to have.

A stall that was selling weapons caught my attention. I was drawn to two daggers, which were almost identical in every way except the engraving on the blade. It reminded me of the brothers. The daggers were not ornate, but a swirl of magic emitted from them. I handed my cup of wine to Tris and picked them up. The weight and balance were good although too heavy for me. The hilt was long, and made for larger hands. The blade was crafted from an unfamiliar metal, and engraved with an intricate design that reminded me of a Celtic knot. Each had a different pattern. What drew me to them were the smooth blue stones about the size of a quarter, and just as flat, embedded in the hilts. According to the stall keeper, they were genuine sapphires. Magic tingled under my finger as I brushed the blade.

"Those too big for you. Maybe nice gift. I give good price. You make someone very happy," the merchant told me.

"I know two men those would be perfect for," Tris said behind me.

"Yeah, me too." I pressed my lips together, continuing to admire the daggers.

The brothers had their own special kind of magic. They didn't need daggers but these seemed to have their names written all over them. I couldn't resist.

Since this was a bazaar, I haggled with the merchant, and, satisfied with the price, I paid him. Before leaving the stall, an older woman emerged from behind the curtains and said, "For you, miss." She pushed a wrapped package into my hands. "A gift."

I was not in the habit of taking things from strangers but her insistence made me pause.

"Please, please," she said.

"For me? Why?" I narrowed my eyes.

"Made by Fae, for Fae," she said.

Uncomfortable heat rushed up the back of my neck. How did she know? I had to at least see it.

I accepted the package and gently unwrapped it. It was a smaller replica of the two daggers I'd just purchased. The magic it emitted was much stronger than the other two. This one had three stones in it. One sapphire and two diamonds. I wasn't betting on them being actual jewels. They were probably glass. The Celtic knot was on one side of the blade, and on the other side, there was an intricate inscription. The dagger fit perfectly in my hand. I twirled it around, stepped to the side and did a couple of thrusts with it. The sheath that came with it was a soft, worn leather that attached seamlessly to the gun holster belt I was wearing. Once it was strapped onto my body alongside my other weapons, it felt like it was created specifically for me. I had to have this beautiful, priceless dagger.

"What does the inscription mean?" I asked her.

She shook her head.

"It's too beautiful. I couldn't possibly accept this. I have money, so I'll pay." I handed over my credit card, prepared to let her choose the amount.

"No, no, it's gift. Very special for special lady." She pushed the credit card away.

I didn't think I was that special, but I couldn't just walk away from the dagger. I had to have it. "Thank you! I love it."

Still, I was not leaving without paying for it. I looked around the stall and motioned to Tristan, "Pick something, please."

"Honey, I wouldn't know where to start." He glanced around at all the blades.

"Help my friend choose something, please. I want to buy him a gift," I said to her.

She nodded and started showing things to Tristan.

Tris picked out a dainty but handy switchblade, and I purchased a couple of sheaths for each of the brothers' daggers. Plus, I bought a bracelet that hid a blade and a matching hair clip that hid throwing darts. I added a heavy tip, which I hoped would cover the cost of my new dagger.

There was still so much more to see. Tris and I continued our shopping journey, laughing, spending money, and drinking. We topped off our wine cups, finishing off the bottle I'd purchased. We were both feeling a bit tipsy. The purple flower was kicking in.

Giggling, we strode down another aisle when I heard someone call my name. I looked around and spotted Brody waving to get my attention.

"Who might that be?" Tris asked, slurring his words a bit. Oh my, the wine was working it's magic. I giggled.

As Brody got closer, Tris looked him up and down and blurted, "He's cute! Did you have sex with him, too?"

"Shush you!" I said with a flushed face as a couple of people glanced at us.

I took a few steps to greet Brody. He lifted me off my feet and pressed his face into my bosom. I let him nuzzle my chest, not that I had an option to chastise him, since my hands were full. Amazingly though, I didn't spill my wine, which was important.

"Hi gorgeous! I'm so happy to see you." He set me back down on my feet.

True to form, Brody brought his lips down to mine for one of his luscious kisses. Mmm . . . *Kisses weren't sex,* I kept telling myself.

"Hi!" I said as we broke apart.

Behind me, Tristan cleared his throat.

I turned around. "Oh! Brody, this is my friend, Tristan."

"Excuse me, your what?" Tris gave me scathing look.

"Pardon me, this is my best friend in the whole world."

Brody chuckled and shook Tristan's hand. "Nice to meet you 'best friend in the whole world'."

He glanced at my full hands and motioned to take my shopping bags from me. "Here let me help."

He was so polite. I was tipsy and happy, so I relinquished my bags but not my cup full of wine.

"I texted you earlier. I have news about that person you wanted info on," Brody said.

"Already?" I swore we had just talked about this yesterday.

"Yes, nothing terribly urgent. I cloned all his stuff last night. It was all encrypted. I need to send it to my tech mage to decode it."

"Last night? How?" I was impressed.

He smiled, showing off his dimples. "I can't tell you all my secrets, beautiful."

"I have a tech mage here, his name is Clay. He could help. I'll text you both now." I texted Brody and Clay. I wanted this situation resolved yesterday.

"Got it. I'll arrange to meet him tonight." He typed into his phone then put his phone back into his pocket.

"What are you doing here?" I asked. Most humans weren't allowed in here unless they were with a supe. I was curious to know his magical contact.

"A friend of mine is looking for a few things. Come, I'll introduce you."

Tris and I followed him.

"What is that?" He looked at my drink.

"It's the best magical wine ever!" I handed over my cup so he could try it.

After adjusting the packages to one hand, he took a sip and handed the cup back to me. "Mmm, not bad."

A man waited nearby, and Brody motioned to him. "This is my buddy, Erik. Erik, this is Mackenzie and Tristan."

Judging by the brands on his forearms, his friend was a top-tier mage.

He didn't smile, or offer to shake my or Tristan's hand. Instead, he gave us a curt hello, sized me up and down and scowled.

Rude. I glowered at him.

Brody gave his friend a questioning look, which his friend openly ignored.

"Erik has been looking for some magical stuff. How about you two?" Brody asked both me and Tristan.

I liked that he was engaging my best friend in conversation. It proved he was interested in getting to know us better. Tristan was telling him about our day and asking him all kinds of personal questions. I tuned out the conversation for a moment and focused on Erik. He was practically seething behind Brody, and giving me skunk eye. What was this dude's problem?

"So, are you single?" Tristan asked Brody.

I rolled my eyes and shook my head.

"Yes, but maybe your best friend might help remedy that." Brody placed an arm around my waist. I leaned into him because it felt natural and, even better, it seemed to bother his friend.

Tristan laughed at him and said, "Well now, I'll need to know a little more about you before I authorize that."

"Deal. How about we get out of here and grab some dinner?" Brody asked us.

"Is it dinner time already?" I pulled my phone out of my pocket to check the time. Sure enough, it was early evening already, which meant we had been shopping for hours.

I turned to Tristan and asked, "Your man good with me keeping you for dinner tonight?"

"My man is always good with whatever I want. Let's grab some food!"

I laughed in agreement. We clinked our cups together and downed the last of our wine, then dumped the empty cups in the nearest trash bin, as we walked out of the bazaar.

Tristan really lucked out with his current beau, Robert. He was a sweetie pie and not because he let Tris do whatever he wanted but because he had good intentions, was genuinely kind, and he loved my bestie.

While Tris was on the phone with his beau, I sent a quick group text to the brothers telling them of my plans with Tris and Brody. If they wanted to meet him, this would be a great time.

Me: Ran into Brody at the bazaar. We're grabbing dinner. Join us?

Caid: That guy again??

Stellan: Is Tris with you?

Me: Yes. And Yes.

Caid: He's in love with you.

Stel: Who else?

Me: Brody's friend, Erik.

Stel: Can't join you Sweetness. Have fun. Be safe.

Caid: Wait one minute! Since you're not coming back, can you at least send us that hot pic we took earlier.

I slanted my head and gazed at my phone. Hot pic? Oh yes, Stel had snapped a pic with my phone. I pulled up my photos and blushed. *Whoa*! It was a shot of my wet, fully exposed pussy and Stel's large dick in me, just the tip. This was hardcore porn.

My pussy clenched.

I sent the pic to both brothers. I've never been shy about my body. Besides, our faces weren't in it. Not that I cared about that.

Stel: Fuck. Soooo hot.

Caid: Gorgeous Love. I'll have my dick in my hand till I see you again.

The texts kept coming, which just made me hot and wet.

Brody, Tris, me, and asshole, I mean Erik, decided to grab dinner at one of the restaurants in The Majestic, but we hadn't decided on which one. Brody was holding my bags while talking to his friend who was still giving off asshole vibes. I asked Tris about it, as we walked toward the area of the hotel that had a variety of restaurants.

"Yep, that guy has a stick up his ass for whatever reason. Maybe he'll decide not to join us," Tristan said.

Glad I wasn't the only one noticing this asshole's attitude. We waited for them to catch up with us. Brody winked at me. He was such a nice guy. Erik still wore a deep scowl. Maybe that was just his face. Permanent asshole face.

"Do you want to go anywhere in particular?" Brody asked us. He was so different from his friend.

"Someplace casual. I'm not picky," I said to him.

"Beautiful and low maintenance. Do you have any other redeeming qualities I should know of?" He winked at me.

"Add flaky bitch to the list," Erik muttered under his breath.

Okay, that was uncalled for and at that point I had enough of his attitude. I pinned Erik on the hotel lobby ground, face down, hands behind his back. My knee was pressed against his spine and my brand-new dagger at his throat. My reaction was a bit over the top, but fuck it, he had it coming.

"What the fuck did you just call me?" I said to Erik between clenched teeth.

He struggled to break free. "Get the fuck off me! Are you crazy!?"

"Apologize, asshole." I pressed a little harder on his spine.

"Fine. Sorry," he spat out.

That was the most insincere apology ever. We were drawing onlookers, and reluctantly, I released him and sheathed my dagger.

"Psycho," he muttered as he stood and straightened his shirt.

Motherfucker. In a flash, I had my dagger out and pressed against his throat again. He stared me down, and his magic flowed into me, probing and searching out my own. What the actual fuck was he doing?

My magic flared, and a protective shield wrapped around me. His invasive magic reached down into me, probing and prodding in places that were private. I shuddered, feeling violated. I didn't like it. Not. One. Bit.

The pressure of Erik's magic was pushing against mine with

harsh, menacing intent. It felt suffocating, the pressure threatening to squeeze every vital organ in my body one by one. I willed my magic to push back and shoved his magic out and away from me.

Using the same trick he'd used against me, I pushed my magic into him. It was odd at first. I'd never done it before and wasn't even sure what I was doing or looking for. I allowed my instincts to guide me till I found the core of his magic located at the base of his sternum. It was beautiful, pulsating. I could squish it if I wanted to.

His eyes widened, and a bead of sweat formed on his brow.

From behind me, Tris said, "Don't get involved, Brody. Kenzie can handle this."

I applied pressure to the core of Erik's magic with my own. "Doesn't feel too good, does it?"

He remained silent and his body trembled a bit, yet he still had an air of defiance in his eyes.

Brody was at my back. "Enough, Kenz, he was wrong and should apologize. What the fuck, dude?"

"I hate flakes," Erik said, my magic still holding him back.

"I don't even know you."

"Of course you don't. You only canceled our training four times now. You should apologize to me."

"Training? What training?" I said, trying to piece the puzzle together. He was a mage. Ah, he must be the tutor I've been dodging.

"Why the fuck didn't you just come out and say so instead of pouting like a bitch. Yes, I admit I canceled training with a mage tutor, but how was I supposed to know it was you? Am I supposed to apologize to every random mage I meet, just in case he was the tutor I canceled on? Seriously?" Yep, I was still pissed.

I put a little more pressure on his magic and growled, "If you try to violate my magic ever again, I will reach down into your chest and smash all that magic in there."

"Kenzie, sweetness, you okay?" a deep raspy voice said from behind me.

Hearing Stellan's protective and sultry voice calmed me. My

anger simmered. I released my hold on Erik, stepped over to Stellan and sheathed my dagger. "I'm fine."

"You sure?" Caid asked.

I didn't know where they'd come from, and I didn't care. Damn it, I was feeling a bit shaky from accessing my magic. I didn't use much, but I could feel the strain. I did my best to play it off.

"It's fine. We'll sort this out." I waved my hand toward Brody and Erik.

I wasn't sure what else to do at that point. Caid and Stellan stood in front of me, and Brody and Erik were behind me.

"We're going to have dinner. Are you sure you don't want to join us?" I asked the brothers.

Stellan stared at Erik and Brody. Caid looked concerned as he came closer to me.

"We missed you, love. Did you have fun shopping?" Caid placed kisses on my cheek and jaw. He licked the corner of my mouth. Mmm.

"Yes, we did. I'll tell you about it later." I gave him a small smile.

"I know you," Stellan finally said, addressing Erik. I turned to see their exchange.

"I did some work for your father, Alpha Reese." Erik nodded.

"And you must be Brody," Stel said, pressing his body against my side.

"Yep. Nice to meet you." Brody adjusted my shopping bags in one hand and extended his other hand to greet both brothers.

Stel introduced himself and Caid, and then reached around me to shake Brody's and Erik's hands. He turned me around to face him and placed his lips against mine, transferring energy to me like he had at the pool. Grateful, I accepted his gift. The last thing I wanted was to show Erik how crappy I was with my magic.

"Enjoy your dinner, sweetness. See you later." He released me and walked off.

His magic swirled through me, restoring my own and boosting my energy.

Before he got too far, I stopped him, stood on my tip-toes and kissed him lightly. "Thank you, Stel."

"Of course, have fun." He bent down and gave me a lingering kiss. My tongue swept through his mouth, and I pressed my body flush against his. He released me, and then walked away with Caid.

After the brothers left, the four of us stood there for a moment in uncomfortable silence. Thankfully, Tristan stepped in, breaking the awkwardness.

"That was entertaining! But I'm still hungry. Let's go to Drummans, I know the hostess, and she's got a table for us." He swooped his hand in the direction of the restaurant.

"Hey Kenzie!" Caid shouted from a couple feet away. "Thanks for the pic!" He blew me a kiss and turned away. *Little shit.*

"What pic?" Tris and Brody asked, while Erik lifted his eyebrows.

I waved them off. I was too shocked and too red in the face to formulate a response. Instead, I shook my head.

After what transpired between Erik and me, I didn't want him around anymore so I turned to him, "I apologize for canceling our tutoring sessions. It wasn't personal. I'm not sorry for putting a knife to your neck though, and I'm not sorry for taking hold of your magic. What I said earlier stands. Stay the fuck away from me and my magic. Tristan and I will go on our way."

I reached out to take my bags from Brody, but he refused me.

"I'm coming with you, Kenzie baby." He stepped toward me.

Not sure why he'd want to be near me, but I wasn't complaining. I liked him. His friend, on the other hand, needed an attitude adjustment.

"You have something to say?" Brody asked his friend with a threatening tone.

"Apologies, I was wrong, all the way around. I shouldn't have judged you, shouldn't have tried to get familiar with your magic. Please, let me make amends. Dinner's on me." Erik motioned toward the restaurants.

CHAPTER 16

KENZIE

A few steps ahead of Brody and Erik, Tristan leaned down and asked, "What did he do?"

"Honestly, I don't know. He reached into my magic. It was like what happens when we were kids and the Registrar's Office assessed our magic."

"He probed your magic." Tris furrowed his brows.

"That, I expected. This was violating. And to make matters worse, my magic responded in kind. It . . . I did the same thing to him." I whispered that last part.

Tristan laid a protective arm around my shoulder. He knew I had problems with my magic. "Don't worry, Kenz, we'll figure it out together."

We reached the restaurant at that point and Tris worked it out with the hostess to get us seated.

Drummans specialized in Southern cuisine. The casual, homey interior resembled a country-style diner. Plastic condiment jars sat on top of wooden picnic tables covered with blue gingham-printed table cloths. Vintage posters hung on the wall, and the old-style jukebox sat in the corner playing classic country music. And the food was always delicious.

During dinner, Erik's attitude changed a bit. He was still frosty toward me but he made an effort to be pleasant with everyone else. He laughed at Tristan's jokes and participated in the conversation. He spoke eloquently, which indicated he was educated and quite intelligent. Without the scowl, he was pleasing to look at. His pale skin and black hair emphasized bright turquoise eyes. His nose was a bit on the larger side but gave him a classically handsome face. He had a shit-ton of experience as a mage and tutor and had spent many years studying different types of magic. I understood why my father chose him as my tutor.

After our meal, we parted ways with Tristan at the valet pick-up area. Brody insisted on walking me to my place, leaving a dejected Erik to fend for himself.

Before leaving, Erik walked up to me and said "It was nice to meet you, Mackenzie. I am truly sorry about earlier and hope you will reconsider me as your tutor."

"Thanks for dinner," I said and walked toward the PH elevators, Brody right behind me.

I wasn't committing to training with him one way or another. Maybe training with him would not be so bad. Gods knew I needed it. However, it wasn't something I wanted to think on right then.

"I can carry that, you know," I said to Brody, pointing at my shopping bags as we entered the elevators.

"I don't mind." He used his muscular body to back me up against the elevator wall.

His mouth met mine with an urgency that took me by surprise. Our tongues did a sensual exploratory dance. As I pressed his face closer to mine, I tangled my hands in his hair.

The elevator door opened, breaking us apart and brought me back to my senses. I got out and walked to my door, pausing in the alcove, lost in thought. Brody stopped and watched me. I had been with two men just this morning, two men I was developing real feelings for. Did I want to be with a different one right now? Did it matter? I wasn't a teenager, I couldn't get pregnant, and I wasn't susceptible to human diseases. There wasn't a single reason I shouldn't do this. Brody was a nice guy, though. The last thing I wanted to do was hurt him. Just when I was about to voice my thoughts, he dropped my bags and lifted me off my feet and pushed me against the wall.

"I don't care about anyone else, Kenzie baby. I just want you, even if that means sharing," he whispered, nipping at my ear.

His declaration stunned me. Before I could question him, we started kissing again. He groped my ass with one hand, the other palmed my breast. My body reacted to his touch; he felt so good. Any hesitation I had went out the window; I wanted him.

The elevator dinged.

Interrupted by the elevator again, Brody put me down on my feet. I peeked around the alcove and glimpsed three men exiting the elevator. They were unfamiliar to me, but perhaps they were here for the pack. They weren't shifters, though, and I could see the slight bulge on the sides of their jackets indicating hidden weapons. This didn't feel right.

We exchanged a knowing look. Brody sensed my apprehension. I nodded and we both drew our weapons. He pulled out a 45 acp and I pulled out my .22. Aww . . . look at us, twins.

Earlier, Stel had insisted I carry my gun and my dagger for my shopping trip with Tris, and for once, I was grateful for his overprotectiveness.

Brody and I peeked around the alcove again. An electrical pulse surged out from one man's hands and fried the lock on the door. They were armed and using magic to break in. Definitely not friendlies. *Fuck me, what now?* Immediately, my magic flared around me like a protective skin. All I wanted to do was protect the brothers.

The magic unlocked the door, and the intruders went inside. Heart pounding, I ran across the hall before it closed, Brody right behind me, and I stopped the door from shutting with my foot. Damn it, Brody was human. He shouldn't be here.

"Go. I got your back." His voice was barely a whisper.

We snuck in behind the intruders.

"Doesn't look like anyone is here," someone said into his phone. "We're coming up," the other person replied.

Oh, for fucks sake! Who uses speaker phone when breaking and entering? Amateurs. Not that I was complaining because now we knew we were having company.

We moved deeper into the penthouse, using the darkness to conceal our movements. Two guys went upstairs and one entered the kitchen area. I motioned with my hand toward the stairs. Brody shook his head, but I was already on the move. Not able to stop me, he followed the other man into the kitchen.

I crept up the stairs. The mage and one of his goons went toward the master bedroom which was dark, and the door wide open. I heard running water in the opposite direction, so I checked that out first.

In the nearest guestroom, I found Jason on the bed. His eyes were closed, his head bopping to music only he could hear through his headphones. He was completely unaware of me. I holstered my gun and climbed on top of him, clamped one hand over his mouth, and pressed a finger to my lips. I climbed off him and slanted my head toward the outside door. He nodded, got up, and then followed me.

Like my place, this room had a bathroom connecting it to the next bedroom. I entered into the bathroom, and found Sandy and Mark. Thanks to the glass shower door I got an eyeful of the two shifters going at it in the shower.

Okay, I thought shifters were supposed to be more aware than this.

Jason made a clicking noise, and the two glanced up. Again, I pressed a finger to my lips and held up two fingers, and then left them to sort themselves out.

Jason and I snuck back out into the hallway. One intruder went into the room Jason had been in. I motioned for Jason to go after that guy while I went looking for the mage.

I drew my gun again and found the mage in the master bedroom. As soon as I entered, he sent a jolt of magic at me. My magic protected me from the hit and absorbed what seemed to be a stream of electricity. Fuck, he just tasered me.

Thanks to my magic wards, this attack felt like a resounding buzz covering me from head to toe. The buzz created a slight numbing sensation, but I didn't hesitate. The mage did though. The fact that I didn't drop to the floor from his hit confused him and made him pause a second too long.

"What are . . ." he started to say at the same time I pulled the trigger. My bullet entered his skull.

I sensed someone behind me and turned, gun ready. My hands were steady, although my pulse was racing.

"Kenzie?" A large figured loomed in front of me.

Stellan. Fuck, I'd almost shot him. He paused, and looked me up and down, to make sure I was okay. I nodded at him and we walked back to where I'd left the shifters. The other intruder was on the floor, his head twisted at an odd angle. He was dead.

The elevator dinged and I met Stel's knowing stare. More bad guys were coming. We silently moved to the stairway.

"Stay here," Stel told me, and then jumped down to the first floor silently, the shifters following him.

I was still at the top of the stairs, about twelve steps or so, looking down at the entryway. One large figure entered, followed by eleven more. Bloody fucking hell. We were outnumbered, and they were armed. Animalistic growls, screams, and gunfire erupted from downstairs. I opened fire.

My .22 was small, and effective for close-range kill shots. Each shot I fired was just enough to slow the bad guys. From the other side of the room, I noticed flashes of gun fire coming from Brody's gun.

Out of ammo, I drew my dagger, and crept downstairs, staying low.

At the bottom of the steps, I reached behind an unsuspecting man reloading his gun. I swiped my blade across his neck and let him drop to the floor. Before I was able to step around him, someone grabbed me from behind, and lifted me off the floor by my throat. I was losing oxygen fast. Flailing, I reached up with my dagger and sliced at his hands until he dropped me to the floor. Gasping for air, I scrambled away, but the floor was slick with blood and I slipped. The guy took advantage of my clumsiness and kicked me. His boot glanced off my chin just enough to send me sliding on the slippery floor, but not enough to knock me out cold. *Ouch*! My ears rang. That one was going to leave a mark. I lay there for a moment, allowing my head to regain focus, and hoped this asshole would think I was out. He stood right above me, and I sliced his inner thigh with enough force to cut through fabric, skin and muscle to the femoral artery. Blood sprayed everywhere.

Before I could recover, someone pulled me to my feet. In fight mode, I ducked under the arm that was holding onto me, wiggled out of his grasp, and slashed out at a wide arc. A hand stopped mine before my dagger connected. "It's me, Kenzie, it's okay," Caid said in a hurried voice.

CHAPTER 17

KENZIE

Caid had to leave me, and I stood in the middle of the wreckage, my body trembling. How the hell did I get to this place in my life?

As part of my combat training, I had worked alongside my father's elite team of mercs after high school. My father thought it would be a good summer job for me before I entered college and used the skills I'd learned.

The first time I had to kill someone sucked. I puked. And cried. He said it would get easier and I'd get used to it. The more jobs I did, the more desensitized I became. Then I got angry. The anger kept my stomach contents down and the tears at bay.

With each merc job, my skills grew. The better I got, the more my father praised me. The job wasn't easier though, not really. I became disheartened. In the end, all the money and praises from my father were not enough to keep me in the family business. In less than a year, I became a shell. I wasn't throwing up nor was I crying, but I wasn't sleeping or eating well either.

One day, I'd looked at myself in the mirror and didn't like the person I'd become. I could clearly remember the day I walked up to my dad and told him I was quitting.

He was disappointed and said I was wasting my talents. He said killing was all I was good at. He said if I walked away, all I would end up being was a wife to someone who would never understand me and never truly love me. He said that we, him and I, were born monsters, and killing was our way of life. It was our legacy.

I liked to think that our shared merc life was his way of trying to create a common ground between us. His parents were combat mages, and their parents before that. He was used to the lifestyle and it was something he wanted us to do together.

As a child, I thought he'd be happier if I had been a boy instead of a girl. At a young age, he'd told me he wished I were different, and I broke. I remember crying so hard and for so long, my eyes were practically swollen shut. His words hurt. They still did. But I had zero regrets about walking away at that time.

When I got married, I had been determined to prove him wrong, to prove to him there was a different path for me. I was a wife, not a killer, or a monster. I had found someone who loved me. And that remained true for a time. As most marriages, the first few years were blissful.

To my disappointment, my marriage didn't work out and maybe part of that failure was because I was a monster. It had been challenging and uncomfortable, but it had also been a valuable learning experience.

After my divorce, I was grateful for my merc skills. My ex had taken all the money we had. He needed it for his new family. I just needed to get on with my life. I took on a mercenary-for-hire contract to survive and used the income to fund my other business ventures.

My father had given me an "I told you so" look when he'd found out I was a mercenary again. I could have asked him to help get me on my feet or to fund my business ventures, but it felt more meaningful to make my own money. So, I'd swallowed my pride and accepted his condescending look with a grain of salt. It wasn't easy but it was a means to an end.

Days ago, I thought I had left that part of my life behind. I was excited to leave the awful business of killing behind me. Tonight, years of training and instinct had taken over. It felt natural.

I had no regrets about my life choices. I wasn't sorry about my role in all this. It was necessary. Justified. Killing though . . . I might be good at, but I didn't love it. And I'll never, ever get used to the carnage. My heart wasn't icy enough to be a merc for life.

I slowly took in the shattered glass everywhere, the bullet holes in the walls, the furniture mangled to pieces. Blood covered just about every surface. Oh, and I couldn't forget all the dead bodies strewn about. The penthouse was a complete disaster.

Lost in my reveries, I must've looked like I was in shock. Maybe I was.

Someone was talking to me, trying to get my attention.

I made an effort to focus on the person in front of me. My senses came rushing back.

The smell of blood and feces assaulted my nose. Killing was messy business.

As if I pressed the unmute button, sound rushed in and bombarded my ears.

Stellan was yelling at someone. Hotel security was talking very loudly and at the same time. I wasn't even sure when they'd arrived. The person in front of me was snapping his fingers, and someone beside him said, "She must be in shock." His voice was muffled.

My sense of touch came alive. Thousands of nerves in my body turned on in one sudden crescendo. *Fuck my life.* My face was aching. Brody came into focus.

I shook my head in response to his snapping finger. It was a bad idea. The shaking made me dizzy, and I sat in the nearest chair, a bar stool that survived the battle. The bar was a complete mess, which made me sad. I truly hoped a bottle of whiskey was spared.

"Whiskey," I said to Brody, my voice coming out raw and

scratchy. *How'd that happen? Oh right, some brute tried to strangle me. Nice.*

Brody smiled and said, "Let's see what I can find for you."

Caid stepped into my line of sight. "Don't worry, love, I got you. You need anything else?"

"No," I said, making the mistake of shaking my head again. "No, just answers and some whiskey."

Stellan approached me and stood between my legs. He didn't touch me though. I could tell he was worried. He placed a gentle kiss on my lips, and I winced. He took a step back.

"I'll explain everything, sweetness. For now, just try to rest. This was an attack on me and Caid. Thank you for stepping in and saving my pack. We owe you."

I shook my head in protest, which was stupid because this time, I swooned while sitting. This was what happened when someone kicked you in the face. *Fucker.*

"You need to get looked at, sweetness." he caressed my tender jaw.

I wanted to protest again but thought better of it.

Brody handed me a glass. I sniffed it and took a deep drink. It warmed my lips and burned all the way down to my belly, soothing my soul from the inside.

"Erik will look after you, love," Caid told me.

"Erik?" I asked, narrowing my eyes.

"He has some med mage training. Unless you'd rather me take you to a human hospital," Brody added.

"No, no, it's fine." Human hospitals were the worst. I had already gone down memory lane once tonight. I didn't need to dredge up more memories.

My magic did a good job of keeping sharp things from piercing my skin and also helped to keep my bones intact. I wasn't worried about a broken jaw or a concussion. Magic burn would be the worst of it.

"Good, just let him take a look, then we'll get you in that huge bathtub of yours, okay?" Stellan pecked my forehead and walked away to deal with the aftermath.

Erik did a quick examination and said, "I can assess you for internal damages if you want, to make sure you don't have a concussion."

He wanted to assess my magic.

"No fucking way."

Erik rolled his eyes and said, "Fine. If you're sure. You may be suffering from shock, adrenaline drop, and magic burn perhaps. Enough whiskey." He took the glass away from me and I wanted to punch his face.

"Do as the wolf says. Take a bath and take this before you sleep. And the other when you wake." He pulled two tonics from his man purse.

I looked at the tonic with raised eyebrows; after all, this guy was a complete douche. First impressions matter.

"I have no desire to harm you, Mackenzie. The tonic has a mixture of herbs and minerals that will help restore the magic burn and speed up your healing abilities. And you may want to ice that pretty face of yours. I expect the swelling to go down, but you may be black and blue for a day or two."

When he handed me the tonics, he grasped my hand and held it. It was awkward. I looked down at his hands still holding mine, and he didn't release them. Instead, he kissed my knuckles. *Hmm . . .* what was with all these men and kissing my hands? They were sweet and gentlemanly, but gosh, I don't think my hands have received this much love in like, ever.

"Thank you," I said sincerely. I wanted to ask him about the jolt of electricity my body absorbed, but I didn't trust him.

He flashed me a genuine smile that made me want to smile in return, except mine ended up being a wince since my face was busted up. *Ouch,* I didn't even want to look it.

I stood up slowly with the intention of getting into the recommended bathtub. Exhaustion hit me. I took maybe two steps before

Caid scooped me into his arms. He was fast and so gentle I didn't even feel any ouchies.

My eyes must have drifted shut as we walked over to my place because when I reopened them, I was sitting at the edge of my tub with Brody unlacing my boots.

"I can do that." I waved him off.

Brody didn't even look up at me as he said, "Yes, you could, but leaning over to your feet would probably cause more dizziness. You don't want that now, do you?" He removed my boots.

Caid helped me get my shirt over my head, and Brody said, "I'm uh, I'm gonna let him get you into the tub and grab you some ice," He was speaking to me, but his eyes were glued on Caid undressing me. Brody wanted to stay, but he was being polite.

"Okay." I smiled on the inside because my face still hurt.

Caid undressed me with gentle efficiency. He turned the faucets and checked the water temperature before allowing me to get in.

Goodness, I wasn't that fragile, maybe a bit banged up. Thankfully, nothing was broken. As sad as it was to admit this, no man had taken care of me like this. And I was married for six years. I was definitely milking all the attention.

Caid undressed while the water warmed up, and then hit the button to turn on the rain forest shower head above. In one swift movement, he stepped under the warm water with me in his arms.

"Sir, you're needed for interrogation," one of the shifters called from outside the bathroom.

"Fuck. Give me a minute," he shouted.

"Love, I hate to leave you by yourself," he said as the warm water rinsed the blood off our bodies.

"It's okay, Caid. I got this. Go take care of business."

"I'll be back soon." He kissed me hard on the lips. It hurt but I liked it.

With my eyes closed, I rinsed my hair and body and got the feeling someone was in the bathroom watching me. I cracked one eye open to find Brody standing there with a bag of ice.

"Umm . . . sorry, I thought you'd be in the tub." He averted his eyes.

I noticed that he too had some blood splattered on him. "Just rinsing off the gore before soaking. You look like you could use a rinse, also. You're welcome to join me." Yes, I had just been naked with one guy, but I really wanted to finish what Brody and I started earlier.

"Nice try, beautiful. You're injured and I'm a gentleman. Next time." He drew my head out of the stream of water and planted kisses around my busted face and down my neck, getting himself soaked, and then he released me.

"Buzz kill," I said, and gave him a small smile.

He chuckled. "I'll leave these here." He placed the bag of ice and a bottle of bath oil on the ledge of the tub, and then reluctantly walked out.

Properly cleaned, I pulled up the stopper on the tub and filled it. Once the tub was filled, I sat back and poured in the bath oil Brody left, which was supposed to soothe sore muscles. It smelled like mahogany and teakwood, just like him. Very masculine. I didn't mind at all.

CHAPTER 18
STELLAN

The fuckers came after us with one mage and fourteen humans. Idiots. Brody, Kenzie's "friend," was smart enough to leave one alive. He was busted up, but alive. Caid was in charge of interrogation. One look at my brother's full-on vamp form scared the hostage shitless, literally. Diarrhea of the mouth and ass.

We learned there was a million-dollar bounty on our heads, mine and Caid's. A million cash each. And an extra hundred thousand dollars for each shifter.

Hotel management had apologized profusely. Someone gave those guys access to the penthouse elevators. They promised to track it down, make it right, and cover all of the damages. *Blah, blah, blah.* Someone would answer for this. We scheduled a meeting for tomorrow, but for now, they had mages cleaning up the mess.

I moved my crew over to Kenzie's place. It was plenty big enough. Hope she didn't mind. Kenzie. Shit, that woman was something. We'd heard her earlier when she came back with Brody. Had smelled her arousal. Yeah, we had been in her place waiting for her without her permission, but she'd never said we couldn't be there either.

Caid had gotten hold of a spare key, the one we'd been using every morning to hunt and let ourselves back in. She knew we had it, I think. I left that up to Caid. Sort of. I had wanted to see her just as much as he had. We fell hard the minute we saw her. The blood song got hold of us both and now we were in it for the long haul. Hopefully, she was on board, too.

We were completely besotted and wanted to be with her all the time. But I knew if I wanted her in my life, I had to give her some space. She was independent, one of the many qualities I loved about her. It hadn't been easy watching her walk away with her best friend and then it hadn't been easy knowing she was having dinner with the mage and Brody. We were determined to do everything we could to keep her happy. So we waited, somewhat patiently.

I had a feeling Brody would be with her when she came home. Not sure what he thought of the situation, but I didn't care. There was something different about that guy, but I didn't know what it was. Plus, it was hard not to like him. He'd gone into our place with her, gun blazing. He didn't know us at all and certainly didn't owe us anything. He did it for her and that said a lot about his character. He'd make a good shifter, maybe he was, but those abilities would have manifested by now. There was something magical about him, even my wolf sensed it. That was another problem for another day.

What really surprised me was her going after the intruders. One minute, she'd been up against the door aroused, the next minute she'd taken off down the hallway to our place. She probably thought Caid and I were there. Brave, too brave.

Instead of saving our asses, she saved my family, my pack. She didn't have to do that, she could've returned to her place, called hotel management, or at least sent me a text, but nope. She'd thrown herself directly into the line of fire. In some ways, that pissed me off. She had been so damn reckless. But I had to admire her bravery and skill. Her aim had been impressive, as well as her knife work. I loved her more for it.

Love. Yes, I loved her and had no intention of letting her go. She thought we were going to leave after the conference. We were, but not without her.

After giving our statements and settling the pack at Kenzie's, I went to her room to find her.

My heart stopped at the sight of her beautiful face swollen and discolored. My wolf wanted more blood from those attackers. She looked fragile sitting in front of the mirror with a bag of ice on her chin. Brody was behind her brushing her hair.

I wasn't pissed at Brody's presence like I thought I would be. He was good to her and a good fighter as well. Having him on our side during the assault had helped us and kept her alive. And now he was taking care of her again.

Turning my head away from the scene at the bathroom, I awaited the person approaching her bedroom. The mage. He was somewhat helpful with his healing abilities. He'd pissed Kenzie off earlier, and I was proud that she'd stood up to him.

"Is she alright?" he asked.

"Should be, unless there's something else we should know."

"If she's anything like her dad, and I think she is, she'll be fine. That guy's a legend."

I raised my eyebrows, "Her dad is?"

"Matthieu Jameson. Legendary combat mage. He hired me to help with her magic. She's part Fae on her mom's side. I don't have Fae blood but I can help her with some of her magic, I think."

"Interesting," I responded. When we'd completed our background check, her lineage had not been readily available, and now I knew why.

"Let me know if anyone needs anything," Erik said, and left the room.

Brody finally noticed me. "Hey, everything sorted?"

"For now." I entered the bathroom, and placed a kiss on Kenzie's forehead.

She was wearing a fluffy pink robe with matching slippers, and she was sexy as hell.

I caught my blood-splattered reflection in the mirror and grimaced. I stripped out of my shirt and removed my sweats. Most shifters must be naked to shift to animal form and back. My magic handed down to me from my parents allowed me to shift on the fly, and I kept my clothes on when going from wolf to human. Still, nakedness wasn't an issue.

Brody left the bathroom claiming he had something to do. I was grateful to have my mate all to myself.

Kenzie stood and pulled me down to kiss her.

I drew away from her. "Time for bed, sweetness, I'll join you shortly."

After my shower, I slipped in beside Kenzie, with nothing but my boxers on. I tucked my nose between her neck and shoulder, and took a deep inhale. Her scent was so familiar to me now. I'd be able to sense her anywhere. Tonight she also smelled like the human, lucky fucker. I wasn't bothered by it. In fact, I liked that he was around to care for her when Caid and I couldn't.

Supes had multiple partners in life, especially shifters. There weren't many females to begin with. My brother and I had shared, not often, but we'd experimented. Having another fella in the mix was odd, but I wasn't feeling territorial or jealous. Anything that made Kenzie happy, I supported.

"Hi." Her sleepy voice and dreamy eyes did something to me. My wolf wanted to mark her right there. And a big part of me wanted to allow it. She was in no shape for that though.

She turned her head to me. "Hi, sweetness." I placed a kiss on her forehead.

"Don't ever run into danger like that again." I kissed her left cheek.

"Come find me first." I kissed her right cheek.

"Thank you." I kissed her lips. "For running in and taking care of my pack."

"Is everyone okay? I hope your pack is comfortable sleeping here," she asked me.

Kenzie was such a sweetheart. Even tired and beat up, she was concerned for people she didn't know.

"Yes, and thank you. I let them sort themselves out in your guest rooms. Hope you don't mind."

"Of course, please tell them to make themselves at home."

They'd probably heard her. The guest rooms were not that far, and the place was practically silent aside from Brody and Erik shuffling around downstairs.

"Is there anything I can do for you, sweetness?" I kissed her lips gently. "I give the best back rubs."

"I'll be the judge of that," she said with a smile.

I got up, grabbed a bottle of lotion from the bathroom and returned. Kenzie was face down on the bed, her long dark hair cascading around the pillows. Her body was absolute perfection. Firm, lean muscles, round ass, and perky tits, and skin that was satiny soft. She wore only pretty pink panties that had bows on them. It complemented her perfect round ass.

I straddled her perfect body, resting all of my weight on my legs. With firm but not too hard pressure, I massaged her shoulders and glided my hands down her back. I took my time, listening to her moan and sigh. By the time I got to her ass, my cock was fully hard.

She noticed and raised her ass, pressing it flush against my cock. I swatted her ass playfully and coaxed her lower body back to the mattress.

"Behave yourself, Kenzie. You're supposed to be relaxing, not getting frisky."

"Where's the fun in that?" She sounded fully awake.

I shook my head and continued massaging her ass, moving around and underneath the narrow straps of her panties. Her hips arched against my touch, and she let out low, breathy moans. The musky smell of her arousal was maddening.

My cock twitched as my hand glided around her silky skin. She moaned a little louder as I massaged her lovely round ass, and she pumped it up and down on the mattress. I groaned.

It took everything in me to stop rubbing on her skin. I had to remind myself over and over that she was hurt and tired. She needed rest not a big brute taking advantage of her.

I made the conscious decision to put the lotion down and walk away, but she tucked an arm under her body, and reached toward her pussy.

"You're torturing me, sweetness," I whispered.

She let out a sensual moan and continued stroking her herself. She raised her ass again, giving me a full view of her bare crotch. That got my attention. Wanting a better look, I nudged her knees apart. My love was wearing crotchless panties. I groaned and my cock was throbbing. Still, I held fast to my restraint.

Her cunt was glistening went. I licked my lips. She slid a delicate finger between her folds, and her hips rocked back and forth.

Like a perv, I stared. My eyes locked on the beautiful, wet cunt in front of me. I was salivating, desperate to have a taste. I moaned with her even though I hadn't touched my cock yet.

When one of her fingers disappeared into her tight hole, I lost all restraint. Growling, I tore her panties in half. She gasped, with surprise and desire. I moved her fingers out of the way. Her juices created a web of moisture between her finger and her drenched cunt.

I bent and slipped her finger into my mouth. She raised her ass again, bumping me in my face. *Okay, I can take a hint.*

My plan to let her rest vanished.

I dove into her sweet pussy, devouring all of her in my mouth. My wolf growled in delight, causing a vibrating sensation on her cunt. She moaned louder and pushed harder against my face. I spread her pussy lips apart and licked alongside her entrance. Her muscles tightened. I plugged her with a thick finger and her breathing grew frantic. With a flick of my tongue on her sensitive clit, she squirted her juices, and covered my taste buds with her sweet flavor.

The nectar of her orgasm dripped in my mouth. I savored every drop while she came down from her release, her body quivering. Her breathing slowed; I was convinced she was sated.

To my surprise though, she wasn't. She rolled over and parted her legs for me.

"I want you inside me, Stel. Now." She reached down between her legs.

"Yes, ma'am." What my mate wants, my mate gets.

Her nipples were hard, and I couldn't resist them. I took a nipple between my fingers, squeezing and pinching. She moaned and spread her legs wider.

I lined up my cock with her tight hole. She was beautiful, so perfect in every way. I rubbed my tip between her lips and around her clit, and then slid in. Her pussy was so tight. With slow thrusts, I made it all the way in, my balls slapping her pussy.

My body was on fire. I tried my best to hold back, but her pussy was gripping my cock for dear life. She screamed my name and I pounded deeper and harder.

She clawed my chest and my arms drawing blood. I smelled the coppery scent and it heightened my arousal.

"Kenzie," I cried out her name, and came with her.

I flopped down on the mattress next to her and gathered her in my arms. She snuggled into my chest and draped a leg over my torso. Her hot and wet core connected with my skin. My juices and hers dripped down. I really didn't mind. In fact, I loved it. My cock stirred again, but I decided not to take her, she needed rest. Her breathing slowed, and her body went limp against mine.

I moved to get up and grab a washcloth, but she grasped my hand.

"Don't go." She tucked her face into the pillow.

I wasn't about to deny her anything. I drew her tiny body against mine. She nestled into my chest and asked, "Caid?"

He walked into the room at that very moment and snuggled against her other side. I could feel her smiling against my chest while she grabbed onto Caid's hand.

"Sweet dreams," she said to both of us.

Life was changing, and I was all for it. There were things though, things that Caid and I needed to discuss.

CHAPTER 19

KENZIE

I woke up alone in my bed, frowning. The bed was warm though and I had remembered Caid and Stellan had slept with me. On my nightstand was a tonic with a note signed by Erik that said DRINK ME. When was he in here?

I sat up with no aches or pains. The tonic must've worked. I downed the one on my nightstand, and then went to my bathroom.

There were no clothes or used towels on the floor. Someone had cleaned up in here. I got a good look at my face in the mirror. I only had slight bruising and no swelling. The cut on my top lip was healing, and the bruises around my neck were barely visible. I was healing in record time.

Still, what had happened next door was troubling. Determined to get to the bottom of this mess, I dressed in stretchy yoga clothes and hurried downstairs. Everyone, including Erik and Brody, were sitting at the dining table.

"Good morning," I said, assuming it was still morning.

"Mackenzie!" Jason, nearest to me, jumped up and gave me a hug. "You saved me! Us, I meant you saved us!"

"Oh, well, I tried my best. Glad you're okay, Jason," I said to him, feeling a bit awkward at this unexpected display of gratitude.

Jason blushed. He was a cute kid, and he really was too sweet to be hanging around this lot.

Everyone started talking and fussing at once. Erik stepped up to me, claiming I may need medical assistance. Caid insisted I have my daily dose of Green Goddess, and he nipped my neck while handing me my drink. Brody kissed my cheek and said something about me needing to eat. Stellan, of course, held his hand out to me, a gesture I've come to love. I smiled sweetly, grabbed his hand and sat my happy ass on his lap.

Looking at everyone in the room I asked, "Is everyone else good? What happened? I need details."

Stellan said, "Eat, sweetness, you must be starving. It's already noon."

Brody set the biggest burger I've ever seen in front of me. It was topped with bacon and avocado and there was a side of sweet potato fries. After everything that had happened last night, I was starving and dug in.

I took a big bite. With my mouth full, I said, "I can eat and listen at the same time. Someone care to fill me in?"

Caid started by telling me that he and Stel had been in my place when Brody and I had come home. I raised my eyebrow, recalling what Brody and I had been doing at the door. My cheeks flushed.

Caid shrugged his shoulders and said, "We've been using the extra key that was in the kitchen since we've been staying here."

I wiped my mouth with a napkin I'd retrieved next to the side of my plate. "Yes, of course, and I don't mind at all. I just didn't expect you to be waiting for me."

Apparently, they'd heard us outside the door. Shortly after noticing my presence was gone, Caid got curious and went to the peep-hole. After not seeing or hearing anything, he'd opened the door and noticed the door to their place busted open. They'd gone in, and discovered I had gone in after the intruders.

Most of what he said thereafter, I knew about. One mage and fourteen human men, had broken in to kill the pack. Thanks to Brody's smart thinking, he'd left one man alive.

Stel had dealt with The Majestic, and Caid had interrogated the man.

The interesting part was someone had placed a bounty on the brothers' heads. I had assumed the break-in was a pack issue. A bounty was a very different situation. At this revelation, I stopped eating to look at them both.

"Okay, so who put out the hit?" I said, playing with my fries.

In response, I received shrugged shoulders and shaking heads.

"He didn't know or he didn't say?" I asked.

"Didn't know. I glamoured him. There was nothing," Caid said.

"Well shit, where's my phone?" I stood up and looked around.

I remembered seeing my purse and the bags from the bazaar upstairs in my closet. Someone had retrieved my belongings from the alcove after the attack. I took the stairs two steps at a time and rummaged through my purse to find a dead cell phone. *Dammit*! I hurried back down searching around for my charger.

Mark, one of the pack members said, "You looking for this? Sorry, I used it to charge my phone last night."

"Yes! Thank you." I smiled. "And no need to be sorry. Are you all comfortable here? Have everything you need?"

"Yeah, we're great. Thanks for letting us crash here."

"Of course!" I went back into the kitchen to charge my phone and resume my lunch.

"Did anyone from the hotel say anything?" I asked Stel and Caid.

"Meeting is set. Higher ups will be here in about an hour," Stellan said.

"Good, they have some answering to do."

"Don't stress it, love, this was an attack on the pack. We don't want you in the middle of our mess. You've done plenty already," Caid said.

"Yeah, right. This is my floor. I bought this place because it's neutral territory. There's no way you're keeping me out of this."

The pack, including both brothers, looked at me and frowned as though I was disobeying orders. I laughed at them.

"Get used to it. I live here. Someone from the hotel gave an elevator key to people that did not belong on this floor. I won't give them a pass. Besides, a bounty for that amount is no joke. There are only a couple of organizations in the world that would administer that kind of payout." I tapped my phone to check messages.

"And you know those organizations?" Stellan was up on his feet, coming toward me.

"Of course," I said absently as I was looking down at my phone, scrolling through messages. "Give me a minute, I need to check something first."

I had four missed texts from Tris. In addition, I had five missed calls from the office and one missed call from Dad.

I couldn't believe my father actually called back in a somewhat timely manner. It usually took a month for him to return my calls. I called him but there was no answer, so I sent a text.

After that, I accessed my Praetorian Alliance app. I had left the mercenary guild on good standing, so I was confident they would answer a direct question. If they wouldn't, my handler would.

Praetorian Alliance, or PA, was one of the oldest and most feared organizations in the world. They were guns for hire, and they were discreet. The trick was contacting Praetorian. Plus, they were incredibly selective on the jobs they'd accept. To be honest, aside from my handler, I had no idea who ran PA, and I was okay with keeping them at a distance.

Their specialty was death. PA was a dark and seedy business. When a high-profile target needed to be killed with expediency and discretion, PA would take the contract then farm it out to their so-called members. They paid well, but I was glad to have that over and done with.

PA had found me, probably through my dad, although he and I

never spoke about it. After that brief stint of working with him as a merc, I was approached. At the time, I had zero intentions of taking that up again. I was in school and had started dating my ex. Encouraged by Uncle Brian, my handler, I went through the acceptance process anyway.

That lengthy process hadn't been easy. In fact, it had sucked. I had taken a series of tests, some painful, some psychologically scarring, but those stories were for another time. Once all that nonsense was done and over with, I had stuck it out. I had to gain something from the grueling hiring process.

With Uncle Brian's guidance, I had been given the occasional job while in school and then I had taken a long break during my marriage. My ex didn't know. I'd continued my training, though. A part of me knew I'd be getting back to it.

Since my divorce, I had accepted few jobs over the years. Only the ones that paid well. My max payout was five hundred thousand. This job on the pack paid a million. Bloody fucking hell. Someone really had a case of the ass for the dominant males that were scowling at me.

Ah, they were waiting for an answer. I couldn't really elaborate too much on Praetorian Alliance. But I had to give them something, so I put my phone down and waited for the app to respond.

"Where'd everyone go?" I asked. I was so focused on contacting PA I hadn't noticed anyone leaving.

The pack had cleared out. Only the brothers, Brody, and Erik were still here. I'd like to think Brody stayed for me, but I had no idea why Erik was hanging around.

"We need to talk, sweetness," Stellan said in a grave tone.

"K, I'm listening." I got up on the counter and sat cross-legged, waiting for a response from PA while my phone charged.

"Do you mind explaining what the actual fuck?" Caid said with an exasperated sigh. "You know the bounty?" he added.

"Ah! Yes, I'm still waiting for a response." I glanced at my phone.

Brody slanted his head and squinted at me. "You're a Praetorian, aren't you?"

"I can neither confirm nor deny my affiliation with that organization or any other organization that might be affiliated with that organization or one like it," I said sheepishly.

"Fuck me," Erik and Caid stated at the same time.

"What? I told you." I motioned at the brothers. "I'm a low-level combat mage, remember?"

Then I made another hand motion to Erik and Brody and said "I haven't talked much with you two."

"Are you able to find out who put out the hit?" Brody asked me.

"I can ask. They may or may not answer. Most clients ask for anonymity, that's a given. But, some don't care. There are those sticky situations where they want you to know they're coming for you. It's a fear tactic. In the meantime, do you guys have any ideas who it might be? The way I see it, the minute you leave this floor, they're coming for you." I pursed my lips. "Although, come to think of it, the men from last night didn't seem like PA mercs."

"So how does this PA thing work? You have an app?" Stel asked me.

"Yes, it's a process. I don't have a ticket, a job, so I'm reaching out to them. It's a slow process. Once you accept a ticket, well, then they're on your ass to get shit done yesterday," I said.

"Kenzie." Brody stood in front of me commanding my complete attention. "Is it possible Avery Knox is involved with this somehow?"

I smacked my palm against my forehead. "Fuck! I forgot about him. Did you get anything from his computer and phone?"

"No," he moved away from me and tapped on his phone. "I'll contact your tech guy now. We met up early this morning. He was supposed to have something by this evening."

"Kenzie! You mind clueing us in?" Caid said, sounding a little pissed.

I didn't blame him. Tensions were running high.

"So... we have a lot to discuss, something weird happened the day we met," I said and explained Avery Knox, the envelope, and Brody's involvement.

"Just for the record, I ended my contract with PA. I completed one last job a few days ago, got paid, and that was the end of it. However, if PA acquired a contract that had a million-dollar payout here in Vegas, I would have heard about it. Or my uncle would have."

I texted Uncle Brian and asked him to meet me.

"Kenzie." Stellan scrubbed a hand over his face. "I wish you would've told us about this. But . . . I get that you didn't know us well enough to say something, and you fulfilled your contract but fuck me, this can't be a coincidence."

"I agree, Stel," I said "I need to check in with Tom, my head of security."

I had missed calls from the office yesterday while I had been with Tristan. Since it was Saturday, Tom wouldn't be working so I called his cell and put him on speaker phone so that the guys could hear.

"Ms. Mackenzie! Finally!"

"Yeah, apologies, I was with Tris yesterday."

"No problem, he told me. I have news about Knox. He's dead."

I drew my eyebrows together, "What? When, where, how?"

"He checked out of the Desert Oasis hotel early yesterday, got on a commercial flight to the Mexico City, and was found dead in some random apartment this morning."

"Foul play, I suspect."

"Yep, knife in the gut. My guy down there confirmed it. No suspects though he was out partying or something, which is odd because he didn't leave his room once while he was here." Tom hesitated a moment. "Your private investigator said he was dealing with the computer and phone situation . . . I apologize if I'm out of line, but Miss, we need to look at the envelope." He paused, waiting for my response.

Fuck. The envelope that was still sitting in my safe at the office.

"You're right. I have a few things to take care of first. Let's plan on meeting in the office later today, I'd like you to be there, and I'll get back to you with the time."

"I'll be ready." He hung up.

I looked down at my phone and frowned. I did not like the way this was going. The envelope was a piece of the puzzle for sure, but what kind of fuckery was this to begin with? I needed more eyes on this. First Knox, then a hit on the guys. I didn't think this was a coincidence considering my association with PA. This was getting messy.

"That didn't sound good, Kenz." Caid ran a hand through his hair.

Stellan was silent and unnervingly calm. He was about to lose his shit.

Yikes!

"We need to see the envelope and the info gathered by your team. Let's set up that meeting, and I'll get Jason to come with. He's good with tech," Stel said in a calm voice.

"Okay, I'm waiting to hear from PA and my uncle."

My phone beeped a message from PA.

> Please contact your assigned pilot for
> available flights in your area.

All communication on this app was encrypted. It was some stupid story that supposedly kept people in the dark. My "pilot" was my handler, and flights were potential jobs. They were obviously not telling me shit. I showed the message to Stel, Caid, Brody, and Erik.

"Well, this could mean a couple of things," I said. "Either they don't have a job or they don't want me involved, or they need to get clearance to get me involved. In other words, it's shit. This could be a while. Sorry, guys. In the meantime, what do we have on the mage? The one that used the electric shock thing."

"Yeah, that was Anton Bard. Tier Four mage. He was working for a group called the Labyrinth." Erik spoke up for the first time today.

Ah, yes, Labyrinth. I knew of them. They came calling a while back as well. The leaders were nut jobs, high on magic and power.

They'd promised to train me and amplify my combat magic if I joined them. The recruiter at that time was a creeper. Something about him had made my skin crawl. My instincts warned me to stay far away. It had been at least a decade ago. I was young, which had been to my advantage. As a way out, I played the young doe-eyed college school girl in love and ready to settle down with her human boyfriend and have babies. I hadn't lied, at the time I was smitten. But I'd played that tune to the best of my ability. It worked though, Labyrinth never came around again.

Now, I had taken out one of their goons. Would they know it was me? Probably not. I didn't think it would matter, and I didn't care. Mages were not immortal. Like most species, a bullet would take them out. Speaking of bullets, I needed to reload.

"So Labyrinth was involved somehow. I can see why the payout is high. Mages aren't cheap," I said. "Brody, did you get a hold of Clay?" I asked as his phone rang.

"It's him," Brody said. "Clay, I've got Kenzie on speaker phone with me."

"Hi Clay," I said. "How quickly can you get that info together?"

"Hey Kenz. I can have it completed in a couple hours. But I did find something that you may want to see right away."

"Email it to me now, please. And meet me in my office in two hours with everything else you find."

"K, it's a large file. Give it some time. See you in two."

"Thanks, Clay." Brody hung up.

"How much longer till the hotel management gets here?" I asked Stel.

"Ten minutes."

"Works for me; I'll go get ready." I got off the kitchen counter and took my phone with me.

This wasn't adding up. I needed answers. For now, I needed to prep. I went to my room and locked the door. Don't get me wrong, the guys were great, but a girl had to have some secrets. In my closet, I pressed a hidden switch to open a concealed door that led to a hidden passageway located behind my closet. It was a vault I'd commissioned to be built. I had one at my home and my office also. This vault was a ten-by-ten space; it was sufficient for what I needed today. I pulled on a pair of jeans, strapped my holsters and slipped in two guns and extra ammo. I was about to put my daggers in and remembered the haul from the bazaar. The new dagger was in my closet, along with the bag of goodies. I retrieved the bag and shelved my new toys along with the gifts for the brothers. I needed to get more stuff from the bazaar before they shut down.

My phone beeped. *Fucking finally.*

> Uncle B: Hey kid. Meet me at G & S one hour.

I sent him a thumbs-up emoji.

The guys were in the entryway waiting for me. Erik arched his eyebrow at me, Caid and Stel furrowed their brows, and Brody let out a low whistle.

"What?" I asked.

"Do you have enough weapons on you?" Brody finally said.

"No, probably not. You all realize that a two-million dollar hit is not just going to disappear because we're holed up here, right?"

They all nodded in agreement.

"Where are we meeting the hotel higher-ups?" I asked.

"Next door." Caid motioned me to follow him.

CHAPTER 20

KENZIE

We walked into a brand-new Penthouse. I wandered the downstairs area that had been in bloody disarray only hours ago. *Damn!* If the guys weren't here to corroborate my story, I'd think I hallucinated the entire thing. The windows were no longer shattered, there wasn't a drop of blood anywhere, and the furniture had been replaced. Thanks to Menders, the terrible smells and stains from such an altercation were gone.

Menders were able to "mend" anything tangible, except the human body. It was interesting magic to hold. Top tier Menders could repair any structure or object. They were great for remodels and repairs. The job they did here was impressive.

The Majestic had hired Menders to do the renovations for all this. Whoever they were, I needed to get in contact with them. I imagined they could renovate my investment properties. I appreciated good, hard-working, hands-on, construction work, but wow, this was incredible.

Stel extended his hand to me and guided me to sit between him and his brother on one of the couches in the living room. Erik and Brody sat opposite us. The rest of the pack stood guard near us, all except for

Jason, who sat on the other side of Caid, a laptop perched on his lap. A few moments later, a Majestic employee walked in as well as their CEO Tarek Gaspari. Tarek was not only the CEO, but he was also one of the majority shareholders of the corporation. He prided himself on being the face of the company. Not sure why. He wasn't much to look at. He was five foot six, balding, soft in the middle, and had bushy eyebrows. He was decent enough if a bit egotistical. He was one of those men that insisted he was always right, even though he wasn't, and everything and anything that was right was because of his brilliance. Quite frankly it was annoying and I personally could only tolerate short amounts of time in his presence. Today though, he had a lot to answer for.

"Mr. Reese, Mr. Reese," he addressed the brothers, shaking their hands.

Stellan introduced the crew, then I stood and shook Tarek's hand. I knew Tarek from our real estate dealings. His family had millions of dollars and was well-immersed in this town in terms of real estate and many other lucrative businesses. I didn't give a rat's ass to be honest. I wasn't the fangirl type when it came to douche bags with money. In terms of magic, the family patriarch was a Tier Six info mage, his specialty was business, which explained their wealth and success.

"Miss Mackenzie." He shook my hand. "You caught up in this mess?"

"Considering I own half of this floor, you bet your ass I'm in the middle of this." I sat back down on the couch. "The mess though is all on you, Tarek. This is supposed to be neutral ground. How the hell did those thugs get up here?" I asked, not even trying to sugar coat the issue.

"It is unfortunate that this happened. I apologize to the Republic. Your entire stay is comped by the hotel. And we have taken every measure to make this right. I have here with me Mr. Mendoza. He is going to go over the details regarding the employee that was involved." He fidgeted with his tie.

If Tarek was nervous, Mr. Mendoza was a split-second shy of a heart attack. Sweat dripped from his forehead. He was a Hispanic man with glasses and a deeply lined face.

Tapping a tablet, he stammered, "Here is surveillance video of a former employee of The Majestic, David West on March second, at sixteen twenty-four hours."

The video showed this West guy smoking a cigarette in what looked to be the back of the hotel property. A black Benz drove up. He and the driver exchanged words as West pulled something out of his pocket to give to the driver of the vehicle.

Mendoza froze the frame on the video and zoomed in to give us a better look. It was clear that West handed over a key card. The video resumed to a shot of the vehicle driving away.

"We've given the plate info to the local authorities and this is what they've come up with." Mendoza scrolled to the next page.

The next shot was of a New York driver's license, Michael Dobrovich, age thirty-six.

"Our database has pulled up what's available on public records," Mendoza said.

Typical dirtbag record. Interesting. If there's one thing I knew about PA, they didn't deal with ex-cons. This guy was basically a low-level thug trying to get in with the big leagues. So fucking annoying.

Stellan barked something to Jason who was typing on his laptop. I was impressed. Jason was a shifter with some tech mage magic. Sweet. I didn't get any tech mage vibes off him, but that didn't mean he couldn't pull off what we needed at the moment.

"Got 'em!" Jason stood up and pumped his fists in the air.

He stood there for a moment until Stellan said, "Don't make us beg for the info, son, what've you got?"

"Dobrovich has ties to the Pacific Coast Highway pack. Says here he's been dating their Alpha's daughter." Jason pulled up the guy's social media profile.

A human dating the daughter of an Alpha. Yep, Dobrovich would have to prove himself in order to be accepted.

Some people thought getting bit by a shifter would make you a shifter as well. Not so. One or both of your parents had to be shifters. If your parents were both wolves, like Stellan's, your second nature would be that of a wolf. If you had one wolf parent and one lion parent, the dominant gene would take prevalence. If a shifter bred with a human, well, that was either hit or miss. Sometimes the child would inherit the shifter gene, sometimes not. The inherent problem with shifters was the ability to procreate. Even if both parents were shifters of the same animal, the chances of conception was very low, and a successful birth was slim to none. Which was why Stellan was a coveted treasure. He was soon to become Alpha, taking over for his father in no time.

Dobrovich had big shoes to fill. He could possibly be trying to gain his girlfriend's father's favor by taking out the largest pack in the US. I wondered if they were setting him up to fail.

Stel and Caid talked to Tarek and Mendoza about the details. I tuned them out, pondering other things. Like, what was this PA meeting about? Were they involved? What was the real motive behind the hit? If the brothers were gone, the Alpha would be left standing. That didn't make much sense. I could understand if the Alpha was taken out first, then Stellan or Caid, or both. What was the deal with Avery Knox paying me a visit? The situation at hand had many layers. And I had zero info to peel those layers back.

I refocused on the situation before me and addressed Tarek. "Pardon the intrusion."

Tarek focused on me, and I straightened my shoulders.

"Tarek, The Majestic has the reputation of being neutral ground for all species. I fully expect your cohorts to get to the bottom of all this. This is preliminary work. The Pack Republic of Texas is here on official business. Your job is to ensure that can happen without further interruption. As an owner on this floor, this situation is not nearly the standard I expected from The Majestic brand. You have clearly provided evidence that The Majestic does not enforce the standards that were promised to all owners and shareholders, and furthermore, your guests received treatment that was far less than agreed upon when they checked in. As you can imagine, one small leak of this info getting to the public would annihilate the brand, which I'm sure your shareholders would not be happy with. Thus, I fully expect you to do better. Make this right. Do you require assistance? Or can we leave this in your hands?"

Tarek paced back and forth, and then faced me. "I got this. I vow to The Pack Republic of Texas, to you, Mackenzie, and all of the other owners and shareholders in The Majestic, that I will personally see to it that the intruders will pay their due."

"By doing what exactly?" Caid crossed his arms over his chest.

"By finding them and making them pay." Tarek fidgeted with his tie again.

"How? How will you find them?" Stellan said calmly.

Tarek cleared his throat. "I recognize that we have some loose ends here in terms of our employees. That will be rectified. For now, to ensure that there isn't another breach, we've boosted security all over the hotel. We are assigning guards to this elevator on the first floor and also on this floor. Our head of security, whom you know, Ms. Mackenzie, has hand-selected guards that will be on duty as well as himself. We've also contacted the Guild; they have agreed to assist in finding Dobrovich. And once found, he is going to be facing trial. The human police departments here and in California have been notified, and the Pacific Coast pack is being investigated."

Tarek was so nervous, I was surprised he hadn't shit his pants yet.

"I ensure your personal safety, Mr. Reese, and you as well, Ms. Mackenzie. No harm will come to you and yours. We have tripled security, and we have made arrangements for the conference to be held here on Majestic grounds. No one in or out will be allowed access without being properly vetted. We have taken extra measures to screen all employees as of this morning, and every employee will undergo further investigation. I assure you, this will never happen again. Even if we have to hire all new staff members."

"And if it does happen again?" I asked him.

I had to admit, he seemed to be doing everything he possibly could. Two million dollars was a shit-ton of money. Whether PA was involved or not, seasoned mercs wouldn't hesitate to take the job. And no matter what The Majestic did, if a merc wanted a million-dollar payout, they'd find a way to get it.

Tarek turned his head to me, understanding about the weight of my question glimmering in his eyes.

"Mackenzie, if there are more issues, I promise you, I will give you this unit free of charge. Both yours and this one will have zero association fees. That is the least we can do. And for the Republic, your stay this week is covered as well as any monetary damages you may incur due to our incompetence. If this happens again, the Republic is welcomed here free of charge."

He'd just dug himself into the biggest hole, in front of witnesses. But I wasn't going to give him the breathing room to back track so I immediately responded.

"For my part, I accept. Stel, Caid, your call," I said.

Both Caid and Stellan nodded. There wasn't much else we could do but get it in writing, which Tarek promised as he practically ran out of the penthouse.

Once he exited, I looked at the guys, "Like I said earlier, we're pretty much on our own in terms of protecting ourselves. The Majestic will compensate you monetarily but you're still very much at risk," I stood.

Personally, I was okay with it. The hit wasn't out on me, but I could get caught in the crossfire. I have always taken responsibility for myself. As long as everyone around me was not affected by my actions.

I wanted to call Tris. He was with me yesterday, and I did not want him caught up in this mess.

Stellan stood and addressed the room "Brody, make sure you and yours are at the airport to pick up the Alpha. And I'm assuming you'll be coming with us to Kenzie's office?"

Brody nodded at him.

Stel pursed his mouth and continued, "Erik, see what more you can find regarding the mages. You both will be well-compensated for your work. Jason and JT, you will come with Caid and me to Kenzie's office to review the new intel her security team has on their end. The rest of you, locate Dobrovich, the vamps from The Catacombs, and apprehend anyone else affiliated with Los Angeles. We'll be conducting our own investigation."

He cupped my face with his massive hands. "What do you need from me?"

Seeing him going all Alpha like that gave me a lady boner.

"I'm good Stel, I've got things to deal with and will meet up with you in an hour or so."

"I don't want you to go alone."

I looked at him with adoring eyes.

"You thought of everything, Stel, I'll be fine. Besides, the hit is not on me. I'll see you at my office soon."

He placed his forehead against mine and whispered, "Mackenzie, if something happens to you, I am going to rip the world apart."

"I'll be fine." I hugged him with my entire body, and added silently, *I love you too, Stel.*

Reluctantly he released me into his brother's arms. "At least let Caid walk you to your car."

"I don't need an escort, but if it makes you feel better," I said and kissed his lower lip.

CHAPTER 21

KENZIE

I left to meet Uncle Brian at G&S.

Brian Sturgis was a retired merc, and one of Dad's oldest friends, hence the reason I called him uncle. He had been in our lives for as long as I could remember. I have been surrounded by mercenaries all my life, a side effect of having one as my father.

When Praetorian Alliance came calling, they assigned Uncle Brian as my handler, or maybe he asked to be. I wasn't quite sure about that. I valued Uncle Brian's opinion as he was a family friend after all, and he never had an ulterior motive.

He was a cowboy, perfectly content to mind the horses on his ranch. He retired from PA many years ago, but stayed on as my handler. He was the best, and he screened all the jobs that came in. He and I had agreed on two things: no details, and we only accepted jobs where the kill was justified, no innocents. Those jobs were easier on the conscience. Plus, he kept Praetorian Alliance far away from me. Sometimes they could be bullies and insisted mercs take a job or else. But not me, not with Uncle Brian in my corner. With my contract now fulfilled, I would always be in good standing with them and I had Uncle Brian to thank for that as well. It would be interesting to get his take on the current situation.

I could have gone back to work with Dad, instead of PA. But I knew that would mean I would never have a way out. My contract with PA had given me options to accept a job or not, and the best part was, my contract time frame had been short.

Uncle B was one hundred percent human. If he was a combat mage, he would still be an active merc, a lifer like Dad. Physically speaking, he couldn't continue. He was dealing with old injuries which made him slow. He never really talked about those injuries or his time as a merc. When I'd asked, he'd given me the same ole answer, "If I told ya, I'd have to kill ya." I knew he wouldn't actually kill me. It was a cop out.

For Dad, having combat magic gave him more longevity in the game. Being magical, he didn't look his age, and he had the physical capabilities of a thirty-five-year-old human, he was nearing three hundred years old. Plus, he genuinely loved his work. He never talked about being with PA. I was certain he had been a member at some point in his long life. When I'd asked Dad directly, he had given me a line similar to Uncle B's. "Young lady, you know better than to ask those kinds of questions."

Dealing with the old timers was often-times frustrating.

Now Dad worked for himself. He ran a crew of black ops soldiers. They did big jobs, the ones that had multiple targets and required a team. I'd worked with that team for a while, but it sucked. It had been overwhelming, or perhaps I had been too young. Either way, I wasn't going back.

I pulled into the G&S parking lot and got behind. G&S was short for Gunpowder & Spurs. It was an old run-down country bar off the Strip. The neighborhood was dodgy, and the building itself looked like it was ready to crumble.

The interior was not much better than the outside. Layers of dust and cigarette smoke overwhelmed me as soon as I'd walked through the door. The owner, Little Mike, had not bothered to install proper ventilation, or perhaps it just needed a good cleaning. The dim lighting did little to hide the layers of dust and grime.

There was a man draped over a slot machine, snoring. He held a burned out cigarette in one hand, a bottle of beer in the other.

In the middle of the dumpy place was a tiny wooden counter bar, which was always sticky and sometimes covered in ashes from patrons forgoing the use of an ashtray. That was where I found Uncle Brian. He was talking to Little Mike.

Little Mike was an old time cowboy. Unlike his nickname, he was not little. He was a huge dude with a rotund belly even Santa would envy. Over the years, I've always asked him the same question whenever I entered, and I did so today.

"Hey Mike! When you gonna renovate this place?"

His response was always the same "And scare off my fancy clients?! Never!"

Fancy clients, my ass, I muttered under my breath. Supposedly, Praetorian Alliance members came here to let off steam. I hadn't seen many regulars aside from my uncle. But again, I wasn't here much.

The back door was open, letting in the cool, clean spring air. The stench of old beer and cigarettes still lingered, but the opened door helped improve the air quality.

I sidled up to the bar and took a seat next to Uncle Brian. The uneven legs of the stool rocked as I sat down. This place was the shits!

"One day, one of your esteemed clients' is gonna fall and break their skull open from these sad sack chairs. The least you could do is buy new bar stools, Mike," I said.

"Once I put in new chairs, those fuckers would never leave. How do you think I get rid of them?!" said Little Mike.

He and Uncle Brian laughed. I rolled my eyes. The only redeeming quality about this place was Johnny Cash playing on the jukebox.

"I got something for you, young lady." Mike pulled out an ice-cold bottle of water. He showed off the bottle like he was modeling a prized jewel.

"Fancy! Just for you," he said with a mocking grin.

Mike looked ridiculous holding the bottle of water and waving his hand around it. I had to laugh.

The last time I'd been in here the glass of water I got had been flat out disgusting. There were floaties in the water, and the glass had lipstick imprinted on the rim. And that was supposedly a clean glass. *Eeeww*!

I happily accepted the bottle and thanked him. My uncle was sitting there with his cowboy hat on and what looked like a clean flannel shirt and clean jeans. Sometimes he dressed up for our meetings. Today was one of those days. His skin was weathered from being in the sun too long with no sun block. His curly gray hair peeked out from under his hat, and his unkempt beard looked especially unruly. My father was certainly older than him but looked so much younger. Uncle B could pass for my grandpa. I loved and respected him as such.

"What's going on, old man?" I asked Uncle Brian when Little Mike moved to the back to give us some privacy.

"I thought you were retiring." He arched his eyebrow at me.

"I am. I am not taking on another job. I was just curious if there was one." I shrugged.

"Hmm . . ." He scratched at his beard.

"So? Are there any high paying contracts out there?" I prodded.

"Is that why you're asking? You need money? I can probably get you a pay increase." He sipped his beer.

I shook my head. "No, no. I'm done. I was just curious."

"Hmm . . ." My uncle was always a man of few words.

"Stay away from The Majestic," he finally said.

I waited a moment for him to elaborate. When he didn't, I asked, "Why?" Sometimes it was like pulling teeth with this man.

He slanted his head and frowned. "Why does there always have to be a why? Can't you ever do as you're told?"

I fixed him with a flat stare. "Have we met? Besides, I've been at The Majestic all week."

It was Saturday and the shifter conference was scheduled for tomorrow night. The Texas Alpha was coming tomorrow as well. Uncle Brian certainly knew all of this. He probably heard about what happened last night. I was curious to find out how he would deal with the situation.

"Mackenzie, you're going to be the death of me." Uncle Brian scratched his beard again. "Were you there last night? At the penthouse incident?"

"Yes, it was on my floor. How did you know? And what do I need to know about it?"

"I hear things." He took a swig of his beer.

On those rare occasions when he did speak, it took him a while. Thank fuck I came prepared with an extra pair of patience.

I could tell by the frown marring his forehead that he was thinking things through. Probably deciding what he could share and what he couldn't. I waited patiently, sipping from my fancy water bottle and did my best not to thrum my fingers on the counter. I really didn't want to touch anything in this place. There was not enough soap in the world to wash off the cooties that were surely living on every surface.

My phone chimed. I pulled it out of my pocket. Clay's email finally arrived. Since Uncle B was still thinking, I opened it and frowned. They were lab reports of some kind. What the fuck? I was going to need help figuring out this nonsense.

"This is pack business. You shouldn't get involved, but I'm guessing you already did." Uncle B finally said.

I set my phone back in my pocket. He hadn't told me anything I didn't already know. *Come on, Uncle B, give me more.*

"Of course you did." He let out a frustrated sigh. "I wish you hadn't gotten involved. This is what I know. The Pacific Coast pack is going through changes. The Alpha is dealing with dissenters, the dissenters want him out, and there are others that want out of the pack altogether. A group of them is looking to take over Texas. Not sure which group, but they have a lot of money backing them. Hence the payload. They will be difficult to uproot. And it will not end pretty."

"It wasn't pretty last night. I need to know who to take out to end this."

"You can't, Mackenzie, this is up to the packs to sort out. Even if the hit is called off, the packs will be at war for some time. The Republic has gotten too big, the Alpha too powerful. Other packs and seethes are gunning for them to make a statement."

"Who ordered the hit? I can start there."

Uncle Brian shook his head and sat silently for a while. He knew more, but he was reluctant to say.

"Uncle, I'm already involved, and may be a possible target. They stormed my neighbors place while they were preoccupied, using a mage to break in. A Labyrinth mage, from what we could gather. The Majestic is accountable, the hired guns who were human are accountable. On top of all that, the strange visitor at my office that I told you about, the one with the made-up seal, he was found dead in Mexico City. I can't just walk away from this. It would be easier for me to go after the source." I leaned back and sighed.

He and I always agreed on going after the source. The hired guns last night were pawns. Any merc that responded to the hit were pawns looking for a paycheck. If we went directly to the person or persons that placed the hit, the contract would end and I would feel better. The pack could handle the politics from there.

"Come on. I'll walk you out." He stood and placed money on the counter. "See ya, Mike."

Little Mike waved at us. I waved back and followed behind my uncle.

Uncle B held open my car door as I got in. Once seated, he finally said, "Praetorian Alliance is not involved in this. And I don't know who placed the order, but if you insist . . . follow the money. People that have the money for this type of high profile hit always want to show off. They want to witness their chess pieces in play. They never want to do the dirty work, but they want to be onsite spectators and gloat as the game plays out."

I nodded, then pulled my phone out from my back pocket, "Okay, one more thing, do you know a good doctor, geneticist, or even a lab tech in town? I need some lab reports deciphered." From my phone, I showed him the email Clay had just sent.

"Where'd you get those?" he said in a gruff tone.

"Avery Knox, the guy with the seal."

"The dead guy?" He handed my phone back and massaged his temples.

"My team found the reports on his computer. There are some other things as well. I'm on my way to the office so that my team and the pack team can take a look at the envelope. My guess is the contents are a hit on the two brothers that are staying with me."

"I'll make a call and meet you at the office," Uncle Brian said, determination tightening his features.

He was putting his game face on. One of the very few things I liked about working for PA was how my uncle would come alive when there was a job. He wasn't out in the field, but he did enjoy puzzling things together, and this Avery Knox situation was right up his alley.

"Will do." I started the engine. "And next time, I'm choosing our meeting place," I said loudly since Little Mike was now in the parking lot escorting the patron that had passed out into a cab.

"I heard that, young lady," he yelled at me with a toothy smile.

I waved goodbye and peeled out of the parking lot.

Stel, Caid, Jason, and JT were getting out of their vehicle when I arrived at the office, a good thirty minutes early.

Jason ran up to my car to open the door.

"Nice digs, Ms. Mackenzie; I knew you were loaded but wow. Impressive!" He whistled at my building, which wasn't that grand, but I was proud of it and liked him more for noticing.

"Thank you. Everything okay?" I asked him as I got out of my car.

"Yes. Alpha, I mean Stellan, likes to be early. He wanted someone to go with you to your first meeting but you gave him the slip," he said with a smile as we joined the others.

After Caid had left me at the elevators, I had noticed someone following me out to my car and put a stop to it. I'd told Warren that I would cut him if he got in my car.

He had been happy to stay out of my car. I suppose the story was I gave him the slip.

"You smell like an ashtray." Jason wrinkled his nose.

He wasn't wrong. Smoke stench clung to my hair and my clothes. I had kept the windows down on my drive over to air out. Guess that didn't help. I swore under my breath. Gunpowder & Spurs was totally out from now on.

I kissed both brothers, and then we marched into my office. Tom was already waiting in the conference room. Clay and Brody showed up a minute later, their expressions grim. *Shit.* I hadn't shared the news about the lab reports yet. Had they discover something worse?

Since we were waiting on Uncle B, I made quick introductions and excused myself to take a shower.

Yes, my private office had a private shower. As I was growing my business, I'd dreamed of owning my own office building. When I'd purchased the land and began working with the architect on design, a private bathroom with a full shower was one of the priorities. It came in handy if I came straight here after a morning workout or if Tris and I wanted to do happy hour.

I was grateful for having the time to myself to think. The hit last night had been a bit of a shit show. But I wasn't bothered by it on a personal level. It had felt natural to pull the trigger. If I was being honest, there was a part of me that liked the adrenaline rush. All things considered, last night had been in self-defense. I had been protecting not killing for money. I felt good about it and had no remorse. Perhaps I was a monster.

Hopefully, Knox's envelope had some answers for us regarding the people responsible for the hit. Fingers crossed it would be that easy.

If not, I would take Uncle B's advice and follow the money. *Hmm . . .* That couldn't be too hard, especially in this town. If there was anywhere in the world where people liked to show off their wealth, Vegas was it. I had to speak with Bunny Rabbit.

Fresh out of the shower and dressed in clean clothes, I made my way to the conference room. Uncle B was ten minutes out so I offered to give the guys a tour. Both brothers were impressed and pride reflected in their eyes. They insisted on me boosting my security team by adding shifters and maybe one or two vamps to the payroll. It wasn't a bad idea.

Once my uncle arrived, we all assembled into the conference room.

"I didn't have time to look closely at the email Clay sent, so we can start there or with the envelope first?" I asked.

Everyone was dying to see what was in the envelope. I had already pulled it out of my safe. I was about ready to tear into the thing when everyone shouted, "Wait!"

"Mackenzie, I taught you to be more cautious than that." Uncle Brian gave me a disapproving scowl.

"What? This has been sitting in my safe for days now." I pointed at the innocuous envelope that was sitting on the table in front of me.

"Love, give us a moment to analyze it," Caid said, eyeing the envelope with caution.

Personally, I thought they were all being overly dramatic. After waving it around like an airplane, I gave in and handed it over to Stel. The brothers and my uncle shook their heads, a judgmental glint in their gazes. Jason snickered. Everyone else stared at me, shocked. At least Jason thought I was funny.

Stel sniffed the darn thing, which was not a horrible idea considering his supernatural sense of smell.

Uncle Brian opened up a satchel and retrieved a magnifying glass to analyze the seal.

Oh my stars, this was going to take hours.

Satisfied with his analysis, which proved nothing, Uncle Brian handed it back to me.

"Are you guys sure? I mean, I don't want to take any unnecessary risks," I said, just to be annoying.

The men in the room, except Uncle B, chuckled.

My uncle shook his head, "Mackenzie, stop messing around."

"Fine, party pooper. Can I at least get a drumroll?"

Jason drummed on the table with his fingers, and I laughed my ass off. Stel and Caid gave him menacing scowls. Uncle B huffed.

I gave Jason a fist bump and opened the darn thing.

I scrunched my face at the puzzling contents, pulling each item out for everyone to see. The first was a hit . . . on Avery himself. Maybe that was why he'd stayed in town. He had been waiting for me to take him out. And maybe he had been annoying me on purpose when he'd sat right here a few days ago. Geez, what kind of monster did he think I was? Anyway, this only created more questions.

Along with his request was a picture of me in the lobby of the Marquis Hotel in San Ramon, California. I had been there almost a year ago on a merc job. I'd checked in, went to my room, and had not been seen again. I'd left the keys in the room to automatically check out. Everything on file would show that I didn't leave the hotel even though I had to complete a job. There had been nothing unusual about the job, not that I could recollect at the moment. I passed the pic over to Uncle Brian.

He knew perfectly well what I'd been doing at that particular hotel on that particular date. By his deep frown, he was none too happy about this info, and I wasn't too thrilled either. Obviously someone was watching me. He took the photo and said he would look into it. Why did Avery have this photo? I couldn't be bothered with this at the moment, but it would be worth investigating.

The last item in the envelope was a key and an address for a bank located in South Florida. Apparently he'd left me a present, one that I wasn't enthused about receiving. The handwritten note was penned on stationery from BioRegenerative Services.

After going through the envelope, Clay and Brody showed us what they'd found on Knox's computers.

Clay started typing away and used the conference room television to project his computer screen, so we could all see the documents.

"It's not good, Kenz," Brody said, shaking his head as Clay flashed the lab reports on the screen. "Knox had a lot of documentation from a company called BioRegenerative Services, BRS. And dozens and dozens of reports, scientific stuff, lab reports, and blood-work from A1Labs, which is privately owned. They don't seem to be your normal lab that runs tests for routine health procedures. The subjects are supes from what I can tell. This could be good news or bad, depending on what they're testing."

Brody's expression was solemn. "And from what I could gather, A1Labs works solely for their parent company, BRS. And BRS has been funding Knox's luxurious lifestyle. All of his offshore accounts lead back to deposits from BRS or one of its many subsidiaries. We were working on locating the BRS owners when we had to leave to come here."

"Fuck," Caid muttered.

"I have a Medmage I can contact. He'll be able to decipher these reports," Brody added.

"If you trust him, yes," I said, absently looking at the reports. It was blood work for sure and DNA sequencing. *Huh? What were they studying?*

"Definitely DNA sequencing. Some of it looks like animal DNA." Uncle B moved closer to the big screen. Old man needed to wear his glasses.

"How long will it take to find BRS?" Stel asked Clay.

"Give me one second." Clay's fingers were flying away on his keyboard.

Clay Watson was a tech mage for hire. Tech mages were often high-strung individuals. Clay was no exception. He was able to focus on a dozen computer screens at a time and was often working multiple projects simultaneously. To counter act his overactive brain, Clay smoked weed . . . quite often.

Clay even looked the part of a pot head. He had shoulder-length dirty blond hair and an unkempt mustache and beard, which according to him, he kept long to hide his brand that covered the left side of his face and neck. There was no way to cover all that ink, not even with make up or laser tattoo removal. He was magically branded. Tech mages of his caliber were rare and in this digital age, lethal.

Despite his appearance and pot habit, he had mega talent. I was glad to have his help. Jason worked alongside him, eagerly learning what he could. Clay was a natural teacher, this could turn out to be a good pairing.

"Here's the website." Clay showed it to us on the big screen. It wasn't much, just an address and a message that read "coming soon." He flashed up another page with the Articles of Incorporation filing for BioRegenerative Services, and a list of corporate officers. The address of record was completely different from what was on the website.

Jason was typing furiously on his end, trying to search the addresses and list of officers. All of it was coming up blank.

"So far, we know Knox was working for BRS. BRS owns AlLabs, who was running some sort of genetic or DNA testing. And Knox wanted to be killed. He was on the run from his employers," Brody said, rubbing his chin as if the wheels were turning in his head. "This is one helluva rabbit trail."

"That it is." Clay still tapped away. "Kenz, this might take me a while. I need more screens."

The screen flashed every few seconds with different information. It was making me dizzy.

"There are several different businesses that use the same address and they all have a different list of officers. You may need to send someone over there." Clay finally looked up at everyone at the conference room table.

It was a stretch to correlate the hit with BRS, but it was all we had at the moment.

Clay was tasked with digging into BRS. Brody offered to check into A1Labs after his job to provide transport for the Alpha when he arrived. Uncle B was going to dig up info on the pic of me in California, while the pack was pursuing the Pacific Coast pack, and I took it upon myself to speak with Bunny. *What a cluster fuck!*

CHAPTER 22
KENZIE

The Majestic was crawling with security when I returned. Tarek was keeping his word. Even the parking garage had a couple of guards patrolling the area, which was usually not the case.

Back in my penthouse, I waited for the guys to show up.

I didn't have to wait long. As I was removing my weapons in my walk-in closet, Caid entered. He stood in my doorway and stared at me. I removed my daggers one at a time, then my gun, then my extra ammo, checking each before placing them on the shelf.

After I finished, he said, "That was one sexy strip tease, love. Don't stop there."

"You're impossible." I rolled my eyes. "How did you get into my room? I locked that door."

"Love, do you really think this mundane lock you have on your bedroom door is going to keep someone like me out?"

"Excellent point. Guess I'll need to update my security system around here."

He laughed, moved behind me, and massaged my shoulders.

Mmm . . . his hands ran up and down my bare skin sending tingles throughout my entire body. I arched into him, encouraging him to continue. Caid pulled my top off over my head, caressed my breasts, and suckled one of my nipples. He unbuttoned my jeans then pushed them down over my hips.

"Ahem." Someone cleared their throat. I looked up; it was Erik. That was weird. When did he get here?

"Stellan says we're running out of time and I have new info. And if you don't hurry, he's coming in to join you." He averted his eyes.

"Don't threaten me with that kind of fun," I muttered. Caid laughed.

"Shit timing, love," Caid stated and kissed me. He must have seen the disappointment on my face. "We will finish this later."

"Fine," I pouted.

"Five minutes." He slapped my ass on his way out.

"Twenty minutes," I shouted

"Four minutes left, love!"

Topless and left wanting, I decided to give him a taste of his own medicine and tease him right back. Why? Because I was feeling petty and my panties were wet, so I had to change clothes anyway. I put on a white halter maxi dress. It showed off my curves and without a bra, my hard nipples would be on full display. I descended the stairs, my head held high, my chest thrust out.

Brody approached me at the bottom of the stairway and enveloped me in his arms. "Hey, Kenzie baby! You look amazing!"

"Thank you." I kissed him on the lips.

He kissed me back, and then went to join the others.

Stellan, Caid, Brody, and Erik were seated on the sofas in the living area.

"Did you kick out the rest of the pack?" I asked Stel.

Stellan nodded and held out his hand. I grabbed it, allowing him to sit me on his lap again. He lifted my dress a little so that I could straddle him, bringing us face to face. He kissed me, snaked his hands under my dress, and grasped my hips.

When he realized I wasn't wearing any panties underneath my dress, he groaned and I gripped the back of his head, holding his face close to me. Our tongues swirled against one another.

"Excuse me! As much as I enjoy the show, we have business to discuss," Caid said.

"Not cool, man." Stellan burrowed his face between my breasts, and I turned to look at Caid.

"You cock-blocked me while we were upstairs just now. Payback's a bitch." Caid smirked.

"He's right," Stellan muttered to me.

"You two have a lot of making up to do," I said to them both while spinning around in Stel's lap to face the rest of them.

"Fuck, I need a drink," Erik said.

"That makes all of us!" Brody said. "Kenzie baby, a box of stuff came in for you today, the purple stuff you and Tris had at the bazaar. Should we have some?"

I drew my brows together. "The purple stuff? Oh Starfish! Yes! Open a bottle or two, please."

"Purple stuff?!" Caid asked.

"It's magically brewed and has twice the alcohol as normal stuff. It works. Tris and I drank it all day and I had a nice buzz going until . . . Well, until Erik over here got on my nerves." I wasn't purposely picking on him, just stating facts.

"Are you one of those girls that brings up shit from the past just to be a pain in the ass?" Erik said to me.

Erik had a handsome face. In the very near future, I would be punching that face and ruining it. Such a shame.

"Call me a pain in the ass again. I dare you." I stood up.

He had that defiant glint in his eyes again.

Brody got up and stepped in front of Erik.

Stel stayed seated and I wanted to kiss him for having faith in me to deal with the asshole on my own.

"All right, let's calm down. Erik, apologize," Caid said from where he was still sitting.

Brody stepped away and went into the kitchen, probably opening the wine box.

"Sorry," Erik muttered.

I stiffened at his half-assed attempt at an apology. He was so not sorry, the asshole.

"Kenzie?" Caid said, waiting for me to say something.

"What?"

"He apologized, Kenz, how about you forgive him so we can move on. Please," Caid implored me.

I wasn't sure why they were protecting him but fine.

"Sure, apology accepted. But someone get him a dial so he can turn down his assholery."

Erik bristled and I could tell he wanted to say something sarcastic to me.

Brody returned with a tray of glasses and an open bottle of Starfish. "Both of you, relax. Here, have a drink." He poured the wine and handed me a glass.

Okay, perhaps I was antagonizing Erik. I didn't trust him entirely, even though he seemed to be helpful. Something about him grated on my nerves. I was staring at him openly. Caid and Brody were looking back and forth between me and Erik, as if waiting for one of us to say something.

"What now?" Erik made a wry face.

"Just curious. I don't know much about you." I sipped my wine.

"You already know, I am a top tier mage. I was hired by your father to tutor you. I have studied magic all my life, which makes me a good instructor."

I waved him off, interrupting. "Yes, yes, I know that part. We discussed that at the restaurant. What are you doing here? Are you staying in The Majestic? Sorry to interrupt, but I'm curious."

I settled back down on Stellan's lap. My crotch rested right above his cock. I leaned back against him comfortably, sipping my wine and watching Erik. I knew the brothers did a background check on him, so I was probably making a big deal out of nothing. Still, intuition was everything.

"Yes, I have a room here. I've been staying here since your dad hired me. Brody contacted me to assist with some healing last night and to identify the mage. Which brings me to the news I have." Erik cleared his throat. "Like I mentioned, the mage Anton Bard was part of the Labyrinth group. Or more like formerly part of the group. He had gone rogue, something to do with practicing dark arts. When they found out, he got ousted. But they were tracking him for a while, monitoring his magical usage."

"They can do that?" I asked. That was news to me.

"Yes. There's an ancient there that can monitor magical signatures. Once you take the oath, she can monitor when you use magic and when you don't, at all times. They let him continue his elicit dealings for a while, which is why he thought he was getting away with things. I was told that he was receiving large amounts of money from an overseas tech company. The amount started out small then increased in the last six months," he said and passed around a file containing the mage's bank statements and basic info on the company that was bankrolling him.

Erik pointed at the file I was currently holding. "As you can see, info about the company is available but nothing on the owners."

I peered down at it, and Stel looked over my shoulder. All the info was from a corporation based in Belize. Missing was a list of officers here in the US. Interesting. This was a shell company supposedly dealing with online marketing.

"I need to get a copy of this over to Clay. Has anyone seen my phone?" I looked up from the file folder that was sitting in my lap.

"Here, Kenzie baby," Brody held out his hand, "I'll do that for you."

I handed the file to Brody. "Thank you."

"Why in the world would they allow him to do anything illegal with his magic for that long?" Caid asked Erik.

"That's where it gets worse. He wasn't working alone," Erik said.

"There was another mage, someone more powerful. They were allowing him to do as he pleased to get to the big fish."

"Do we know anything about that mage?" Stel asked.

Erik shook his head. "No, nothing yet. It seems he was another rogue, but not a Labyrinth member. I'm having my contact send me records of anyone that was either let go or denied membership."

"Great, now we have another player involved," Brody sighed.

"You think this other mage is in on the hit?" I asked.

"Could be. We can't rule it out." Stellan rested his head on my shoulders. I loved being this close to him.

"I wouldn't be surprised if this company was connected to BRS." Caid ran a hand through his hair.

Well, wasn't that the shit.

"At least we know for sure PA is not involved." Brody handed the file back to Erik.

"Yes, that does help. PA is a huge organization and for the most part, fair in their business dealings," I said, trailing a finger across Stel's hand.

"For the most part?" Erik asked me.

"Honor amongst thieves," I replied, shrugging my shoulders.

"PA is a nefarious organization that deals with death. How can anyone really trust them? The info I got is good, though. They wouldn't have any reason to hide or lie when it came to a two million dollar paycheck. Their cut would be significant. They'd send that out to every merc on their payroll, including yours truly," I added.

"It looks like this is as much as I can do for you right now." Erik patted the file he was holding.

"Thanks, man. This info helps. Keep us posted if you hear anything about this other mage," Stellan said.

"Sure." Erik nodded, and then looked over at me "Hope we can schedule that training, Mackenzie. After you're done being petty, of course." He gave me a small smile.

Whether he had been joking or not, I stood up intending to junk punch the asshole.

Brody ushered him out and closed the door. I was not satisfied with the answers he had given regarding himself. He had been evasive, and his attitude toward me sucked. My father wouldn't have hired someone that was a threat, but Erik could be involved in this hit. If he was involved, wouldn't he have made an attempt on the brothers by now? I decided to stay clear and let the guys handle him.

"You okay?" Caid stood up to comfort me.

I nodded. "I'm good. I need to go down and speak with Bunny. You guys work the tech mage angle, and we'll figure out a plan. For now, is your Alpha still on his way?"

"Yeah, Brody's company is assisting with that," Caid said, "The pack is en route bringing the two vamps. The ones you overheard at the club."

"Nice work." Whoever tracked them and brought them here should be applauded. Vamps kept their hideouts private for good reason. Employers that hired vamps knew that they could only expect to get their PO box info, not an actual residence. There were known hives here in Vegas, but you'd have to have balls the size of Alaska to go into one of those even during the daytime.

Stellan stood and followed me out. "You're not going anywhere in this place alone, sweetness"

In the corridor, Greg, a security guard with The Majestic, and a shifter named Warren both stood guard. We didn't need both but more was better in this situation.

Greg Chistokoff was head of security. I've known him for years and always wished I could hire him to work for me. I remembered what Stel had said earlier about hiring a shifter or vamp to my security team. I'd have to ask him about it, see if there was an opportunity there. I'm sure The Majestic treated him well, but perhaps there was something in my organization that was better for him. He was a bear, literally, a bear shifter. His human self was built like one, too. He was tall and wide and hairy. He was built like a professional wrestler, with a broad chest, wide shoulders, and large arms, but he lacked cut corded muscle like Stel. He was a good family man, and he absolutely adored his wife and their four children.

"Greg! I didn't know you were posted outside my door," I said to him.

He hugged me with one arm. "Aw, you know how it is, Ms. They send the best when something needs doing."

"Glad to have you here. How's the family?"

"The wifey is good. The kids are getting bigger every day and keeping me on my toes."

His wife was a doll and always made the best baked goods. I was determined to get her to open a bakery one day. She always declined when I brought it up, her children were small and kept her plenty busy. One day though, I'd be happy to front the cash for her bakery.

"Well, that's what happens when you keep feeding them," I said with a teasing smile.

"Don't I know it, my wife's cooking has me putting on too much weight." He rubbed his belly.

"You love it! Just chase those kids around. That'll keep you in shape." We both laughed, and then I turned to Stellan.

"Oh, sorry to be rude, this is Stellan Reese. Stel, this is Greg, The Majestic's head of security because he's the best."

The two shook hands and exchanged pleasantries while I said hello to Warren and called the elevator. When it arrived, I turned to both guards, "Don't hesitate to ask if either of you need anything. And thank you both."

As the elevator door closed, Stellan backed me up against the wall, enclosing me with his large body.

"I love watching you work, sweetness. Love watching you interact with people." He kissed my neck and chest. "You're well-liked and people respect you. You treat everyone like equals."

"I'm no better than anyone else, Stellan. We are equals in my eyes."

"No, sweetness, you are so much more than that."

He kissed me hard, and groped my body. The door opened but we didn't stop kissing, until Mark spoke up.

"Umm . . . boss?"

We separated and walked out of the elevator into the main lobby of the hotel, and a group of people stared at us. *Oops.* Sorry but not sorry.

Stellan's wasn't sorry either. He grasped my hand, and we approached the concierge desk.

CHAPTER 23

KENZIE

Bunny was not at the concierge desk. Apparently, she was working in the office today. I didn't know she had one. A human employee guided us to an office area that housed a small lobby with a couple of chairs and three equally small offices, all with glass windows. Aside from the muffled voices coming from the offices, it was relatively quiet.

Bunny sat at her desk, phone to her ear. She noticed me and gave me the one-minute hand gesture. I took a seat next to Stel and leaned into his body.

"Tell me, sweetness, what is it about Erik that you don't like?" Stel asked.

"Aside from he's an asshole?"

Stel chuckled.

"We started off wrong. And it's put me on guard around him. He umm . . . he accessed my magic, which I did not like." I scrunched up my face.

Stel nodded. "He told us about that."

"He did?" I arched my eyebrow. I was surprised Erik would admit to that.

"Yeah, he apologized to us. Said it was wrong. Said it was instinctual. Fae magic is a mystery. He said he was overtly curious." My wolf put his arm around me.

" Huh? Still makes him an asshole. What do you think about him?" I asked.

"He's worked for the pack before so we have history. I had my crew back home check into him, and he checks out. His connections to the mage world are valuable. Plus, he is skilled. He might make a good tutor." He gave me a sidelong glance. "We've had your human checked out, too, and he's good. We ran the security checks while you were out to dinner with them. If we found anything that was even slightly disturbing, we would've got you and your friend out of that restaurant. And we checked their financials. Both men are loaded. They don't need two million dollars. Still, we're on our guard for now. Don't worry, sweetness, we're covering all our bases."

I had suspected the brothers had ran background checks on both Erik and Brody. Still, it was a relief to get confirmation from Stel. Two million dollars was no joke, but if neither of them needed it, perhaps they were okay. It really sucked to be suspicious of people like this. But if Stel was good with it, I'd rely on his judgment.

"And Brody is a good guy. As you advised, we're working with him on investigating the shifter and vamp disappearances in California, and when he's up there, we'll have him visit that A1Labs place. And his company is providing transport service for Dad when he arrives. Even though Dad doesn't need it. Brody's useful in many ways."

"Good to know and I trust you Stel." I trailed my fingers over his hand that was draped around my arm.

"I'm not concerned about either of them." He kissed the side of my head. "Sandy followed Erik while we were at your office, nothing unusual reported. Something is different about Brody, I don't believe he's entirely human."

"What do you mean?" I tipped my head to look at his face.

"I'm not sure what it is. His scent is human and other. Not Fae, like you but something. Something ancient. Maybe Dad will know. And my wolf likes him. Any male around you makes me testy, with the exception of my brother and Brody and even Erik. Anyone else, including my pack members and your best friend and the tech mage . . .” He shook his head. “No more male friends, Kenzie.”

“Stel, if you told me that you didn’t want me anywhere near Brody ever again, I would do as you ask.”

“I know, sweetness. Thank you for saying so. You don’t have to stop seeing him. Shifters are different. Female shifters have difficulty conceiving so they take many partners. It’s not unusual. And it’s weird to say, but Brody watching is kind of hot.” Stel nibbled my ear.

My heart melted, and my panties got all wet. Bunny chose that exact moment to open her office door.

“Freaking interruptions,” I muttered under my breath.

Stellan huffed out a laugh as we both stood to greet Bunny.

“Mackenzie!” Bunny exclaimed and pulled me into a fierce hug. “I heard what happened! Are you okay? Well, you must be with muscles over here. Where’s the other one?”

“We’re fine. And muscles over here is Stellan. Stellan, Bunny.”

“Yes, we spoke over the phone a couple days ago about your neighbor. I see that worked out,” she said.

“Nice to formally meet you and yes, it did work out.” Stel shook her hand.

“I need details,” she said to me behind her hand in a whisper and gave me a wink.

“Come sit, both of you.” She waved us into her office. “Tell me how I can help,” she said in a louder voice even though Stel surely heard her last remark.

“I need a favor, please,” I said to Bunny.

“It is my pleasure to help you anytime with whatever you need. You are the best resident we have in this place! Girl, the stuck-up bitches that come in here are fucking awful! Excuse my language. Just because they have a lot of money, they think they own us.

Fucking annoying! You are always a joy to have around. It makes me sick this happened on your floor."

"That's my sweetness, everyone loves her." Stellan placed a kiss on my knuckles.

Bunny tried unsuccessfully to hide her smile. *Oh dear!* I could already hear the gossip mill going crazy.

"That makes you a lucky man and don't you forget it!" Bunny said.

I loved this girl. I really needed to spend more time with her.

I focused on why I came here. "Anyway. As I was saying, I need some help. I need to find the most expensive party going on tonight. There's got to be a VIP event going on in this city somewhere. Some corporation or celebrity or athlete must be throwing a soiree that costs an obscene amount, perhaps?" I said, getting us back on task.

"Oh well, that's just too easy! There are three going on that are exactly that!" She went on excitedly, and then proceeded to print out the details we needed.

Since we didn't recognize the names of the party throwers, Stel decided to split up the team. He gave Bunny the list of who was going where, and she set us up on the guest lists accordingly and sent the info to me via text. Bunny even offered to accompany us to one of the parties. Stel told her what would be expected of her, which was nothing. She would just show up with a couple of the shifters, then go about her merry way.

Bunny was incredible at her job. She had everything we needed done in less than an hour. I thanked her, and then Stel and I left.

Stellan and I got handsy in the elevator ride up to the penthouse. When the door opened to our floor, my nipples were sticking straight out, my hair was disheveled, and my pussy juices dripped down my inner thighs. We stepped into the corridor, Warren's nostrils flared and Greg regarded me with wide eyes making me blush. Shifters and their damned heightened senses. I waved at them and walked by quickly, keeping my chin down to hide my red face. Stellan, on the other hand, didn't care, his hard cock strained against his jeans as he strutted to my door with a smug look. Both men gave him a nod of approval. Men and their fucking egos.

Caid and Brody were playing some sort of video game in the living room, and two bottles of wine had been emptied. It looked like the boys were bonding.

"Kenzie baby!" Brody dropped the game controller and greeted me in his usual way. His eyes were a bit glassed over, and his words were slurring together.

I glanced at Caid who shrugged his shoulders, "Humans. Can't keep up with the big boys."

Ah, purple stuff was working its magic on our unsuspecting human. Poor Brody baby. It was early afternoon, giving us plenty of time to sober his ass up. Parties around here didn't start till nine P.M. at the earliest. We had plenty of time till then. And since we had three parties to cover, Brody had a part in all this. Fuck, how do you sober up a human drunk off of magic wine? I didn't know. Perhaps another trip to the bazaar was needed. Or maybe Erik could earn his place amongst the group. If he wanted to that is. Or maybe not. That man was a pain in my ass.

While I was thinking about how to sober Brody up, he and Caid were busy smack talking, and of course Stellan got involved. Okay then, there was too much testosterone in my living room. It was kind of fun seeing them get along so well and I wanted them to like Brody. After what Stel had said earlier, it was great watching it all playout. I poured myself a glass of wine and smacked Brody's hand away when he tried to reach for it as I sat cross-legged on one of the chairs.

"Oh, no you don't. We need to sober you up before nightfall," I said to him as he knelt down in front of me. I allowed him to lay his head in my lap. I couldn't help running my fingers through his dark brown hair, massaging his scalp with my nails.

"I'm not drunk." He slurred his words with a big drunken smile on his lips

"Sure, I believe you."

"You're sooo beautiful. I think I looove you."

Goodness, how much did he drink? How long were we gone? I laughed and continued massaging his scalp.

"I think it's naptime for Brody baby," I said.

His eyelids were closing slowly as though they were heavy. He was trying his best to keep them open but losing the battle.

"No naptime, playtime," he said sleepily.

"Naptime now, playtime later." I continued massaging his scalp and bent down placing gentle kisses on his forehead then his lips.

In a matter of seconds, he was snoring.

The brothers stared down at us with expressions I didn't really understand.

"What?" I finally said.

Caid gave me a big smile and walked over to kiss me while Stellan rubbed his hand over his face as though he was trying to wipe away the grin he wore. I wasn't sure what that was about but whatever, I didn't have time to figure it out. I needed help getting the human off the floor and in bed.

Stellan set up a pillow on the longest portion of the L-shaped sofa and draped a sheet over the leather.

Caid offered to move Brody off my lap. I knew I wouldn't be able to move the big lug onto the sofa so I let the guys sort it out. If I thought watching them joke around moments ago was cute, this was downright precious. Both brothers hefted Brody up and carefully laid him out on the sofa. Caid took his shoes off, and Stellan covered him with a blanket. Brody continued snoring contentedly. *Aww.*

"What are you smiling at, sweetness?" Stellan whispered to me, not wanting to wake up Brody.

I just beamed up at him. I didn't want to say anything that would diminish their masculinity by pointing out their sensitive sides. Plus, I couldn't get the dumb smile off my face.

Caid scooped me out of the chair and the three of us made our way upstairs.

I kissed and sucked on Caid's neck as we went up the stairs. Stellan was behind us, a wine bottle and three glasses in his hand.

Caid placed me at the foot of the bed. I knelt before him on the mattress, hiking up my dress, my knees apart. He reached out, pinched my hard nipples, and massaged my breasts, and then bent to lick my hard buds through the fabric. I tilted my head back, moaning his name.

He released me for a moment to let his brother take his place. Stel slashed at my dress, slicing it down the middle with a big hairy claw, exposing my breasts and bare pussy. Did he just partially shift?

Before I could ask how he did that, Stel's phone rang. *Son of bitch!*

Stel answered. Both men paused and listened intently to the person on the other end.

When Stel hung up, the brothers looked at each other.

"Let me guess, shit timing?" I said to them.

"Shit timing is right," Caid grunted.

"Dobrovich has been found. We'll be back as soon as we can." Stel kissed me.

Dobrovich was the moron who was involved with the hit next door.

I kissed them and let them go. This was a big deal. They couldn't pleasure me all day while there was important work to be done. I understood perfectly. I had lady blue balls now, but I understood.

CHAPTER 24

KENZIE

With the brothers and the pack gone and Brody still asleep, I did a quick cleanup of the place, and then went to the gym. I needed to work off this sexual frustration.

After my workout and a shower, the guys were still gone and Brody was still asleep.

I sat next to him and stared like a creeper. He looked so peaceful and young. Gosh, how old was he? The brothers looked about twenty-seven, which was not close to their real age, but magical beings didn't age like humans. Brody was human as far as I could tell despite what Stel had said earlier. I caressed Brody's cheek, but he didn't even stir. I kissed his lips, nothing. He was still snoring away. This guy slept like the dead. Or maybe I was not his true princess.

He needed to rest so I left him alone and went into the kitchen and started cooking.

As soon as the food was ready, the guys arrived home, pack in tow.

Jason zeroed in on the food, the rest of the pack gathered around the dining room table.

"Brody hasn't woken up yet?" Caid asked me.

"Not yet. Should I be worried?"

Stel and Caid shrugged their shoulders.

I sat next to Brody, petting his head again. This time he stirred.

He smiled up at me with sleepy eyes. I couldn't resist caressing his dimples.

"Kenzie baby," he said in a soft voice. I almost felt bad for waking him. "Time is it?"

"Time to wake up, Sleeping Beauty, we're making plans for tonight."

"Okay, okay, I'm up." Instead of getting up, he brought me down to his chest and held me close.

I wiggled my body to fit against his more comfortably. "You don't have to be involved in this, you know. The pack has it covered, and this really isn't your fight."

"No baby, I'll see this through, if you'll have me of course," He kissed me on my forehead. I raised my head to kiss him on his jaw. He tugged my chin up to kiss me lightly on the lips. *Mmm*, I liked kissing him.

When I pulled away from the kiss, Brody had a sweet smile on his lips. He and I would need to have a conversation about the situation, but this wasn't the right time. For now, we needed to deal with the bad guys.

"Yes, we'd love your help with this situation. I don't even know what to call it," I said to him.

"Operation Follow the Money?" He stretched his back and sat up. That made me giggle.

"Would you like some coffee?" I offered, while standing up.

He shook his head and smiled. "Thanks babe, I'll join you guys in a minute."

I watched him leave the room to sort himself out. A little concerned, I sent off a message to Pierre, the wine guy from the bazaar. He might know of a hangover cure for humans. He responded right away with a potential answer, so I popped out the door, letting the guards know Pierre was on his way.

The pack were still in the dining area eating the food I'd prepared. They feasted on fajitas, with Spanish rice, chips and salsa, a Mexican salad, and fresh guacamole.

They murmured their thanks to me between bites. It made me feel good that they enjoyed my cooking.

"Ms., if you keep feeding us like this, we'll never leave," Mark stated, which earned him a glare from Sandy, and growls from Stel and Caid.

"I only meant that we'll gladly stick around as long as the bosses will have us," he amended, keeping his head down.

I was having a tough time keeping track of their possessiveness.

Brody joined us, and he stopped behind me, resting his chin on my shoulder. He looked a little green, poor baby. I petted his head.

"Will food help?" I asked him. He nodded so I made him a plate while he took a seat.

To their credit, the pack didn't make fun of him. Stel even poured him a big glass of water, which he downed.

The pack cleaned the kitchen after dinner, and then we all went into the living area for our debriefing.

Stellan started the meeting.

"First up, just an update. Dobrovich was apprehended earlier by the human police and handed over to the Guild. Caid and I went down there to interview him, but he couldn't say anything. Someone put a spell on him. Every time he mentioned anything about The Majestic, our pack, or the Pacific Coast pack, he fell over in pain. Erik is down there now, working with the mages to see if they can break the spell."

This was not good news. A geas like that could kill him before he could say a thing.

Stel met my uneasy stare then continued. "Since Dobrovich may not prove to be useful, we're going to continue our own investigation. We have reason to believe the guys that put out the hit are here in Vegas. We narrowed down three potential places they could be tonight. There are three VIP parties to attend. We're getting help from Kenzie, Brody, and Bunny, another friend of Kenzie's. I want two people going into the party, and two to remain outside as lookout and extraction. Warren, Stedman, and JT: you'll attend Crystals, along with Bunny. She has already been debriefed. Sandy, Mark, Jason, and Brody: you're at Nacht Residence. Me, Caid, and Kenzie will be at Cloud Nine."

"Sir, you'll be short one person at Cloud Nine," Jason said.

"That's on purpose. We suspect them to be there and want them to make their move. And that's why my brother and I will be sticking together. But since we can't be one hundred percent certain that they will be there, the rest of you will cover the other parties. Your mission is to make contact with the VIP guests and find out any info on who may have put out the hit. If you suspect the culprits are there, text back code word *Treasure* and stay on them until the rest of us arrive. Do not engage until you get back up. Clear?"

Everyone gave Stel their acknowledgement.

Sandy asked about Bunny, or more importantly why she was a part of this in the first place. Stel did not appreciate her line of questioning and quickly shut her down. She was a troublemaker for sure. She was the type that was drawn to drama and reveled in causing dissension. Stel was ever the patient leader when dealing with her. I knew she was only questioning Bunny's involvement because she was my friend, but I wasn't worried one bit. Sandy could be a bitch about it all she wanted. I was there when Bunny had volunteered to help. Stel had debriefed her when the three of us were together, and he assured her, and me as well, that her part was small. And more importantly, the three shifters he assigned to her would keep her safe. It was a good plan. As a concierge, she was expected to be at parties now and then. Having friends with her was not all that unusual, and no one would question it. All she needed to do was show up and introduce Warren and JT to the host. It was sweet of her to volunteer to do this with us. And Stel made sure that she knew enough to keep her safe but not too much where she might be a target. He was looking out for her, and I trusted the shifters would look out for her as well. I really needed to do something special for her once this was done.

Caid pulled up a dossier on the big screen, which gave detailed info on each host at these VIP parties. He and Stel had info on everything from what they looked like, their preferences and the drinks they liked, their businesses, and their family lives as well. BRS was hosting a party, the one Caid, Stel, and I would be attending. Clay was able to identify the owners of BRS, but they were not listed as hosts. Hopefully they would show. Caid had thorough info on them as well. Impressed with their work, I gazed at the brothers with adoration. Those two could rule the world.

After everyone acknowledged their role, the pack members cleared out to prep. I had a meeting of my own.

Pierre Morceau showed up, with a case half his size. I guided him to the living room, while Caid, Stellan, and Brody went into the dining room to discuss other details.

Pierre surprised me with the apothecary of tonics and potions in his case. Apparently, he wasn't just a wine maker, he was also quite the alchemist. The case opened up like an accordion, containing rows of neatly organized little jars. It must've weighed a ton, another surprise because I had him beat by five inches in height, and he couldn't have weighed more than I did.

He had so much in his case it was a tad overwhelming. Pierre took his time, taking the vials out one by one and explained each one to me. The bottles themselves were completely different. Some were plain, some were intricately designed, and some were different color. I was interested in all of them.

The first one he handed me was the one I wanted to cure Brody's hangover. I set two aside. The next was a delicately designed bottle that was a pheromone enhancer designed to attract a lover. The bottle had a pretty delicate flower etched into the glass. I thought it would make a good gift for Bunny. He had a few more bottles that helped restore magic burnout. I bought every bottle he had of that one. I certainly planned on learning more about using my magic, but this would help in the meantime. He had truth serums and anti-aging potions. He even had one that would extend a man's erection. I had to get that for Tris as a gag gift. He'd laugh and swear he would never use it, then use it and tell me all about it.

Brody came in and took a seat next to me. His leg brushed up against mine. He still looked a bit haggard, but the water and food must've restored his energy.

"Look?!" I showed him the bottle of hangover cure. "A special blend just for you!"

Pierre explained the benefits and how it worked. Brody didn't hesitate to swing it back. Damn, this guy was trusting. He thanked Pierre, and then kissed the top of my head and went back into the kitchen.

"How long will it take to take to work on him?" I asked Pierre.

"Mere moments, Miss." Pierre bowed his head, and then continued to show me other things.

"Pierre, this is all incredible. Why didn't you sell this at your booth downstairs?"

"This is a hobby. My family is in wine business," he said with pride.

Thank goodness he spoke English because my French was shit.

"Is your wine popular in France?" I was surprised I hadn't heard about it before.

"Human wine, yes. Mage wine, no." He shook his head.

"Not yet. It will be. I'll do my best to help. I'd like to speak with you further about these tonics and potions. Perhaps I can retail them with my skin care."

"Really?" His eyes widened.

"Yes, and the wine too. Maybe we can set up a distributorship agreement for me to sell here in the US." I had to run the numbers, but it would be a great opportunity. Besides, with all the other shit going on in my life, why not add more to my plate?

"*Mon dieu! Merci beacoup!*" This must have been exciting news because he ranted in his native language. Other than those few words, I had no idea what he was saying.

Pierre continued going on and on with a big smile on his face. At least he was smiling. I sat patiently and allowed Pierre to get whatever it was out of his system when Caid walked in and started communicating with him in French. My jaw dropped. Of course the hot vamp would be fluent in French. And oh my, hearing him speak the love language made me hot.

Caid placed an arm around me and said, "Pierre is very excited about doing business with you. And I told him that he needed to treat you fairly, or else."

"Please tell me you didn't threaten the nice man, Caid." I wanted Pierre to feel comfortable about working with me.

"Maybe just a little. Did you buy enough stuff?" He pointed with his chin to the huge pile of bottles sitting near me.

"For now," I said unapologetically and smiled.

Forty minutes later, Pierre left me with a bottle of just about everything and promised to send up another case of wine. I took notes and pics of everything because, goddess forbid, I mixed up things. I paid him handsomely, and he kissed me on each cheek and left.

CHAPTER 25

KENZIE

With just about an hour to get to our designated party, I went to my room to get ready. Cloud Nine was a decadent pool club located on the rooftop of Majestic Tower One. Most places that offered bottled service started out at three-thousand dollars per table. This place was three times that amount, and the waitlist was a good three to six months out.

I was betting we'd find our target there. If I was right, we could have this all done without much bloodshed. We'd find our target, get them to call off the hit, and everyone would be happy. Then I could spend the rest of the weekend between the sheets with my guys. That would make my weekend.

For once, I took my time getting ready for this pool party. Seated at my vanity in the bathroom, I added beach wave curls to my hair and carefully applied waterproof mascara and a light layer of makeup, just enough to highlight my cheekbones and accentuate my lips and eyes. In early April, the night-time weather would be on the cooler side but not too cold to where I'd be uncomfortable in a dress.

I chose a turquoise ombre strapless dress that had an asymmetrical high-low hem line. The bodice showed off my cleavage while

205

the hemline flowed delicately over the curves of my hips. The front of the dress was just long enough to conceal my dagger, while the back grazed the back of my knees. Underneath, I wore a gold string bikini that had a gold chain-link detailing embedded with turquoise gems as straps on the bottoms. The top was strapless and had the same gold chain-link turquoise gems in the middle. It was flashy, perfect for a nightclub pool party. The colors accented my tanned skin and would reflect the light. To draw more attention, I rubbed my entire body with a lotion that had a gold shimmer and slid on five-inch gold Louboutin heels. I added a few gold bangles on my wrists, gold hoop earrings, and the gawdy ring I'd bought from the bazaar. Matched with the dress, the ring didn't look half bad. I glanced at my reflection in the bathroom mirror, and added final touch-ups to my make up.

"Wow!" Brody admired me with an impish grin. "I can't believe I'm not on Team Kenzie tonight. So not fair!" He pouted. He showed no traces of a hangover. I should've bought more of the cure.

"Looks like you're feeling better."

Brody was a casual dresser like Caid. This was the first time I'd seen him dressed up. Damn, he looked good. He wore black dress slacks with a light gray button-down shirt and a matching black sports coat slung over his shoulder.

His face was cleanly shaved, and he'd added gel to slick his wavy locks back. I was pouting over him not being on Team Kenzie tonight also.

He placed kisses on my neck, and I gripped the countertop to keep me steady. I pushed my ass back against his crotch and groaned. The guys had clit-teased me all day long, and it was driving me insane.

I turned to face him and sucked on his bottom lip, leaving mauve lipstick all over his face. He gently traced his fingers down my arms, to my fingers.

I slipped away a bit, grabbed a tissue and wiped the lipstick off him, "You're going to get gold shimmers all over you."

"Don't care." His lips came crashing down to mine and hard cock pressed against me.

I broke our kiss and turned my back toward him. Time was short and we had things to do.

Brody pulled me to his chest. His lips were all over the back of my neck and bare shoulders. His hands palmed my breasts.

"Brody baby, I don't think we have time for this."

"We don't." He snaked a hand under my dress.

I pushed my ass back, grinding harder against his cock. "Maybe we should stop," I said unconvincingly.

"Maybe." His voice was deep and husky.

I caught our reflection in the mirror, mesmerized by what we we're doing.

He looked at the reflection, and our eyes met. He unzipped my dress, dropping it to pool on the floor around my feet.

He stared at my reflection for a moment, running his hands all over my body. I wanted to be completely naked for him, and I wanted him to see all of me. I wiggled out of my bikini bottoms while he unclasped my top.

"You are so fucking beautiful, Kenzie. I absolutely adore you," he said with hooded eyes.

I loved the way he was looking at me.

He squeezed my nipples then ran a finger down my slit. Juices soaked my lips and coated my inner thighs. I gasped.

"I love how wet you are."

Desperate to feel his skin, I turned and yanked on his tucked in shirt. While he unbuttoned his shirt, I snaked my hand underneath it and glided my fingers on his flat, muscular abdomen. Our kisses become more heated. My pussy was drenched, my core pulsating. I unbuttoned his pants and reached down to stroke his hard length. He tilted his head back and moaned.

"Come here." He led me out to the bedroom, taking off his sports coat and shirt as he walked.

My room was dark, the only light filtering in came from the city lights outside my window. During the day, Vegas was like any other concrete jungle. But at night, it was almost magical. The lights went on for miles down the Strip, and lit up like the Milky Way. The peaceful silence of my bedroom enhanced the city's beauty.

Brody passed the bed and led me over to the floor-to-ceiling glass window. He placed my hands on the glass. Behind me, he hooked my jaw, turning my face to devour my lips with his mouth, while he reached down to rub my throbbing clit with his other hand.

He gripped my hips, and then pushed my chest against the window. My hard nipples pressed against the cool glass. My naked body was on full display for the entire city to see.

He tapped each foot with his, forcing me to spread my legs farther apart.

"I've been wanting to fuck you since the day we met." He stared at my pussy in the window reflection.

Brody lined himself up with my cunt, and kept his gaze on my naked body as he sank himself inside me. My pussy eagerly accommodated his girth and length, and squeezed him slowly as he slid all the way in to the base of his shaft.

Moaning, I bucked my hips against him. He took absolute control. He fucked me hard against the window, making me scream out his name. My breath fogged the glass. I loved that he was fucking me in front of the whole city. Having an audience made me come hard and fast. The intensity of my orgasm made me lightheaded, and my legs quivered.

"You're so sexy," he whispered. "I've been dreaming about you every night and thinking about you all day long. Can you come for me again?" He reached around to flick my clit.

His thrusts become more and more persistent, and he fucked me like this was the last thing he would ever do. I didn't want this to end. Knowing that anyone could see me getting fucked took me to new heights, and my pussy juices dripped all over his balls.

"You like being watched, don't you baby." He yanked my hair, forcing me to arch back toward him, all while his other hand was pressed on my lower back, bracing me in that perfect position.

"Fuck yes, I want the world to see me being fucked."

Brody roared when he came, filling me with his hot cum. He didn't slow down. His hips kept pounding into my core while he snaked a hand over my belly and down to stroke my swollen clit, another orgasm ripped through me and I screamed out his name.

We were both panting, our breath fogging the glass. Brody held me up between his big, heavy body and the window, and I closed my eyes, savoring the moment.

"That was fucking hot," Caid said from behind us.

I snapped my eyes open. In the reflection of the glass, Caid and Stellan stood on either of side of us and they were openly staring.

"Really? You guys couldn't give us a moment?" Brody said, his voice still deep and husky.

"Like you didn't notice us standing here." Lust glimmered in Stel's eyes.

Brody tried to hide a smirk. The brat had known we had an audience. Not that I cared.

"Sorry . . . not sorry," he said to me, leaving a kiss on my shoulder.

He straightened and slid out of me. I felt empty, and his cum leaked down my leg. Feeling a little shaky, I braced myself against the window. He placed a hand at the small of my back, supporting me but stepped away and allowed Caid to step at my side. My sexy vamp steadied me on my feet. I could see the outline of Caid's cock through his pants.

"We need to get going." Stellan kept his eyes focused on me.

"I'll take a quick shower. You good, baby?" Brody cupped my face and kissed me reverently.

I kissed him back and nodded, still leaning on Caid. Feeling empty, I watched him walk away.

Stel stepped directly in front of me, and lust stirred in my belly. Fuck me, I was so depraved. I was completely addicted to these guys.

My pulse was racing, and my pussy was throbbing. All I wanted was for both brothers to stick their cocks in me. They'd turned me into a sexual deviant, and I absolutely loved it.

"Sweetness, we don't have time," Stel said, unconvincingly.

Heat emanated off Stel's large muscular body. He was standing so close, but didn't make contact. Caid stood behind me. Both men had their hands at their sides, minimizing contact, resisting the temptation.

Stel's swept his gaze all over my body. He fixated on my pussy, and his nostrils flared. He smelled my arousal, and for once, I was glad. I was hoping my arousal incited him to take his clothes off.

"Not even a quickie?" I asked, pleading with my eyes. My breasts were heaving with every breath.

Brody was out of the shower and half-dressed. He sauntered up to us, turned my cheek to him and kissed me fiercely, leaving me breathless. Without warning, he plunged his finger into my needy cunt.

I cried out, my hips involuntarily rocking to meet his thrusting finger.

"Kenzie baby, if I could stay, I would. You two take care of this sweet, tight pussy; she wants to be fucked again, don't you?" Brody removed his finger abruptly and shoved it in my mouth, then kissed me again.

I moaned out my agreement. He groaned, then left hurriedly as though he had to make a quick exit or he'd never leave. My legs wobbled, and my cunt ached with want. I fingered myself while Caid and Stellan stripped out of their clothes.

CHAPTER 26
KENZIE

Ouchy, my love box was feeling extra sensitive, and I had no complaints. My body, although tender, was tingly all over. My skin was radiant with the afterglow of multiple orgasms; I was in heaven. This was what being dick drunk felt like. Best high ever.

Caid and Stellan met my demands and then some. After Brody left, they satisfied my need. I was being greedy, but I was utterly consumed with them. The fact that Stel, Caid, and Brody were on-board with sharing created flutters in my belly. I was already dreaming about being with all three at the same time.

Thanks to my insatiable needs, we were fashionably late to the party. It actually worked out, considering we had a short walk to Cloud Nine.

I strapped my brand new dagger to my thigh, my gold Chanel clutch was too small for anything aside from my phone. It wasn't ideal, but the strap fit comfortably around my shoulder freeing up my hands. I could make it work. The brothers insisted they would protect me and I didn't need to bring anything. Of that I had no doubt, but a girl couldn't be too careful.

Brody hooked us all up with mics and earpieces that were nothing but clear-colored round stickers no larger than a dime. They were practically invisible. The earpieces wouldn't work across town, but they would be fine within our smaller groups. The plan was to infiltrate the hosts' inner circle. This was something I was good at so the guys were going to stand back. I arrived seemingly alone, after Stellan and before Caid.

On the rooftop pool deck, I paused to admire the view of the entire city. It was spectacular, you could see the dark silhouettes of the mountains on the west side of the valley, all the way to the untouched desert heading north past the motor speedway. The infinity pool faced east, darkness creeping at the edges of the city toward the lake.

Crisp, cool air teased my skin. Fire pits were lit along the pathways and surrounded the pool, providing a bit of warmth. Loud EDM music pumping out from the speakers muted the sounds of voices and laughter. Patrons writhed to the music, or engaged in some sort of sexual act. My body stirred as I glimpsed a couple making out on a lounge chair. The female's skirt was hooked up around her waist while the man pinched one of her nipples. My pulse sped up, and my thighs involuntarily clenched.

"Focus, love," Caid said in my earpiece.

"Your arousal is distracting, sweetness," Stellan added.

How did they sense that from so far away? I shook my head, clearing the lust haze in my brain, and I continued walking. I scanned the crowd and located the brothers. Stellan was at one end of the bar doing his job to blend in. He wore a tight black t-shirt and black slacks that gave off the illusion of being part of the security team. Caid was reclining back on a chaise lounge near one of the fire pits casually sipping on amber liquid from a snifter glass. Cognac. Good choice. Where could I get one of those?

My musing about getting a glass of alcohol ended as I noticed a human female propping her ass on the arm of Caid's chair. Her black leather skirt barely covered her long legs that she stretched out before her. Short blonde hair accentuated the slim line of her neck and highlighted her perfect features.

Oh hell no. A knot in my stomach was blooming, and my hackles were up. I'd never been jealous, until the brother's walked into my life. Before I could get my emotions under control, I headed straight toward them. I was pissed as fuck. They were MINE.

"Easy, Kenzie. He doesn't mean anything to her," Stellan said in my ear. "Caid, get rid of the skank," he growled.

"I'm waiting for my girl," Caid said to the bitch.

Blondie didn't move away from him. Instead, she leaned in closer and spoke into his earpiece. "She's not here now, is she?"

I was going to cut a bitch. I was ready to throw my dagger and take her eye out. From where I stood, it would be an easy shot.

"Leave. Now," Caid said and all but pushed her off him.

She stumbled and walked away looking offended, as though he had the audacity to reject her.

"Sweetness, focus," Stel said in a stern voice.

I rerouted my steps and headed for the nearest bar. What the actual fuck was wrong with me? I was ready to rip her fucking head off. Still annoyed with myself and what I'd witnessed, which was nothing, I turned back and saw her walking toward the opposite end of the bar, farther away from Caid. The bitch better move.

A cocktail waiter stopped in front of me with a tray of champagne. "Glass of champagne?"

I picked up a glass and downed it. *Mmm*, Cristal. Fancy. I placed the empty glass on the tray and snagged another before he moved off and gave the waiter a wink.

"You okay, love?" Caid asked me with too much smile in his voice.

"Sorry, guys, not sure what the fuck is wrong with me, but if either of you start talking to any ladies, I am likely to lose my shit," I replied, hiding my lips with my glass.

Jealousy had never been my thing. I hated that I was being so irrational. And I hated that I was losing focus, and I hated that I allowed some skank to unsettle me like this.

We had a job to do, a rather important one. This was not the time for me to get emotional. Fuck, I needed a minute to gather my thoughts. I found a corner near a pool towel cabinet to stand next to.

"Hi, beautiful," Stellan said from behind me. I took a deep inhale.

"We're with you, sweetness, no one else." He traced a finger along the backside of my shoulder.

With my free hand, I reached back toward him. Our fingertips touched. "Thank you."

"You need a break?" His voice was barely a whisper.

"No, no, I got this. Make my way into the hosts area, confirm they're responsible for the hit, and signal you for extraction," I said to him and to myself to remind me of what I needed to do.

Fuck, when did I become so unprofessional? Stellan's words and presence grounded me, renewing my determination.

Still hidden behind the shadows, he moved my hair to plant a kiss on my neck, and then he disappeared into the crowd. I downed the rest of my champagne and made my way further into the party.

I traversed the rooftop to the VIP section. It looked like all the pretty people were up here. If my magic senses were correct, they were mostly human. I was about to grab another glass of champagne from another waiter's tray when I heard my name.

"Kenzie!" A guard waved at me trying to get my attention. "Hi! It's been a while!" he said to me. I looked over at the guard, dressed in a tight black shirt and tight black pants. Who was this guy? I smiled as he approached. I could smell his cologne from six feet away. Ah yes. I remembered him. We had sex once, and it wasn't very good.

"Brett! Good to see you." Of course, I lied.

"You too. You look great! What brings you out?" He kissed my cheek.

"Thank you! I'm just making new friends and enjoying the free champagne."

Laughing, he said, "Follow me. I'll introduce you to one of the bartenders."

He pushed his way into the crowd and introduced me to a fella behind the bar. As Brett continued to speak, the bartender handed me a glass of champagne from a freshly opened bottle. I thanked him and smiled, pretending to be involved in the conversation.

"Yes sir, be right there," Brett said into his wrist, and then turned to me. "The hosts want to meet you, gorgeous."

I followed him through the club to a roped off area that over-looked the pool. The crowd grew thicker the closer we got. Everyone wanted to be near the hosts it seemed. Instinctively, I searched for both Caid and Stellan. I couldn't see them, but I felt their presence close behind me. It was comforting to have back up even though I didn't need it.

Brett stopped suddenly, and I bumped into him. He turned and whispered, "Let's hook up later."

"You better tell him no," Caid said to me in my earpiece.

His statement made me smile, but before I could respond to Brett, he moved aside, revealing the two men we were here to see.

The owners of BRS, Carlos de Rosa and Wilfred Bates, sat in the VIP lounge area surrounded by four bodyguards and a half dozen sycophants. Women in bikinis and topless men were draped over the lounges, drinking and doing drugs. Some were dancing.

Carlos was wiping white powder from his nose, smiling sugges-tively as he stood and placed my hand in his. "Welcome, welcome, welcome! You, gorgeous, belong here with us! Please, sit!"

His sweaty hand grossed me out, and I discreetly wiped my palm on my dress. According to the dossier Caid and Stel had briefed us on earlier, Carlos de Rosa and Wilfred Bates, both human, were tech billionaires from Silicon Valley. Their startup company was mostly involved in gambling software and crypto mining. The intel said that Carlos was the brainiac. He was a bona fide genius. He graduated from MIT when he was fourteen and became a self-made millionaire by the time he was only eighteen years old. His solo success continued at a steady pace until his early to mid-thirties. During that time frame his life became tabloid fodder, which coincidentally started when he'd partnered with Wilfred Bates.

Wilfred Bates had a humbler past. He'd worked for a major tech company as a software engineer for a good decade. He had designs on starting his own company, which is where Carlos came in. They started their company five years ago, and its success recently put them on the billionaire list.

Carlos could not have been more than thirty-eight, but he looked like he was pushing sixty. He was unhealthily thin with thinning hair to match. If it wasn't for the money, this guy would not be mingling with this type of crowd. He wore white linen drawstring pants paired with a multicolored satin button-up shirt that was left open to reveal a narrow hairy chest and a too-thin torso. Drug use was rearing its ugly head and marking his body.

Bates, on the other hand, was complete opposite. He was tall and slim, with raven black curly hair, and almost feminine features. He would be considered attractive if not for the sinister glint in his dark eyes. He had the posture of someone holding in a grudge, cold and very distrusting. He was ten years older than Carlos and was believed to be influential in his young partner's life. Unlike Carlos, he wasn't partaking in drug use and looked to be nursing a beer. Bates wasn't a partier. He was here to observe. He beckoned me over. Although he made my skin crawl, I took a seat between them.

We started with small talk. Who are you, where you from, what do you do? I laughed at their jokes and pretended interest in whatever it was they had to say. I politely declined drugs or drinks, sticking with my champagne. I sipped my drink very slowly so I wouldn't need a refill. I poured alcohol for them both, and their appreciation for my act of subservience became apparent as they ignored the other guests. Bates scrutinized me. He was interested in me but wanted me to grovel to him. Doing so would make it too easy, and it would turn him away. Bates was competitive, and he wanted more of what he couldn't have. If his partner got the attention from someone he was interested in, Bates would fight harder to prove he was a better catch. A song with a slow beat played and Carlos and I got up to dance. We danced off to the side, blocking Bates's view of us.

In my heels, I was a good foot taller than Carlos. It was too cute. We swayed to the music. His body was close but not touching mine.

"You should come back to our room," he said, trying to get closer to me.

I raised my eyebrows. "Our room? You and your partner share?"

"No. I mean yes. We are both in the penthouse at The Dragon. But no, we don't share anything else."

"Just business and hotel rooms."

"Yeah, something like that," he said.

He looked lost in thought, so I said nothing. After a minute, I asked, "Did I say something wrong?"

"No! No, you're, you're perfect. It's just . . . Between you and me, I liked it better when I called all the shots."

"Oh?! Why? You two seem to have the perfect synergy. Your business is super successful."

"It is but, fuck, he's intense. We have plenty of money, enough to last generations, but he wants more. And more power. I like to enjoy myself." He shook his head.

"Are you enjoying yourself tonight?" I asked, swaying my hips to music.

"With you, yes." He smiled.

Whether it was the drugs or the fact that he was overwhelmed and out of his element, Carlos just wanted to unburden himself. This was my opportunity to get him to tell me all about it, so I danced a little closer, holding his gaze.

His eyes brightened with desire, his guard falling further. "Bate's has got some shit going on this weekend, things I don't want any part of. I like having you here."

"Well, that sounds ominous. Promise to tell me when it's time to take cover?" I said with a coy smile.

"You're fine. I won't let nothing happen to you." Carlos puffed up his narrow chest.

"Are you going to be okay?" Fake concern laced my words.

"Yeah, yeah, should be. He's got us involved with the pack in L.A. It's a new business venture involving some of our genetic sequencing and DNA alterations. It's fucking scary, you know, dealing with supes. But he insists. We're helping the pack, and the pack is offering up test subjects. It could be really cool, you know. We got next level genetics testing and stuff," Carlos said.

Damn, it was too easy to get him to open up.

"That sounds intense. It can't be safe making a deal like that with shifters." I tried to keep the tone of my voice soothing.

"Don't worry, he gave the order to take out the biggest threat." I shook my head like I didn't know what he meant, encouraging him to continue.

"He paid people to do the dirty work. Hit men," he said in a whisper.

We have ourselves a winner! I couldn't believe he just admitted that to me.

"We'll be partying and nowhere near it when it goes down," he said in a louder voice.

Bates moved to a lounge chair directly in front of us, making the couple that was sitting there leave. He glared in our direction, a calculating look in his eyes. He may have heard Carlos, but I continued with the ruse. All I needed now was to lure them out.

"Partying sounds good to me!" I smiled. I held one of his hands overhead and twirled.

He laughed, and we continued dancing, the bass of the music thumping in my chest.

Bates was still glaring at us.

"I think your partner is feeling left out. You mind if I drag him onto the dance floor with us?"

"Go get him! He needs to loosen up." He turned around and motioned to Bates to come join us.

I laughed and approached Bates. "Come on! This is a good song!"

Reluctantly, he got up, drink in hand, and danced with Carlos and me. Carlos was having the time of his life. Bates was pretending to enjoy himself.

"Carlos said you're staying at The Dragon," I shouted to Bates over the music.

"I told her she should come check it out. She's never been," Carlos added.

"Let's not waste any time. Let's go now," Bates said leering at me.

"Really? You wanna leave?" Carlos' eyes widened.

I shuddered. These two were so gross but I'm a professional so I sucked it up.

"Yeah, let's get out of here. Everything is lined up. Be better if we got far away from here." Bates grabbed a champagne glass from the table and handed it to me.

"Do NOT drink that, love," Caid said in my ear piece. He didn't need to tell me. My magic ring flared hot, warning me of danger.

"We got eyes on you and will follow. The rest of the team are back and in place. Keep it up," Stellan added.

Swaying, I looked at Carlos and Bates with arched brows. "We out of here?"

"Let's go. Our limo awaits!" Carlos reached out to me, tipping my glass and causing the contents to spill. He laughed and offered to grab me a new one on the way.

Bates was scowling again. He noticed me noticing. I stepped up right in front of him, and gently patted his cheek.

"Smile, Bates. It's a party, your party. Aren't you having a good time?" I slurred my words and wobbled a bit.

He thawed a little, smiling shyly at first.

"There it is! That billion-dollar smile."

His smile got wider. I linked my arm in his and we followed Carlos out.

"I think we should get you more champagne," he said to me.

"Yes!" I stopped to speak with the bartender I had been introduced to.

He noticed me and asked, "More champagne?"

"Yes, a bottle please. I like to share!"

This brought a genuine smile to Bate's lips. Finally the fucker was starting to thaw. I needed him to keep his guard down until my guys snatched them up.

"Good work, Kenz," Stellan said in my earpiece as we stepped into a vacant elevator.

Carlos was still dancing even though there wasn't any music, and Bates was now drinking champagne directly from the bottle. We were all laughing carelessly as the elevator started its descent. Midway down, the elevator stopped. In a matter of seconds, Stellan and Caid burst in, knocked out both guys, hauled them over their shoulders and exited the elevator. I followed closely behind them as they entered the stairwell, running down a couple floors. I was proud of myself. I wasn't doing any heavy lifting, but I was keeping up with them in my five-inch heels.

We exited the stairwell, and the guys deposited the still-unconscious bodies into a large laundry cart.

JT, who looked nothing like a maid, walked off with the cart and entered a service elevator.

Caid picked me up and took me into another elevator, kissing me feverishly. I wrapped my arms around his neck and my legs around his hips. Stel entered the elevator right behind us. Caid turned to lean up against the elevator wall while Stel's chest pressed against my back, and he nipped and sucked at my neck. My tender over-used pussy was wet and throbbing. I was moaning, and wanted them to take me right there.

The elevator dinged as we reached the lower level.

"Oh my God!" A woman shrieked at the sight of us groping each other.

We broke apart and exited, and the woman still stared at us, mouth agape, hand to her chest.

Oopsy! She was an older woman, grandmotherly. I almost felt bad. Almost.

Before too long, we were at my place. The brothers dropped me off and left for their interrogation. They wanted to keep me safe, and had insisted it was better to keep me out of it. I'd resisted at first, but Caid reminded me that Carlos and Bates thought I was a party goer with no ties to the pack or that I was a supe. True enough, it was best to keep it that way for now.

THE PENTHOUSE WAS empty and I had mixed feelings about that. My body was riding the high of adrenaline and lust. And for the first time in days, I was all alone. I'd been entrenched with the brothers and their problems. Truthfully, I enjoyed every moment with them, Brody included. It wasn't just the sex. Working with them, going out to clubs with them, and even the quiet moments all meant something to me. They were a welcome change to my single independent life. Companionship was something I secretly wished for. *Uh-oh*, I felt the strings of attachment forming, and I didn't know how to reel them back in, or if I really wanted to.

CHAPTER 27
CAID

Kenzie's jealousy had hit me like a punch to the face. It had taken everything in me to refrain from marking her as mine, right there and then. My brother had felt it, too. When she'd confessed her possessiveness over us, his wolf had been ready to make his mark as well.

Watching her work our targets to get the info from them had made her even more appealing. She had a way with making people feel comfortable. Shit, Carlos was willing to give her anything she asked, even though she hadn't. Bates was all ice. Cold as fuck and calculating, yet she'd defrosted that iciness and brought them both to us without a fight.

We had to leave her in the penthouse to go down to the basement. She could hold her own, no doubt, but the info she'd obtained from Carlos revealed a more sinister plot. Stel had insisted on keeping her identity anonymous as much as possible. I had to agree. She was out here, we lived in Texas. If the Pacific Coast pack got wind of her involvement, this could be bad for her. We didn't want that. I wanted her to come home with us to Texas.

I looked over to Stellan, the brother of my soul. She was ours. One couldn't have her without the other. It just wouldn't work.

He noticed me staring at him and said "I know, I know, I don't want to go home without her, either."

I wasn't surprised he knew my thoughts. All our lives, we always knew what the other was thinking. However, I was surprised he wanted to take her home with us.

"Do you think she'll come?" I asked. "If we ask nicely?" She was not the type to uproot her life for any man. Let alone two.

"I hope so. I don't think it will be that easy for her. Or for us."

Ah fuck, sometimes I forgot the responsibilities we were saddled with. Stellan would become pack Alpha soon, and he would be expected to mate and perpetuate the bloodline. I already had an arrangement, sort of. It was in no way a marriage, so I wasn't lying when Kenzie had asked the question over dinner. I hoped she would understand. Plus, I had the master vamps in Texas to deal with. That would be grueling. I was strong, but the ancient ones were stronger. They were not inclined to acquiesce to a young buck like me. This hit was nothing in comparison to all the hits that came at me when I was at home. I was used to it and was able to manage it so far. In order to lead, the vamp masters would expect me to prove myself. They were gunning for me, and they made it clear. That meant Kenzie, my love, would be an easy target.

Truthfully though, the issues with the master vamps weren't all that worrisome. Kenzie could handle herself. It was the other arrangement with a female vamp that had me scared. It would break me if Kenzie walked away because of it.

"I love her," I said out loud.

"Me too," Stellan said.

We were fucked as far as she was concerned. Maybe we were pussy drunk.

"No, it's not just the sex. Although, that does help," Stel said, finishing my thought.

We entered the basement, both of us smiling. Considering we

were about to interrogate two morons that had paid to have us killed, our smiles were inappropriate.

The pack and Brody were here. Once we'd confirmed Carlos and Bates were at the pool here, Stel called them all back. Brody was here helping Jason with the surveillance. They were scrubbing our faces and eliminating all traces of us being down here, as well as deleting the footage that showed Kenzie walking out with Carlos and Bates.

For a human, he sure was helpful. And seeing him with Kenzie, fuuucckk. My dick twitched.

He stood up as we approached. Good, Stel and I needed to speak with him.

"How's Kenzie?" Brody asked.

"We dropped her off at her place," Stel said.

"About Kenzie . . ." I started to say. Brody crossed his arms. Motherfucker. He had balls. Kenzie would never forgive me if I killed him. So, I restrained myself and continued. "Relax, we know you're not going away, but we plan on marking her before we leave."

He raised his chin at Stel and me. "She okay with that?"

"Yes," Stel and I said at the same time.

"Fine, I'll give you guys some space." He paused a moment, rubbing his chin. "I plan on heading to California after the Alpha's arrival to look into those disappearances and those labs."

Brody was having a team pick up our dad instead of the transport company we had hired earlier. Dad wanted to come in stealth-like, which made it easier with Brody's involvement.

"Thanks for looking into that. Invoice the pack, not Kenzie," Stel told him.

"Something about it is not sitting well with me." Brody shook his head.

He was working on the puzzle, which helped us out a lot.

"Everything looking good with the surveillance?" Stel asked him.

"Yeah. Kenzie's tech mage is freaking brilliant. He created a backdoor entrance into The Majestics' security system. He could take this whole place down. Jason and I are working on it. It'll get done,"

Brody said, and then walked back over to Jason who was sitting at a table with his computer gear. After taking a couple steps away from us, he turned back around.

"Just so you two know, I will choose Kenzie every time, without question. Don't hurt her. You're lucky she loves you." He stalked off.

Stel and I looked at each other. "She loves us," I said. My brother and I smiled.

"They're awake, boss." Warren said, getting our attention.

Nodding to Warren, I followed Stel to where Carlos and Bates were tied to chairs.

Carlos saw us. "Where's Kenzie?! What did you do to her?!"

Aww, the guy liked her. This could work to our benefit.

"Hotel security found her knocked out in the elevator and got her medical attention," Stel said.

He sputtered nervously, looking back and forth between us. "What did you do!"

"Relax, she was knocked out and that's it. For now," I told him.

We'd never hurt Kenzie, not in a million years, but he didn't need to know that. Carlos, released a breath, relaxing. His partner sneered at us.

"You know who we are?" Stellan asked, looking directly at the silent one who wisely cast his eyes down.

"No, no, of course not. We, I, we didn't do anything," Carlos said.

"Really? You're telling me you had no part in the hit on my brother and me," Stel compressed his mouth.

A flash of realization crossed Bates' face. He kept his head down focusing on the floor.

"No, I wouldn't. I didn't. It wasn't my idea. We can undo it! Tell them, Bates!" Carlos was panicking.

Good. He was going to sing like a canary.

"Shut up, you fool!" Bates spat out, anger reddening his face.

"Oh no, Carlos, please do continue," Stel said.

"Fuck you, you filthy shifter, you think you're so much better than us humans. Think you can control everything! Because of us, the Pacific Coast pack will take over the whole country. We will be stronger and more powerful," Bates blurted.

Stellan backhanded the fucker like a fly, knocking him out.

"You were saying?" I said to Carlos, getting his attention.

"Yes, yes, we did put out the hit. He did it. It wasn't my idea. I don't like his plans. Never did! I, I can fix it, give you everything you need. Please don't hurt me!" Carlos began sobbing.

The fear that had radiated off him when we'd first started was now amplified to nerve shattering panic.

"First, cancel the hit. Now." Stellan said.

"You need to text Bronson. He used to work for Labyrinth. He's the one that we paid to place the bounty. Check Bates' phone. Or mine."

I made quick work of Bates' phone, using his finger to unlock the device. I found Bronson in the messages, did a quick read through, and then typed "Cancel the hit." I hit "send to the group" option.

> Bronson: Are you sure? First try failed but our second attempt is all set for the Alpha and his sons tomorrow at the conference.

> I responded: Affirmative. Change of plans. Cancel the hit immediately. Payment is off the table.

> Bronson: We're not refunding the deposit.

> I responded: Fine

> Bronson: Group text URGENT!! Republic job cancelled immediately. No payment granted.

> Sasha Cohen: WTF? Who authorized this?

I knew Sasha. He was the beta in L.A., another wolf. Motherfucker. I showed Stellan the messages between him and Bates. His Alpha didn't know about the hit.

I texted to the group: I canceled it asshole.
Don't question me. Our deal is off.

Unknown: Affirmative

Blake Reynolds: Affirmative

Son of bitch, Blake was second to the master of the seethe in L.A. County. Those fuckers were all making moves against us.

"Is it done?" Carlos asked nervously.

"What kind of deal did you have with the shifters in California. Tell us everything," Stel said.

And so, he did. Like we'd gathered from his conversation with Kenzie, they had a lab in California that was doing testing on supes, shifters, and vamps. They were studying our blood and DNA. He thought it was possible to give humans super natural powers by altering their genetic structure and combining them with that of a supe. Bates was one hundred percent human and was interested in the alteration. He wanted powers. Money was not enough. Greedy fuck. The beta in L.A. wanted to overtake the Alpha, typical. And he wanted to come after us once his powers were amplified, which was possible according to Bates. Carlos was not on board with that last bit. He said they didn't have any proof of that and he was in charge of the labs and research. To further his research though, they needed volunteers. Volunteers both Sasha and Blake were willing to provide.

We spent hours going over every detail. Brody continued working with Jason doing what they could tech wise. Jason was good with tech, but he could use more training. Together, they were manipulating Majestic's security system. After Carlos told us about all their shenanigans, they got to work, tracking the lab. It wouldn't be long before we had access to everything. With his help, we were even able to gather more intel on the Pacific Coast supe community's involvement. It went deep. There were layers of criminal activity, thanks to Bates's manipulations.

Bates woke up halfway through Carlos's confession. When he

realized he'd been made, he had a fit. He swore profusely, strained at the cuffs, and bucked in the chair, which only caused it to topple to the floor, his face making acquaintance with the concrete. Moron. His frantic screams were nothing but an annoying waste of time. Without remorse, I flashed to him and ripped his carotid artery with my teeth, putting him out of his misery.

Wide-eyed and trembling all over, Carlos pissed himself. Brody saved the day again by calming him down and getting the guy to focus and spill more info.

It was an interesting dynamic having Brody on our team. Obviously, he had feelings for Kenzie. We watched them have sex, which had been better than porn and yet neither of us had been bothered by it. Brody was good to her, and he would care for her. She was also softer around him, nurturing in some ways. Perhaps Stel and I were okay with this because as far we could tell, he was human. His life was temporary. And he was young, even in human years. If I was being completely honest with myself, what Stel and I thought about him didn't matter. Kenzie would do as she wanted, and we'd have to toe the line, or she would tell us to fuck off. Brody was helpful and he made her happy. If that changed, we'd change right along with it.

We pressed on, gathering all the info we could possibly get from Carlos. He was wiped out, the fear-based adrenaline had sapped all of his energy. I wasn't sure what we'd do with him. For now, we were busy packing up computer gear, and cleaning up what was left of Bates. We made quick work of removing any evidence of him.

"What should we do with the little guy?" I asked Stellan.

My brother tipped his head to one side and rubbed his chin. "He could be useful if we get him cleaned up."

"You want to take him back with us?"

"Yeah, I think so. His partner will have an unfortunate accident, and Carlos will check himself into a rehab aka Wild Oak Ranch. If he sobers up, he might be able to work with us on all that genetic stuff instead of against us."

"And that's why you get to lead the pack." I clapped him on the back.

He was a natural leader, and the pack would follow. I was proud to have him as my brother. I just hoped I could lead as well with the vamps.

"And you will make an even better leader than I with the vamps," he told me, reading my mind again.

CHAPTER 28

KENZIE

Being alone in my place had never been an issue. Up until this week, I had always been alone in here. Yeah, I had occasional lovers but unlike the brothers most weren't invited to spend the night. Those two had practically moved in, and I didn't mind at all.

My home would not be the same without them. I cleaned up everywhere I could, and took extra care to primp before getting into bed. I even laundered the sheets from today's playtime, except the pillow cases, which still smelled like the brothers. Stellan's scent was on the right and Caid's on the left. I was secretly thinking that I'd never wash these pillows ever again. That was absolutely pathetic.

It was nearly midnight, but sleep evaded me. I tossed and turned for what felt like forever. I finally gave in and sat up, thinking of ways to occupy my time till they returned. Returned? Was I seriously waiting up for them? Will my absurd attachment never cease? Yes, I was already becoming attached. How did that happen? This was new for me. I was happy with my single life, wasn't I? They were clear that they had responsibilities at home and moreover, they loved it there. But maybe, just maybe, they felt the same way I did, and we could figure out what would happen after the conference was over. After all, we did have a conversation about me being their mate.

Plus, how did Brody fit into all this? I knew very little about the guy, but what I did know I liked. It seemed he got along with them well, and I could tell there was a bond forming as well as a business relationship. What would happen when the brothers left? Would Brody leave, too? Did I want him to leave? I couldn't decide. I really didn't want to. If Caid and Stel left me for good, would I have a relationship with just Brody? That didn't sit well with me for some reason. My phone dinged a text. It was from Brody. Had he read my thoughts?

Brody: Thinking about you Kenzie baby. Hope you're sleeping soundly.

Me: Thinking about you too. Not sleeping, restless.

Brody: Wish I could do something about that restlessness. Helping the guys. Try to sleep.

Hearing from him made me relax a bit. I was thankful they all worked well together. Still, what would happen next? The conference was tomorrow. Time here was running out. Maybe a long-distance relationship might work? I was making myself crazy.

Frustrated, I decided to divert my fanciful thoughts of a life with the brothers and Brody. I got out my laptop and went to work. I sent and replied to emails, analyzed numbers from inventory to shipping to expenses, and did the payroll. I researched more properties and made a list of things I needed to do for the recently acquired property in Texas. The Texas property was twenty-five acres of prairie land with a patch of wooded area, a small house smack dab in the middle, and a creek not terribly far away. It was perfect. I longed for a place that was remote, quiet, away from people, somewhere I could openly practice my magic. I wanted to have horses and the freedom to run around naked outdoors, if I wanted to. Thinking about the Texas property made me smile, mostly because I wondered if the brothers lived close by. There I went again, making plans with men I shouldn't be thinking about. I kept getting ahead of myself.

An hour or so later, I was beyond caught up with work stuff. I even had tasks and projects for the staff that would last a couple weeks. My thoughts kept returning to all three guys. It was nearly one A.M. and they weren't back yet. Or maybe they were next door. That thought fired me up. I threw on my robe, and marched downstairs determined to get some answers.

I flung open the door, and JT was sitting there on guard duty. I stopped short, unsure. Like I was caught doing something I shouldn't have been doing.

"Miss. You should go to bed. They're not back yet. Try to sleep."

He rarely spoke. I almost forgot what his voice sounded like. It was hoarse like his vocal cords had been damaged.

"Um . . . are they okay?"

"Yes, of course, you don't need to worry about them. They'll be back soon." He grimaced, which I guessed was his version of a reassuring smile.

I tapped my foot on the floor. "Have you heard anything? From anyone?"

"The pack is fine. We all have our jobs. The brothers work well together and will always make good choices. They'll come back to you. I promise." He turned his head to face the elevator doors.

Feeling dismissed, I closed the door. I wandered into the kitchen, still too restless to sleep and opened the fridge. My refrigerator was full and I couldn't sleep so I decided to cook. The pack had big appetites. They would probably be hungry when they returned. I got to work preparing two breakfast casseroles, filled with cooked sausages, and veggies. These could be easily warmed when they returned. I rolled out dough for cinnamon rolls and popped them in the oven to bake alongside the casseroles. There were a couple bags of potatoes. Whoa, who ate this much? I had a big appetite but I certainly wouldn't eat all of this food on my own. I decided to roast them since they would go nicely with the casseroles. There were packs of bacon, and I cooked them as well because shifters seemed to like extra protein. I also squeezed oranges to make fresh orange juice. I stepped back to look at the food that was spread over the counters, dabbing my damp brow with a paper towel. This was a lot of food, and luckily, I had the bakeware for it all.

After I cleaned the kitchen and breakfast or brunch was all set, the guys still weren't back yet. I peeked out the door. JT was still sitting there so I offered up some food.

"Yes, please. It smells so good," he said, absently rubbing his belly. "I can't leave my post, though."

"I'll bring you something to eat and some coffee. Sound good?"

"Yes, thank you, Miss."

I delivered a plate to JT who said, "Thank you Miss. It won't be much longer. I'll make sure they come to you as soon as they return. Try to sleep."

Fatigue finally settled in and I went back to bed. I snuggled up to the pillows now named Caid and Stellan, and I focused on JT's promise. A contented smile curved my lips. He would send them to me as soon as they returned.

CHAPTER 29
STELLAN

Greg, head of Majestic security, was standing at the elevators leading to the Penthouse. A feeling of dread tightened my chest. Why was he here? My thoughts immediately focused on Kenzie. Was she okay? She must be. JT was up there guarding her door.

"What happened?" I asked, not even bothering to say hello.

"Nothing. Everything is good. I was on my way up. I wanted to introduce you to Kevin, my second. He is going to stand guard today until this afternoon. Kenzie knows him."

I nodded at this Kevin. We didn't need the extra security, not for ourselves, and especially not now since the hit was called off. But we wanted to take extra precautions for Kenzie's sake. She had quite the network. Greg was definitely an asset. He'd helped us take care of things in the basement with zero interference or repercussions, and now he was offering this guard. I wondered if he'd be open to relocating. He'd be great to have back on the ranch.

Her little friend Bunny was also incredibly helpful. She'd put together VIP access to all the parties last night, which showed we were nowhere near the BRS partners. Plus, she'd given us all alibi's that were solid should anyone ask.

Kenzie's alibi was that she'd left the party with Carlos and Wilfred, and they'd parted ways at the elevator. She'd gone home alone. JT, the guard on duty, would support her alibi.

The sun was up, and we all had been up for more than twenty-four hours now. My wolf wanted to run, but was more anxious than I was to see her. It had been a long night.

Exiting the elevator with the new guard, I barked out orders, sending a couple pack members to ensure Carlos was situated. Mark and Stedman brought him up earlier and secured him in one of the guest rooms. He was coming with us to Texas after all. I intended to sober him up and make use of his talents somehow. He was smart and not a bad guy, he just got caught up in his partner's schemes.

I was turning toward Kenzie's door when Jason spoke to me.

"Sir, we'd rather stay with you...all of us together. If you don't mind." He kept his eyes on the floor.

Shifters took comfort in numbers. After the night we had, that would be expected and welcomed.

I nodded. "Secure the package and make your way back . . . quietly. I don't want Kenzie to be disturbed."

I reached her door and JT said, "Sir," He almost never spoke. This must be important and about Kenzie.

"Is she okay?" I interrupted him before he could finish. Being away from her was making my wolf restless.

"Yes, great, sir, I think. She did come out this morning looking for you, both. I think she finally fell asleep around three A.M. That's all, sir."

"Why do I smell bacon?" Caid muttered.

My nostrils flared I noticed it also but was to focused on my sweetness to bother asking.

"She cooked; I think she wanted to have food prepped for when you came home. Breakfast food. The cinnamon rolls are great. I hope she made extra." JT smiled and rubbed his stomach.

That was the most I'd ever heard him speak. He liked her. Of course he did. Everyone liked her. A hint of jealousy rolled through me; a low growl rumbled from my chest.

"Sir, forgive me, she offered. I didn't go near her." He quickly looked down, hands in the air in submission.

"It's fine. Thank you for standing guard. Kevin will take over. Get some rest."

He didn't move, waiting for my signal allowing him to come in. I nodded my head toward her door, which made him relax. "Be quiet."

Caid went straight toward the kitchen. The pack followed in behind him. My pack was hungry so I allowed them to go in and eat. I followed them, curious to know what my sweetness was up to. I widened my gaze. She had prepared a feast. Brunch food. Something tugged on my heart.

"You okay, sir?" Sandy asked. "Your chest," she pointed to where my hand was rubbing the area over my heart.

I didn't even realize what I was doing, and it made me a bit self-conscious. This sensation was odd. Kenzie genuinely cared for me, for us. After years and years of taking care of the pack, it was nice to have someone taking care of me for a change.

"You like her, boss. Can't blame you. She can cook, and she's not bad to look at either," Warren added.

My claws elongated, and I was a split second from ripping his throat out for that comment. My wolf was at the surface pushing to get out.

"Whoa! No offense, sir." Warren amended, and everyone in my pack knelt in a submissive position.

Bloody fucking hell. I quickly, reigned in my wolf. Should I apologize? Probably, but I didn't.

"None taken. Eat, clean up, and keep quiet." I swiped a cinnamon roll and a handful of bacon to take upstairs. "Now get up."

My pack rose and grabbed plates.

I wasn't hungry when I'd entered the kitchen, but the spread made me ravenous. The snacks I'd grabbed on my way out of the kitchen were in my belly by the time I reached the top of the stairs. I probably should've eaten with the rest of the pack and had an actual meal, but I wanted to be with Kenzie more. Plus, Caid was down there. He'd make sure they stayed quiet and cleaned up after they ate.

I walked quietly into her room. Kenzie was sleeping soundly, her long dark hair cascading over the pillows. She looked like an angel. One pillow was between her legs, the other smashed against her chest. A naked thigh peeked out from under the covers. I caressed her silky skin, wanting nothing more than to remove the tiny boy shorts she was wearing and bury myself deep into her pussy. If I slipped a finger in her, I bet she'd be all wet. Before my curiosity got the better of me, I noticed the dried blood under my nails and caked on my clothes. Only a caveman would get into bed like this. After taking a quick shower, I threw on a clean pair of boxers. Caid and I moved in here, and everything we'd packed was in her closet now. Had she noticed?

Trying my best not to disturb her, I slipped in next to her as quietly as possible. I pulled one of the pillows away, and she grumbled in her sleepy voice. I gathered her small, barely dressed body and drew her against me. She sighed softly and squirmed around, making herself comfortable on top of me. She nestled her face into my neck. At first contact, I bristled. For most supes, this was the most vulnerable area of the body. As a fighter, this was a primary target. Rip out the neck and take out your opponent. That was how it went.

With Kenzie's soft body against mine and her face nuzzled into my neck, the feeling was entirely different, and I relaxed. At that moment, having her touch my neck spread peace and contentment through me, something so foreign. I'd never experienced anything like it. Life as I knew it would never be the same again. Before I could question my feelings, she stirred.

"Stel. You're home, finally," she whispered in her sexy sleepy voice.

Her lips puckered and she kissed my skin.

I kissed her forehead and whispered back "I'm here, sweetness, go back to sleep."

Her breathing deepened, and I grinned. She was already sleeping.

Caid entered, smiling as he gazed at us. He approached the bed. I focused on his blood splattered shirt and shook my head. No way was I letting him in bed like that. Vamps were messy eaters. He looked down, realized his error and hopped into the shower.

I was still awake when he slipped in on the other side of the bed. He hovered over Kenzie and planted kisses on her cheek. He'd better not wake her. His nostrils flared as he inhaled her scent from the top of her head to her neck and down her back. He was going to wake her, and I would have to punch him.

She repositioned her body, keeping her back on my chest and one leg draped over Caid's waist. Caid rested his head on her breasts. She lazily reached up and ran her fingers through Caid's still wet hair. The droplets of water wet her tank top and exposed her nipples through the fabric. Despite my exhaustion, my cock stirred.

"Caid," she said sleepily, acknowledging his presence.

Kenzie didn't stir again, and her breathing slowed. She started to snore softly. It was adorable, and sounded like she was purring. She was unaware that she was doing something to my heart.

Caid sensed my mood and whispered, "I'm in love with her, Stel. I know you are too."

"I am. We cannot lose her," I admitted to him.

"What are we going to do?" Caid asked me, his voice sounding uncertain.

I knew what he was asking of me, but I didn't have an answer.

Our roles did not allow us to make a choice such as this so freely. My father expected me to provide him with a wolf heir. The probability of that happening with Kenzie was unlikely. She briefly mentioned that she was unable to conceive, causing a sadness that weighed heavily on her. My childhood had been full of expectations. My father was a good man, he raised Caid and I well. I wasn't complaining. But I didn't want the same for my children, if I had any, and I didn't dislike them, I just didn't care if I had an heir.

Caid, on the other hand, was in a similar situation. Day walkers were created in the traditional human procreation way. His parents were both day walkers. Our father had made an agreement with his sire to keep him with us when we were just boys. The promise was that he would mate with another day walker. An arrangement was already in place. That would be tricky to get around. But we would find a way. We had to.

Me and Caid lay there thinking over our options. Our bodies exhausted, but our minds refused to be quiet and we were determined to come up with something. We could mark her, physically. She was already ours, I had imprinted the moment I saw her. I was pretty sure it was the same for my brother.

The physical mark would make it official to other supes. It would signify to all others that she was ours and we were hers. It would be dangerous for her though. She would become a target. Our father would not be happy, and we'd probably be ostracized. Caid's sire would send vamps to us non-stop. This weekend's bounty would be minor in comparison. We would never find peace. Fuck it, she'd be worth it.

Caid lifted his head and looked me in the eye, "Let's mark her."

I swear we had one mind.

"I was thinking the same thing," I admitted.

"I know. She may not like it and what it will mean for her. It won't be easy," he whispered.

"No but..." I ran a hand through my hair.

"She's worth it," we both said at the same time.

With a plan in place, I fell asleep.

CHAPTER 30

KENZIE

I woke up sweaty, tangled up between Caid and Stellan. It was hot, yet oddly not uncomfortable. My guys were home safe that's what mattered most. I sighed.

They were both snoring, their faces so peaceful. I wiggled my legs free from Caid, and moved a hand he had conveniently draped over my crotch. Then I gently raised my head off of Stellans' chest, lifting his heavy arm that was wrapped around my torso. As I sat up, I stared down at them. Affection stirred in my heart. I brushed a stray strand of hair from Caid's face, and his lips turned up into a smile. Stel was also smiling in his sleep. I caressed his lower lip with my finger. They both wore boxers with matching blue pinstripes. Aww, they were twining! I fully appreciated their muscular forms. Stellan was thicker, his body frame denser. Caid was slimmer but not less muscular. They both had zero body fat, and their defined muscles looked like they'd been chiseled by the gods, every inch perfection.

Needing to pee, which is what woke me up in the first place, I squirmed away from the brothers and discovered Brody sleeping at the far end of the bed. Aww...he did his best to squeeze himself in with us, in what must have been the most uncomfortable position.

There was something about watching him sleep that calmed me. I'd noticed this the other the day. I sat there for a minute admiring all three of them. My heart was full, brimming with love, adoration and lust. Their perfectly sculpted bodies begging to be touched. Caid turned over, his head facing the other way, and I snapped out of my fantasies.

I craftily hopped out of bed as silently as possible, even though I wanted nothing more than to pull down those boxers and Brody's tighty-whities. The clock read nine-fourteen A.M. At least I got six hours of sleep. The guys rolled in later. I wasn't certain what time but they must be exhausted. After I finished in the bathroom, I decided to leave them to rest. I got dressed and tip-toed downstairs with my cellphone in hand.

The rest of the pack were all asleep in my guest rooms and snoring peacefully. They must be completely zonked because my shuffling around didn't wake them. I made my way to the kitchen and noticed they'd eaten all the food I'd prepped for them. Sticky notes with "thank you" messages were plastered all over the fridge. I smiled while reading them, cherishing each word.

I reached in the fridge and grabbed a green drink with my name on it in Caid's handwriting. I was smiling from ear to ear and glanced at my phone.

There were missed texts from Tris. I couldn't wait to speak with him. I had a lot to tell him about everything I was feeling, and everything that had happened since I last saw him. I was falling hard for the three men asleep in my bed and needed him to ground me.

This wasn't the place to talk, so I grabbed my wallet and daggers and headed out. In the corridor, Kevin was standing guard. Hmm...I guess all was not resolved. When he noticed me, he nodded a greeting.

"Hi, how long have you been out here?" I asked.

He thought about it. "Um...not long. I started my shift when they all came home, since six, maybe sevenish."

No wonder they were still asleep.

"I'm going downstairs for a bit. I have my phone if anyone needs me."

"Where to, miss? I think the vamp and the wolf would want to know, just in case."

"Oh. I'm going to the bazaar pick up a few things. I won't be long." I headed to the elevator.

In the elevator, I decided to go straight to the bazaar and call Tris later. It was still early, and he probably was still asleep anyway.

Last night, Brody had given us incredible mics and earpieces. They were discreet and they worked well. He had bought them here, and I wanted to see what else that vendor had. I wasn't sure where he got them so I was darting in and out of aisles, trying to cover as much ground as I could. Erik suddenly appeared in front of me, and I took a wary step back.

"Hey," he said, looking down at me.

I had never realized he was so much taller than me. He was lofty like the brothers and Brody.

"Oops, excuse me. I wasn't paying attention," I said, a little embarrassed.

"You here alone?" He glanced behind me.

"Um yeah, I am. I was looking for the vendor where Brody bought a few things."

"Ah, the tech magic. Yeah, that's where I met you." He focused on my confused expression and then said, "Come, I'll take you over there."

I hesitated a moment, but decided to follow him. I wanted to get home to my guys as soon as possible, and this would speed things up. Otherwise, I'd get lost in here. I couldn't help but feel uncomfortable around Erik though. He was helpful, but I was at a loss for words.

After a few moments of uncomfortable silence, I attempted to break the ice. "Thank you for helping the other day."

"No problem. It was the least I could do. You guys have a good night?"

"Yeah, we did." I replied, not wanting to offer more.

He cleared his throat. "Look, I know we got off to a rough start, but I do hope you take me up on that training. You have untapped powers that could do incredible things."

"Maybe I like things exactly as they are." I wasn't sold on having him as my tutor.

We weaved in and out of the aisles. The bazaar was more crowded than when Tris and I had been here.

"That might be true. But I suspect you get a locked up feeling deep in your gut every now and then, like there's something there weighing you down. If you don't expend the energy, that feeling becomes overwhelming. And, when you finally use a burst of power, it drains you."

"That might be true," I said, stealing his words. "Perhaps I've already figured out a way to neutralize the energy."

"Fair enough. But...what if I could teach you a way to turn that energy into something amazing and productive and something that could help others? Wouldn't it be worth it? Just for curiosity's sake." He had an inquisitive look in his eyes.

His eyes were beautiful, captivating. He placed a hand on the small of my back and guided me to the stall I was looking for.

He said something to the vendor in a language I didn't know, possibly Mandarin. The vendor looked at me and said something back to Erik. It's rude to talk about someone in a language the other person didn't understand, but I ignored the slight.

Erik laughed and turned toward me. "He said that you're quite beautiful."

"*Che che*," I said to the vendor with a smile.

Their approving laughter relaxed me.

"Don't get too excited. That's the only Chinese I know." I added. That earned me more laughs.

I told the vendor, who of course spoke English, what I was looking for. He showed me the mics and earpieces and a few other interesting items. Tech magic was the best and made a merc's life much easier. I wasn't a merc anymore but I still loved these magical gadgets.

There was a tracking device, that looked like a bar code sticker. Sync the code with the app, place it on someone's skin and it embedded itself. Turn on the app and that person could be found anywhere. I wasn't in the habit of tracking people, but it could be useful. He showed me a voice modulator. A neuro translator, which was weird but cool. This one is embedded in the back of the skull and it allowed you to speak and understand over twenty languages. Whoa!! I also grabbed several teleporting devices, which were rare and expensive as all hell. Erik assured me they were the best, even though I should be able to teleport myself.

I paid for the lot and planned to head back, but Erik insisted I stop at another stall. This one had different potions and tonics. Even though I'd picked up a dozen different things from Pierre, I was curious to see what else was available. Erik showed me a couple of potions that were too good to pass up. One was a healing tonic like the one he'd given me a day or two ago. There were some other nifty things like power amplification tonic, a magic nullifying potion, and one to restore magic burn-out. Erik, insisted I didn't need the last one if I would start training. I ignored him and bought it anyway.

Despite my doubts about him, Erik turned out to be a great shopping partner. I enjoyed his company as we made our way through a couple aisles. He was intelligent, and our conversation was light but interesting. We agreed on most things thus far. I didn't think it was possible but maybe, just maybe, he wasn't a bad guy.

After a couple of hours, I insisted on taking my leave. He walked me to the elevator but didn't ask to go any farther. He planted a kiss on my cheek, taking me by surprise and said, "Call me, Mackenzie, for training."

I got back upstairs and found everyone still snoring away. It was almost noon, but I was pleased that the pack was comfortable sleeping at my place. I peeked in on my guys, and they were still in the same position I left them in. The brothers were hugging pillows, and Brody was still at the bottom of the bed faced down on his stomach. I didn't realize how big my bed was, and I was certainly glad to have it. I snuck back downstairs to the kitchen and started cooking knowing the pack would be hungry again. They'd wiped out the food I'd prepared last night, or was that this morning? In any case, it was gone. I got to work on making fried chicken, sweet potato fries, coleslaw, apple pies and a healthy green salad. When did I become so domesticated?

Tris and I texted back and forth while I cooked. I wished he was here. I wanted him to join us, but it wasn't exactly safe with everything going on. We promised to have a sleepover, soon. My emotions over the three men sleeping in my bed had me torn, I was both happy and anxious. It was a conversation I wanted to have face to face with my bestie over cocktails.

Erik texted and told me how much he'd enjoyed being with me today. I wasn't sure what to make of that guy but, I sent a cordial text back anyway.

I texted Bunny and thanked her for her help. She responded that she had a great time and asked if JT was single. I giggled, and then promised her that I'd ask and put in a good word for her if he was. She had the next few days off, and we planned on grabbing lunch soon. I was looking forward to that since I'd found some other things at the bazaar that I wanted to give her.

I pulled the apple pies out of the oven, sat them on a rack to cool, and was startled to discover Stel standing a few feet behind me.

"Hi, sweetness," he said in that deep, raspy voice I loved.

I didn't know what came over me, but I lunged and jumped into his arms. Yeah, I couldn't help myself. I was that happy to see him. We were kissing each other like we'd been apart for months. Before we could get down to business, voices floated in from the living room.

"Smells good in here!" Jason yelled. When he saw us, he said "Eww, get a room."

Still holding me in his arms, Stel glared at him over his shoulder.

"Just kidding." Jason ducked his head.

JT came into the kitchen and sat at a barstool at the kitchen counter. "Good morning Miss Kenzie, what you got to eat?"

I thought of Bunny, and I blurted, "JT, are you married?"

His eyes got big, and his face turned red. He shook his head.

Stedman came in and clapped him on the back. "This one married? He's been looking for Mrs. right for a long while."

The smell of food must've woken everyone. The rest of the pack entered the kitchen, and then Brody and Caid. Stel set me down on my feet to say hello to his brother and Brody.

Everyone seemed to be enjoying the food and all were in a good mood. Although Sandy, still hadn't warmed to me. Every time I asked questions or try to engage in conversation with her, she gave me short, clipped answers. I wasn't hoping to be her best friend, but I was hoping to diffuse the awkwardness between us.

Stel and Caid briefed us on the mission and what was to happen going forward. The hit had been called off, and Brody and a couple of the pack members were going to A1Labs to collect any and all info that would shed light on what they were up to.

Brody got on with everyone rather well. He was a likeable person, no doubt, and it was comforting to see him fit right in. He only stayed for a short while though. Unlike the brothers, he hadn't moved in. His room was downstairs in the poor section he called it. I giggled. I was sure there was no such thing in this hotel. His room had to be much more comfortable for him than sleeping at the end of my bed with a wolf, a vamp, and a half Fae. His team of security guards were responsible for the Alpha's arrival, so he promised to see me later and took off to do his prep.

CHAPTER 31

KENZIE

Green foliage and tall trees surrounded me, and cool breeze prickled my skin. I spun in a slow circle, hardly able to believe we were still in the desert. How did the mages, create this? Pine trees this tall took decades to grow. I was speechless.

Stel, Caid and the rest of the pack brought me to a special area where they could hunt.

When the magical community had taken over Vegas from the humans, this paradise had been one of the biggest changes. A group of mages specializing in earth magic had created forest areas in the desert. It was unfathomable, but they'd achieved it. The magical community acquired acres of land that housed either commercial or residential properties. This had created contention. Many businesses and people had been displaced or paid to leave.

Large plots of land had been turned into forest areas, specifically catering to the magical community. The Enchanted Woods was the first and largest supe park. What used to be concrete and desert sand was now acres of forest land, like something that would be found in the Pacific Northwest. Dense foliage and trees reached as high as the eye could see, and there were creeks, rock formations, even wild game. I couldn't believe my eyes.

The Enchanted Woods was for shifters and vamps only. No humans allowed. It gave them somewhere to shift and hunt wild game. Only so many shifters and vamps were allowed at a time, and reservations were required. It was walled and gated of course. No one wanted an innocent human wandering in here and mistaken for prey. However, all of the hotels here encouraged supes to hunt. The Majestic had a wooded area that guests could use, but this was the largest and the most popular place to hunt in Vegas. The magical community and the human government figured if they allowed supes to hunt in a natural environment, human patrons would be safer.

Stel wanted to show off his wolf form. Well, okay I asked to meet his wolf. After lunch the pack talked about their second nature, and the conversation was intriguing. They were all of a different animal species. Shifters were mostly predator animals. How they coexisted in one pack was beyond me.

Jason was set on shifting in the house, but Stellan forbade it. Caid had recommended we come here, where they could shift and hunt and he could stand by and keep me safe while he got a dose of sunlight. Being a day walker, he wanted a power boost after whatever had happened last night.

I didn't get details on what happened with Carlos or Bates, which was fine by me. I didn't need to know everything. Sometimes it was better not to know it all.

As I had never seen the Enchanted Woods or any other mage created forest areas located in Vegas, or anywhere for that matter, I had certainly been onboard with coming here. Stel had agreed as long as I promised to stick with Caid, and we were not allowed to go in very far. He would hunt, and then come back to me to relieve his brother, so that he could hunt, too.

Here I was, spinning in place, taking in the forest around me. It was incredible. The dense tree line blocked out the sky. Sun filtered in through the leaves, and birds sang and flittered above, moving branch to branch. Other small creatures scurried through the woods. I bent down to touch the soft mud and green moss ground covering. It even smelled like a forest; damp, mossy and earthy, with a touch of pine.

My mind was blown This was once concrete, asphalt, and desert sand. Now it was fertile earth. Where did they get the water? I was so curious about my surroundings I wanted to know more. When these were being built, the answers to the obvious ecological questions were always the same . . . its magic. Boy, it sure was.

"Sweetness, the pack is ready to hunt," Stel called to me only a few feet away.

I walked over, and grasped his outstretched hand. He was shirtless, wearing only sweatpants and his broad chest was on display. The view distracted me and he noticed me staring.

"Do you want to take a picture?" he said with a smart-ass smile.

"No!" I planted kisses on his chest instead.

"We have an audience, sweetness."

Right, the pack. I turned around, and they were removing their clothes. Oh yeah, I forgot shifting meant no clothes. Except Stel. He could keep his clothes on when he shifted. Some supes had other gifts, and keeping his clothes on while he changed forms was one of his. Yet, he was topless. He and his brother liked to tease me with their sexiness. Stel rubbed up against my ass, his cock getting hard. Mmm...I wouldn't be able to keep my hormones in check if he kept doing that.

It took a few minutes for the pack to shift. It was amazing how their magic worked. Sandy, was a beautiful honey colored wolf, I remembered her form from the pool. She was not as large as the others, and looked more feminine but no less powerful. True to her character, she didn't give me the time of day.

Jason's wolf form was covered in copper fur with white patches on his paws, muzzle, and around his neck. He was larger than Sandy but younger. He eagerly bounced around like a puppy and nudged my hand with his nose. I patted his head.

JT was a large black gray wolf and his shoulders came up to my hips. Wow, this one was scary. His eyes were the same blue-green color as his human eyes. His approach to me and Stellan was respectful.

Stedman's shift looked like a tornado, and out of that tornado emerged the largest bear I had ever seen. He was a giant, standing nearly ten feet tall. One swipe with those paws could take a head clean off. I widened my gaze as he came near, but with Stel at my back I wasn't fearful, just amazed. Stedman sat at my feet, which was kind of funny because even sitting he almost matched my height. I scratched him behind the ears to let him know I approved of his scary form. He leaned into my hand, and then shuffled away.

A black panther strutted up to me next and I could tell by the light brown eyes that this was Mark. Like a true cat, he waved his tail at me and strutted off.

Warren stepped up to us next in a coyote shape, his fur the color of desert sand. He looked as though he'd be at home here in Vegas. He flashed his teeth, which I assumed was a coyote way of smiling.

Stel motioned to the pack to go ahead without him and they all loped off into the forest, going for a run, or hunt, or whatever.

Caid remained his fangs fully extended, his skin was pasty white, and was covered with streaks of black veins. He wasn't naked so I'd assumed those black veins were everywhere. He approached me slowly, his eyes no longer the intriguing grey I was used to. They were completely black, no white sclera. Whoa! This was one scary mother fucker. Despite the change in his appearance he was still my guy, my vamp. I stepped away from Stel and pressed my body against Caid's and touched his face, tracing the veins. I traced my finger over one fang and he abruptly pulled away.

"Sharp, love. It will cut you," he said in his normal voice.

I rose up on my tip-toes to kiss him. In a flash, he reverted back to his human form, bronze skin and all.

"You good?" Stellan asked Caid, and he nodded.

The other pack members had shifted slowly in comparison, the process dragging out in minutes, rather than seconds, so I was unprepared for Stel's speedy shift. In the blink of an eye, an enormous white wolf stood before me. Holy fuck. He couldn't be real. He was so large, I would easily be able to ride him like a pony. His fur was snow white, his eyes silver with flecks of blue. I approached him slowly, and ran my hands through his fur, then wrapped my arms around his large neck. His soft fur covered corded muscle underneath. He sweetly rested his head on my shoulder. It felt as though his wolf was embracing me. For some reason, tears filled my eyes. I quickly rubbed them away, and moved around to admire him.

How are you real? Stel licked my face, making me giggle. He stared at me, cocking his head to the side, as though asking if I was done. "Go. I'll wait with Caid."

After Stel loped away, Caid held my hand and we walked a bit. "He's incredible huh? I used to be envious."

I tilted my head to look up at him, "Really?! Why? You all vamped out is the scariest one of the bunch."

"You think so?"

"Absolutely. I would not want to be on the wrong side of that." The pack was out there, but it seemed like we had the entire Enchanted Woods to ourselves.

"Well, thank you. I guess. The shifters have a way of working together. That is what makes them so powerful. They bond differently than other species. There is a hierarchy that is respected. I envy that. My kind, not so much. We kill each other because we want to always be the one and only. Even our children, the ones we sire, end up wanting to take over. It's pretty fucked." He compressed his lips.

"Do you have children?"

"Yeah, the two from the Catacombs, the ones we went out chasing. They're mine now," he said.

I nodded. "I thought they were already vamps."

"Yeah, some bonds between a vamp and their sire can be broken.

I broke theirs. I don't do it often, but I can and have. It can create some complications. I have sired a couple others, back in Texas. They're loyal and useful in most cases." He ran a hand through his hair.

"You sound conflicted. Like there's something about being a sire that you're not so sure about."

"It's complicated. And a lot of responsibility. Newly formed vamps go off the rails most of the time. It's a headache. Plus, the downside is that it doesn't always work. Humans think it's glamorous, to be changed. They don't understand the risk. Most die in the process."

"I did not know that." I hadn't realized how much responsibility he and Stel shouldered on a daily basis.

"Yeah, the downside, makes me not want to try. Even if it works, it's a pain in the ass. If it doesn't, you could lose someone you love." He sounded defeated.

Ah, he was talking from experience. My poor vamp. I snuggled into his side a little more, and then growls, yelps, and the sound of tearing flesh, erupted in the Enchanted Woods, and it was much more than hunting noises. What the fuck? Caid and I exchanged stunned looks.

"Something's wrong," Caid said, all vamped out.

He picked me up with one hand and hauled my ass toward the exit of the Enchanted Woods, but we didn't make it out. We were knocked aside from what felt like a freaking freight train, sending me flying out of his arms and a good twenty-five feet into the air. I hit the ground with tremendous force, and blacked out.

CHAPTER 32

KENZIE

My head felt like it weighed two tons, and I hurt all over. I was sure there were a few bruises forming on my body, but my vision was blurry, I couldn't make out anything. The sounds around me were muted like I had cotton stuffed in my ears. Where was my dagger? I realized I was on my side, my hands were tied, and my ankles were bound as well. My dagger was gone. I was fucked. My heartbeat thundered in my chest. I couldn't afford to panic though. I took slow deep breaths and counted to ten.

I was able to regain my senses and my heartbeat slowed to a normal tempo. My vision cleared, not that there was anything to see, it was dark all I could make out was a hard, dusty concrete floor in a tiny room. Judging by the shelves lined up on one side of the wall, it was probably some sort of closet or storage room. There was a mop in a bucket with the handle propped against the wall and a couple of cleaning products. I needed something to cut through these ties.

The door opened. Ah fuck. A vamp and a mage?? I lay there and pretended to be unconscious. My hair covered my face but I was able to get a glimpse at one of my captors. Average height, slim build. He didn't look intimidating, but he was a vamp, and I wasn't going to underestimate him. The last thing I remembered the sun wasn't due to set for a couple hours, so what was a vamp doing out at this hour? Shit, I must have been out for at least two maybe three hours. Caid and Stel would be heading to their conference, unless...

I stopped my thoughts right there. Worrying wouldn't help the situation. Hopefully they escaped capture and were looking for me. Yeah, I was hanging on to that small glimmer of hope. I needed it to get out of this place.

"What should we do with her?" the vamp at the door asked someone behind him.

He peered at me, flipping something over in his hand. My dagger. Motherfucking thief! It was the new dagger I'd bought at the bazaar. I was definitely getting that back, with interest.

"Leave her! We need to get upstairs to the meeting. She'll make a good victory meal," said the mage, as he peered at me.

"Fine," the vamp muttered, and then they left without closing the door all the way.

Before it could swing shut, I shuffled to it and held it open with my foot. I lay still like that for a few minutes, listening, waiting to make sure I was alone again.

After a few long minutes, I sat up and looked closely at the plastic tie straps. Hmm, all I needed was something to cut through these bad boys and I was home free. I scooted to the door and peeked outside into another storage area stacked with cases of soft drinks and bottled water. Where the fuck was I? The one guy mentioned a meeting upstairs, and I was hoping that meant I was in The Majestic's convention center.

I focused on the old-style mop with a metal contraption on one end to replace the mop head. It was a bit rusty but perhaps sharp enough. I tipped the bucket over to get access to the mop and rubbed the plastic tie strap against the sharpest edge. Ten long ass minutes later the plastic started to split apart. I kept working it till my hands were freed. I massaged my wrists, and then worked to free my legs.

With the use of my hands, I was able to finally free myself much faster.

I crept out of the room. The only door I came across opened to a narrow corridor. I ran down the corridor and climbed a small staircase that led into a vast open space. Ahh, this was the convention center. I was standing in one of the convention halls, which was now empty. I noticed two shadowed figures farther down the hall. Yep, I was following them, sure they were going to lead me to my guys.

They went down another set of stairs. According to the sign, they led to bathrooms. Curiosity overtaking caution, I got closer. I hid around the corner close enough to hear them. There was an obvious humming similar to the hum of a large electrical appliance, maybe a commercial refrigerator. I couldn't make out what they were saying over the humming. Frustrated, I took a few steps closer, sticking to the shadows.

"This is fucking eerie. Can we just wait outside?" I recognized the voice coming from the other side of the door. It was the vamp who had stolen my dagger.

"The boss is a powerful mage. He has them under control. Don't be a wuss."

"Look at them, they're feral, their beasts are at the surface. He can't contain them much longer. You know what? Fuck this. I'm waiting outside till it's time."

The door opened abruptly and almost knocked me into the wall behind me. When it closed, I jumped on the vamp's back and twisted his neck with a sickening crunch. His vamp blood would heal the cracked vertebrae in about twenty minutes. Not wanting to deal with this asshole again, I took my dagger off him, planning to plunge it in, but the door opened again. It hit the downed vamp's leg and couldn't fully open.

"What the fuck? Sam!" the mage said.

Ah, shit! I slammed the door on him, smacking him in the face. He cursed again, stunned. He forced the door open but didn't see me yet, so I sneak attacked him like I had done to his friend. This time I drove the dagger in hard and pierced his heart. Blood bloomed from his wound, and he dropped dead at my feet.

The door was still open, so I took a look inside and found dozens of shifters and vamps. All of them swayed on their feet, murmuring something I couldn't make out. So, this was where the humming came from. A silver brace was affixed to their necks. This was not good. Their eyes were blood shot, and drool dripped from their mouths and fangs. What the actual fuck?

I closed the door and used the padlock to lock them in. I did not want to deal with a bunch of feral supes. No thank you.

The thieving vamp was still on the ground with a broken neck, so I plunged my dagger in his heart, turning him to ash, and then I hauled ass to another set of stairs leading to more bathrooms.

Several cages imprisoning unconscious animals lined the hallways between the men's and ladies' room. I recognized a black panther, three wolves, a bear, and a coyote. Fuck me.

As I approached the nearest cage with caution, I heard voices from further up the hall. I walked past the cages. Four men were dragging two silver bound bodies up the stairs, leaving a trail of blood behind them. One body had familiar blond hair, the other body had dark hair. Stel and Caid. My gut tightened and a shudder tore through me. I started to follow them out, but a whimper behind me caught my attention.

The sound came from Jason, in his wolf form. His eyes were sleepy and unfocused. I couldn't leave him or the others. I approached the cage he was in. It was pad locked. Shit.

With nothing on me but my dagger, I jammed it into the keyhole and wiggled it, hoping it would magically open. It didn't. Fuuccckk!

In frustration, I slashed out at the lock, and my blade cut right through the metal. Hell yes! I kissed the magic dagger.

I dragged Jason out of the cage. He wobbled at first and shook his head. I looked him over, searching for wounds or embedded silver but he appeared to be unharmed. After a moment, he was standing on his own.

"I have to go, Jason. Help the others."

They were still asleep. I wasn't sure if he understood me, but he yipped, and I took that as a yes.

As I ran past the cages, I sliced open the metal locks. Determined to find my guys, I followed the trail of blood that led into the meeting area.

CHAPTER 33
KENZIE

Angry shouting filled the meeting room, and the crowd was no longer in their seats. Anyone in their right mind, would have run away from this madness but not me. I just knew the two bodies that were carried out belonged to Stel and Caid. My senses were on high alert, and my magic flowed over my body like a protective skin.

The Guild mages donned their usual garb of long, flowing purple robes with the Guild crest and gold stitching. They stood in the middle of the meeting space like referees, using their magic to hold people back. A naked man, raving like a lunatic, held up a severed head by its hair.

"California is mine!" said the mad man in the middle of the meeting area. He was around my height but wide. He had dirty brown hair and wild, crazy eyes.

The mages were trying to keep the incensed attendees from mauling each other to death but they were barely holding on.

When the four men that held Caid and Stellan captive arrived in the middle of the meeting, the crowd went silent.

"You see Joseph, California is now MINE, and now you WILL step down from your role as Alpha of the Republic and succeed all of your claim to me!" the crazed lunatic holding the head screamed.

He must've been the beta of the Pacific Coast pack. I think his name was Sasha. He threw the decapitated head to the floor, which I assumed belonged to his former Alpha.

A young-looking man calmly, stalked toward the center like a predator. No more than six feet tall, and sinewy like a cyclist, he could've been a collegiate athlete. He wore slacks and a light gray cable knit sweater and cowboy boots. Despite his casual appearance, power radiated off him. Shifters began transforming and falling to the floor in submissive crouches. Joseph Reese was in charge, and he was fucking pissed. The only similar physical trait he shared with Stel, his biological son, was hair color.

The Guild mages focused their powers on keeping the two shifters away from one another but Joseph Reese fought their magic.

"You will die at my hands insolent pup." Joseph wasn't shouting but his words were heard loud and clear.

With the showdown between Joseph and the crazy shifter from California taking center stage no one was paying attention to me. I used the distraction to get closer to Stellan and Caid. From just a few feet away, I could see their injuries. Silver chains bound them to a table and silver glittered around their wrists and their ankles. Thorny silver crowns topped their heads, and embedded into their skulls. Droplets of blood oozed and streamed from those horrible crowns. I cringed at the disturbing scene.

My heart cracked at seeing them like that. I crept toward them. No one paid attention to me. All eyes were on the two shifters. I glanced back and Joseph had shifted into a large wolf. He had a patch of silver on his chest and behind his ears marking his white fur. The other shifter, had transformed into a smaller snarling wolf, his coat brown and spotted gray. He was smaller but no less ferocious, and his eyes had that same blood shot tinge, like the feral supes I'd locked up downstairs.

A gun shot rang out, and one of the Guild mages crumpled to the ground. Who the fuck brought a gun to a supe conference? Before that question could be answered, the crowd exploded. Shifter against shifter, vamps against vamps, vamps and shifters against one another. It was utter chaos, which worked in my favor.

I didn't know where the Texas Alpha was, but I focused on releasing his sons. I used my dagger to cut through the silver chains around Stel's wrists. The sharp crowns would be a challenge. How would I remove those without hurting my guys?

Stellan's hand reached toward me, and his mouth moved like he wanted to say something. I leaned over to listen. "I need to shift . . . head."

With shaky hands, I lifted up on the chains and discovered they were embedded into his head a good inch. My stomach lurched as I worked gently and lifted the silver. My effort made the wounds gush blood. Stel hissed, and I stopped, worried I was making it worse.

Stel growled out, "Rip it, sweetness."

Bloody fucking hell. I didn't want to but I needed to release him. I woman up and ripped the fucking thing off.

He let out a gut-wrenching scream, then shouted "Behind you!"

I ducked, and a clawed hand barely missed me. Stellan caught said claws and twisted. I scrambled out of the way and swiped my dagger across the enemy's thigh, hamstringing him. He doubled over allowing me to sink my dagger in his heart and he turned into ash.

Stellan sat up and ripped the other chains away from his ankles, so I made my way over to Caid. A shifter was there blocking him from me. Shit, I wished I had my gun. Fighting with a dagger only worked for me when my opponent was up close, and he wasn't. I danced to the side and tried to get closer to Caid. The shifter was still in human form, which helped me. I'd fought shifters before in their animal form with more weapons. This time, I would just have to make do.

The shifter lunged for me lazily as though he deemed me unthreatening. The lack of judgment on his part allowed me to side-step and deliver a round house kick to his stomach. Thanks to my magic, he staggered a few feet away and gave me time to swipe and loosen a couple of the chains around Caid's ankles. He shifted into a mountain lion and charged at me, only to be intercepted by a large white wolf. My wolf. Smiling inside for being saved, I worked to release Caid.

After cutting the silver chains that bound his wrists and feet, I tore the silver from around his head, but he didn't stir as quickly as Stel had. He lay there, unconscious. I was starting to get frantic, checking his body for more silver and Jason ran up to me.

"He needs blood, Kenzie. Someone alive is best. Never a good idea to feed off the dead." He shifted while running and joined the melee.

I was about to slice my wrist for Caid to feed, when a half-shifted Stellan, stayed my hand. "You need your strength, sweetness."

I barely dodged a swipe of claws belonging to a female vamp. Her fangs protruded and black veins popped out over her skin. She was probably beautiful in her human form judging by her long red tresses and voluptuous curves. The she-vamp went on the offense, slashing wildly at me. Trying to match each of her claw swipes with my dagger, I got too close, red welts seeped blood from my arms. I pulled on my magic. With more speed, I launched a spinning back kick and connected my foot to her head, knocking her off balance, and then followed through with a flurry of dagger jabs. Right before sinking my dagger into her heart, I remembered needing a blood donor for Caid. She was bracing to meet her true death and I turned the dagger and hit her on the temple with as much physical force and magic I could muster. She fell to the ground out cold.

I dragged the female vamp to Caid, and then sliced open her wrist, letting her blood dribble over his mouth. A few seconds of that and nothing happened.

"Caid, please. Wake up!" I shook him, but he didn't stir.

I started crying, and shaking him and pleading with him.

"Please." I pressed my forehead to his.

He reached for the wrist pressed to his mouth and sucked down on it savagely. The female vamp let out a pleasurable moan and the hair on the back of my neck prickled. I did not like this exchange. Not at all. I wanted to sink my dagger into her chest. Caid was still feeding though, so I couldn't pry her off him yet.

He drained her blood in less than a minute. The red-haired vamp was nothing but an empty husk. Caid got to his feet. He pushed me to the side and extended his arm behind me, tearing a shifter's throat out. It was disgusting, but I was grateful to be safe and in his arms.

"Thank you, love," he said.

Bodies and ashes were everywhere. Stellan returned to us, still in his wolf form. Carnage surrounded us. The brothers, got back in to the fray, all while remaining close to me.

A thunderous animalistic roar stopped everyone in their tracks. Joseph Reese was stalking the newly claimed Alpha, who was covered in blood from several injuries.

The California beta was in human form, limping badly, and screaming like a maniac. "Release the ferals NOW! You will not survive this! I die you die."

Joseph shifted back to his human form. One moment he was standing in front of Sasha, the next he was holding on to a human spine. What remained of Sasha was slumped on the floor at his feet. Fuck me. That was so intense and so fucking gross. I gagged. It took everything in me to stop myself from vomiting.

Joseph barked out orders about organizing the packs. The vamps were organizing themselves as well. Another shifter approached him, his stance submissive.

"Alpha," he bowed and waited for Joseph's acknowledgement.

"My name is Cal. I was a beta in L.A. I offer my allegiance to you, our new Alpha."

"Gather the rest of your pack. And what is the feral this one mentioned?" Joseph asked still holding the spine.

Eeeewww! I wished he would put that thing down.

Stellan, Caid and I, stood closer together. When Cal, the L.A. beta shook his head about the feral, it dawned on me that the supes locked up downstairs were what the dead beta had been referring to. I didn't want to speak with Joseph, especially since he was holding that spine, which was dripping blood and goo. Yuck.

Under my breath, I sputtered, "There are a bunch of supes locked up downstairs. They look feral."

Caid and Stellan glanced at me. Caid opened his mouth to say something to me, but his father interrupted.

"Who is this son?" Joseph asked him, coming closer to us.

Stellan, shifted to human. He pressed his body into my back in a protective gesture I found very comforting at the moment.

"She's our mate, Dad." Caid replied, standing close and blocking me from his father who was still holding that damned spine.

"Tell us what you saw, sweetness," Stellan said into my ear.

"A vamp and a mage kidnapped me, and they were supposed to stand watch over a group of supes..." I sensed a wave of magic barreling toward us.

Instinctively, I pulled on my magic with everything I had, creating a wall of magic to shield us. The vile magic hit mine, with the force of a hurricane pushing against me. I could see its shimmer. My shield was pearl white, almost iridescent, while the other magic was a sickly putrid color. I dug in my heels as my body strained alongside my magic, keeping it back. Sweat dripped from every pore from the exertion.

"Hold on Kenzie!" Stellan yelled, his hand on my shoulder, Caid's hand was on my other.

A surge of energy flowed through me giving my magic an extra push forcing the other magic back, and snapping it in half.

I slumped from the exertion and said, "There's a mage here. Someone was helping that Sasha guy, and they're still out for the Republic."

I was bent over at the waist and gasping for breath. Joseph ordered his shifters to secure the feral supes and find the mage.

The brothers were organizing shifters and vamps, while I caught my breath. And then I saw it, a very faint, very indistinct shimmer rippled the air behind the Texas Alpha. In a flash, a hooded man appeared holding a sword aimed at Joseph's head. It was a familiar strike, one I'd known my whole life.

"No!" I screamed at the top of my lungs, my magic flared and created another shield around the Alpha, absorbing the sharp hit of the blade.

"Daddy! No!"

"Mac?!" My father dropped his sword and moved toward me catching me as I fell. I was completely drained from using too much magic, and my body gave out.

CHAPTER 34
STELLAN

Bloody hell, what an absolute mess. Without Kenzie's help this would've been seriously bad for my family and my pack. We were forever indebted to her for the countless times she'd saved us. We owed her our lives.

After the shit show of a conference, I left my father and brother there and had brought her unconscious body back to her place at The Majestic. Caid and Dad were more than capable of the clean-up.

I didn't want to leave her side. Caid didn't want to leave her either, so we had been taking shifts. Brody had also been helpful until he went to California on business. He was beside himself when we brought her home. She had been unconscious for days.

Right now, I was with her on her bed. Her head rested on my chest. It worried me that she hadn't awakened yet. I'd tried transferring pack magic to her, but her body wouldn't accept it. If not for the steady thrum of her heart, I'd have lost my mind by now.

The mage Erik said she'd drained her magic. He went on about how she needed tutoring. I was sure he could help but also knew he wanted to spend time with her, just like the rest of us. He had a long way to gain her favor though. Understanding how she felt about him, Caid and I weren't about to leave him alone with her. Not that he would do anything to her, but if she woke up to his mug and only his, she'd be pissed.

My brother and I appreciated having Brody and Erik around. They were careful with her, loving almost. We had so much on our plate that having the backup was necessary. It was nice having a team.

The whole Pacific Coast Pack mess was a complete shit storm.

Calling off the hit was a minor achievement. Sasha, the ambitious fuck of a beta, was determined to take down his Alpha and he'd succeeded. He could've had a large pack of loyal shifters if he hadn't been so greedy.

The mage in his employ was working with BRS, and they were determined to take over the entire country, starting with the biggest and baddest . . . us. It was a pipedream for sure, but I guessed they got brownie points for trying.

The vamps had come at us in the Enchanted Woods. The mages had figured out a way to mask their scent, and we hadn't realized the vamps were hunting us until we'd been caught. They'd drugged the pack, and they'd encased my brother and I in silver chains. Thankfully, Kenzie had come to our rescue.

Caid and Dad were dealing with the master vamps in L.A. They claimed they had nothing to do with BRS or the hit, and that the vampires involved were acting on their own accord. They would get a pass...for now.

BRS had done all that so my father would step down giving up his territory, even though in the end it wouldn't have mattered anyway. Sasha had been unhinged. He was consumed with the desire for power and control. His reign wouldn't have lasted very long. My pack would have never tolerated a scum bag like that. They would've revolted.

The mage that he had been working with was no doubt crafty. He had escaped, which didn't sit well with my father, or any of us for that matter. We were under pressure to track him down.

According to Erik, the rogue mage was identified as a Malcolm Johnson. Labyrinth had disassociated from him long ago. Yet he'd amassed large amounts of power, dark magic. Erik's connections to the mage world were certainly helpful. It was one area we were sorely lacking. He was doing some research for us and keeping us apprised of any new findings. I sure hoped he and Kenzie would work things out. I liked having him around, but if she wanted him gone, he'd be out on his ass.

Carlos shared some helpful info since he had been working with the same rogue mage. He was still not coherent most of the time though. The drugs were still in his system. The only saving grace that we could glean from his info so far was that Malcolm Johnson, was selfish with his spells and magic. Apparently, no one was able to do what he could do, and he insisted he was the most powerful mage. I didn't give two shits about his mage abilities. Hubris like that would bite him in the ass.

In any case, between the rogue mage and Sasha, those fuckers had been relentless in their pursuit of power. They'd cooked up magic that nullified shifter and vamp magic. Their silver collars made supes feral, practically zombies, and controlled by the mage that synced his magical signature, his blood, with the collar. It was a lot of spell casting and a lot of silver. And it was enough to take out several shifters and several vamps. It was disgraceful for Sasha to serve up his own kind for this experimentation. It made me sick. To say it was a big concern was the understatement of the year.

And on top of all that, we had Kenzie and her dad, to worry about. He was a legend in the merc world, and had some serious stealth magic. He heard about the hit through the merc grapevine and didn't get the memo about it being called off. Good thing Kenzie had stopped him right before she'd passed out. My dad was none too happy about the attempted hit. Yeah, that was fucked up. For Kenzie's sake, Caid and I held him back from going after her dad. He knew how we felt about her, and was willing to comply. Kenzie's father ensured ours that he spread the news about the hit being called off through all the necessary merc channels. At least that was one less thing to worry about.

As far as we could tell, Matthieu Jameson was not a bad guy. He came from a long legendary line of combat mages, and he was definitely a badass. If it weren't for Kenzie's quick thinking, he could've easily wiped us out. What a great way to meet your mate's father.

Kenzie sighed in her sleep and snuggled closer to me. I held her tighter. Caid and I had talked about her and what to do now that the conference was over. We wanted her to come home with us. Somehow, we'd convince her. She was ours.

"Stellan . . ." she whispered.

"I'm here, sweetness" I held my breath, waiting to hear her voice again.

"Caid?" her voice was weak, but at least she was speaking.

"He's fine. He's taking care of things. We're worried about you." In my head I added, *I love you, Kenzie.*

"Hmm . . . I'm sleepy." Her voice was barely a whisper.

"It's ok, you can sleep," I exhaled. She was going to be ok.

She slept for a while, and I did as well.

My vibrating phone woke me. Caid was checking in. Beside me, Kenzie stirred.

"How long have I been out?" She asked in a sleepy voice.

"You've been asleep for almost two days."

"Two days? Oh shit! What happened?! My dad was there at the um, the thing." She struggled to sit up in bed.

I tugged her back toward me. "It's okay, sweetness. We worked things out. He's at your place, your house. He's been checking in. You should call him soon. Everything else is working its way out. Thank you, Kenzie, for everything you did for us. First the incident across the way, and then the meeting. You've been incredible," I said, while kissing her everywhere there was accessible skin.

"Um . . . Stel, this feels amazing. But I really have to pee."

"Of course." I rolled out of bed, and held out my hand to help her up.

Kenzie was a little wobbly, so I placed a hand on the small of her back to steady her.

She must be hungry and thirsty, too.

"I'll get some food and water up here. Do you want me to run a bath?"

With a faint smile, she rose on her tip-toes placed a kiss on my bottom lip, then nodded. The small movement made her sway. I picked her up and carried her into the bathroom.

She took a few steps into the water closet and closed the door. I ran the bath and texted Caid to let him know she was awake, and then I went to the kitchen.

CHAPTER 35
KENZIE

I sat on the toilet for what felt like twenty minutes, peeing. Sleeping for two days straight will do that to you.

I was sure a lot had happened while I'd been out. Fucking magic drain, totally sucked. I brushed my teeth running the electric toothbrush for three cycles and sunk into the tub that was filled for me.

The water was too hot, but it felt divine. Miraculously, I didn't feel terribly beat up, although areas of my skin were still discolored from bruises that were already healing. After all this, I needed a vacation. Maybe Tris and I could do a girls' trip.

Stel returned with a glass of water. He handed me the glass and kissed my forehead. "Food will arrive shortly. Do you need anything, sweetness?"

"My phone, please and thank you." I drank the glass of water.

Stel retrieved my phone and set it on the edge of the tub. I gave him the empty glass and he left the bathroom claiming he needed to make a few calls himself.

I dried my hand and tapped my phone. The time read eleven P.M.

Oh my gods! There were dozens of missed texts, calls etc. Regardless, of the time, I had to call a couple people.

I called Dad first. "Daddy, are you ok?!"

"I'm good. You? I was worried. How long have you been awake? I told them to call me as soon as you woke up." He sounded worried.

"Yes, I'm fine. Just woke up. We have a lot to catch up on. How long are you in town? Do you need anything?"

"No, I'm fine, I made myself comfortable at your house. Are you planning to stay at The Majestic? You're not living there full-time, are you?" Dad had a key to every one of my properties.

"Good. Yes, make yourself at home. And no, I'm not living here full time. I'll try to make it there tomorrow. So, tell me, what happened?" Despite all the drama, I was glad he was hanging around.

"Yeah, about that. Sorry Mac, if I had known they were friends of yours I wouldn't have taken the hit."

"Guess we need to talk more often." I said with a bitter tone. A girl could dream.

"Guess so." He replied.

"You need anything?" I asked again.

"No, I'm fine. Take care of yourself, see you when you get back, honey. I love you."

"I love you too, Dad."

My next call was to, Tris.

"Bitch! You disappeared! Those men better be taking care of you."

"I'm good, Tris. I just used too much magic. It knocked me the fuck out."

"Girl, I know you don't want to hear about this, but maybe those training sessions are a good idea. I can't bear to lose you, Kenz. If something happened to you, I would lose my shit!"

I smiled. "Don't lose your shit. I'll get some training in, I promise."

We talked for a few more minutes, and then Stellan poked his head into the bathroom. "Food's here."

My tummy let out a rumble.

"I need to go Tris. I will be back in the office soon."

"Don't rush, doll. Take care of yourself first. We'll plan on doing a girls' night when you're ready."

"You're the best! I love you!" I hung up and got out of the tub.

I dressed quickly and took one of the tonics for magic burn out, then found Stel in the bedroom. He had a dozen different dishes on the bed.

"I could've gone downstairs to eat," I said to Stellan.

"No, sweetness, you shouldn't be out of bed yet. Settle in."

The food smelled delicious; my tummy rumbled again. He got everything pastas, Chinese food, salads, and desserts. He'd brought up a buffet! It was amazing. I ate as he told me about what happened.

Wow. That was the only reaction I had after Stel recounted what had transpired at the pack conference. The plot was a convoluted, sickening mess. And I'd voluntarily stepped right into it. Yay for me.

I could see why the Republic was the largest pack in North America. They had good leadership and between Stel, Caid, and their father, they'd left no stone unturned. They worked tirelessly to help the Pacific Coast pack get back on their feet. I was also happy to hear that Brody and even Erik were being useful.

Everybody was worried about my magic drain. My impressive shield saved many lives, even though it'd kicked my ass. To be honest, I was worried as well. I'd never amassed that much power and had no idea how I did it or if I would be able to do it again. Erik was ready to help. It was time for me to put my big girl panties on and give magic training a try.

After eating, Stel and I went down to the kitchen to clean up and grab some wine. I needed a drink. Stellan had wanted me to eat before consuming alcohol. After straining my body, he was probably right. The tonic I had taken was potent. I was feeling loads better, so we headed back up to the room. Now that I had a full belly, I was permitted to indulge in this wonderful purple stuff, Starfish. I preferred calling it purple stuff. Yeah, that name was going to stick. After one glass, I was already tipsy.

Stel finished his third glass, and poured his fourth. Luckily, we brought up another bottle. He looked a bit nervous as though he wanted to say something. It was interesting to see this big man looking so unsure of himself. I didn't want to push but somehow, I needed to help him. It seemed important.

"So, big fella, is there something you'd like to tell me?" I straddled his lap.

"Ah, sweetness, with you on my lap like this, I think I'd rather do something else instead of talking."

He grasped the back of my head, held me still, and kissed me deeply. Our tongues did a slow dance as he palmed my breast, and pinched my nipple through the thin fabric. He burrowed his face in my neck, nipping and licking. His touch was exquisite. I was desperate to move things further, but I remembered, he had something important on his mind.

I drew away from him, gazing directly into his eyes, "Stel, you can talk to me about anything, now and forever. Ok?"

"I...I, I don't want to lose you, sweetness. I want you," he said tenderly.

I didn't respond at first, he seemed to have more to say. When he didn't say more, I kissed him conveying my passion and then said, "I want you, too. And Caid."

For a second, I thought my heartfelt admission was going to ruin the mood. There was something about each man as individuals that I was drawn to, but I couldn't have one without the other. If we were having a heart-to-heart, then I wanted him to know.

"I know, sweetness, we both want the same. We don't want this to end. It's not just the sex. That's absolutely incredible, but we want to make this more permanent. And fine if you must, you can have the human, too," he said all this sincerity.

"You and Caid have talked about this? And Brody?" It made me wonder how that conversation went.

"Yeah, we talked about it. After the day at the pool, we both knew we were in it for the long haul. We just didn't know how we'd go about it. You're very independent, which we both love and admire. As far as Brody goes, he seems to fit right in. And he loves you." Stel kissed my nose.

"Does he now? Where is he?" I asked.

"He's still around. We hired him to help with the lab mess, the disappearances, and locating that mage. He's been checking in on you."

I did get a few texts from Brody, but I hadn't had a chance to respond.

"You're keeping him busy." I said. I was glad Stel heeded my advice and hired him.

"We don't have anyone else qualified. Thank you, for recommending him."

I swear he and Caid could read my mind.

He cupped my face and gazed deeply into my eyes. "There is nothing in this world I wouldn't give you. If you wanted two hundred men, I would give them to you. Yes, Brody made me jealous at first, but he makes you happy. Because of that, I will set my ego aside, so you can have him. I will kill him if he hurts you though. One tear drops and I will eat his heart."

He wasn't even joking about that. Yikes.

"He's human, sweetness, he won't live as long as you and I," he said softly.

I hadn't thought about that, and it made me sad.

Stel caressed my cheek. "One day you will have to say goodbye to him. But not anytime soon. I will do everything I can to keep him alive for you."

His words sunk in. He would keep Brody safe, for me. Stellan loved me. My heart swelled in my chest. I loved this man more deeply than I have ever loved anyone. I stared into his eyes and almost L-bombed him, but instead I kissed him hard.

"Thank you, Stellan," I said when we broke apart. "How is this supposed to work long distance?"

"Somehow, we'll figure out a way to be together. Maybe we'll come here, move in with you." Determination furrowed his brow.

"I'm not married to this city. I'm open to moving to Texas."

Both brothers would never leave Texas. There was too much at stake.

"Seriously? You'd move to Texas?" His face lit up.

"Whoa! Down boy! I am willing to consider it."

"I'll take it, sweetness. One visit and I'll convince you to stay, you just watch." He flipped me over on my back, eagerness gleamed in his eyes.

I hadn't felt this happy in, like, ever. There were things to work out, but just knowing they were interested in prolonging this relationship was making my heart sing.

"How are you feeling?" Stel asked in a serious tone.

"I'm good. Food and the tonic helped a lot."

"Maybe you should rest."

"No, no more resting. I want you. Now. I need you." I brought his face down for a blistering kiss.

Our kisses became more intense. We needed each other at that very moment as though he was my oxygen and I was his.

Stellan's hard cock rubbed against my core, and my hips bucked against him. Since we were alone in my Penthouse, we were both in our undies. He was wearing boxers, and I was in a small tank and tiny boy shorts, but there was too much between us. He knew what I wanted, and started tearing off my clothes.

Caid walked into the room as Stel dragged my boy shorts over my hips. Despite Caid's presence, Stel didn't stop, he focused on my body. He trailed kisses from my ankles to my inner thighs, spreading my knees apart. My wet pussy was fully exposed. Caid approached the head of the bed and kissed me full on the mouth, gliding a finger between my folds.

"I'll be right back, love." Then he vamp-speeds into the bathroom, I heard the shower running.

Stel was between my legs, sitting back on his knees. Precum seeped from his hard and throbbing cock. I bolted up. I wanted that cum in my mouth. Gripped by arousal, I bent over in front of him, my ass in the air. I opened wide taking in as much of his cock as I could. His enormous length barely fit in my mouth.

I sucked and stroked his cock at the same time, my hand and mouth moving in perfect rhythm. Eager for an orgasm, I used my other hand to rub my pussy, and my juices escaped down my leg, my clit swollen and pulsating.

Caid was out of the shower, and pressed up against my ass. He slapped my hand out of the way, lined up his cock up with my pussy, and slammed in, making me cry out. He fucked me hard. I could barely catch my breath.

Stellan grasped a fistful of my hair, and fucked my mouth, moving in sync with his brother's thrusts. His enormous cock grazed my teeth as he forced himself down my throat. My guys were punishing my body in the best of ways, and my first orgasm ripped out of me almost immediately.

"That's it, love, squirt all over my cock." Caid slapped my ass.

My body quivered with my release. Stel dragged me off of Caid's dick, laying me back on the bed to eat my pussy again. He flicked his tongue over my clit.

Caid shoved his cock, still covered in my cum, in my mouth. I eagerly licked my juices off, pushing Stel's face harder against my pussy. Another orgasm rose within me, and I was about to blow, when they both pulled away.

Startled, I looked up at both of them. A sheen of sweat covered their muscular chests, and their swollen cocks stood proud. Stel hauled me up to kneel in front of him, his pale blue eyes bore into mine. He searched for answers deep in my soul. Caid held one of my hands. Before I could get nervous about what they were thinking, Stel touched my wet pussy rubbing gentle circles on my clit.

"We want to mark you, sweetness," Stel said.

Caid plunged his fingers in my cunt, working it while his brother massaged my clit.

"Would that be ok, love?" Caid asked.

"Yes, do it." I wanted this. Been wanting it. I was theirs and they were mine, there was no doubt about that, and I had zero hesitation.

Stellan drew me on his lap and lined his cock up with my core. He pushed up while pulling me down, impaling me on his huge cock. I tossed my head back and screamed his name, rocking my hips back and forth.

"This might hurt, sweetness, I'll go first. Then Caid, his venom will help to ease the pain."

I didn't care about pain. I had full confidence in my guys. They would take care of me, now and always. All I wanted was to ride their big dicks and chase down another orgasm.

From behind me, Caid held my hips still. He rubbed himself against my filled hole. "Can you take both of us in your pussy, love?"

That made me pause for a second. My pussy clenched around Stel, intrigued by the idea of having them both in me.

"I don't think you'll fit," I said.

"We'll fit, love, just relax." He kissed my shoulder.

Stel laid back onto the mattress and brought me down on top of him. He massaged my back, helping me relax my body against his while Caid threaded his cock in me slowly. He stretched my pussy, somehow fitting his massive dick alongside his brother's. Oh, my gods.

When they were both buried to the hilt Caid started pumping into me setting the pace. The feeling was all encompassing, the sensations overwhelming. I moaned and screamed uncontrollably, loving how full I was with both of them in me. The pleasure started between my legs and traveled through my entire body. In that moment I felt complete. This moment, with them, was everything.

Just when I was ready to come, Stel said, "I love you, Kenzie," then he bit down hard on my shoulder. The sharp pain startled me for a moment. It felt like my shoulder was about to be torn clean off my body. I cried out. My breathing ragged. Before it got too intense, Caid whispered, "I love you, Mackenzie Jameson," then he bit down on my neck. The dual pain in my neck and shoulder simultaneously made my eyes roll back in my head. The discomfort was short lived and replaced by an overwhelming amount of pleasure. Every nerve on fire.

The exquisite pleasure continued rising inside me. One of my arms was wrapped around Stel, holding him to my shoulder while the other was hooked around Caid, keeping his head to my neck. I held them close and forced them to take their fill of my blood. Caid's hips rocked back and forth, keeping that sweet friction between my legs.

They both drank deeply, and I could feel them drawing from me, taking my blood and a part of my soul. Caid's venom swirled through my veins, inciting pleasure I've never experienced. I felt like I was floating above my body, with both of them floating with me.

Something deep within me unfurled, and latched onto them, creating an anchor. Our very existence sealed, binding us together forever. From deep within my core, my magic surged out, traveling through my body and around, then enveloping my wolf and my vamp. My magic glowed around us, it danced, sparkled, and cemented an unbreakable bond between us. This unwavering connection locked securely into place at the same time my orgasm exploded out of me. Caid and Stel must have felt it too. They came in perfect sync with me. I screamed both their names, telling them how much I loved them. I saw stars, and then I must have blacked out.

I was completely breathless, my body limp like a wet noodle. I was lying flat against Stellan, his and Caid's cocks still in me. My pussy squeezed a little, causing them to groan. I wanted so much to fuck them again, but my body was completely useless. Aside from the aftershocks from our intense orgasms, I couldn't move an inch.

Caid slid out first, then vamp speeds into the bathroom and returned just as quickly with a warm, wet washcloth. He swiped the cloth against my tender neck and shoulder. Then he helped slide me off of Stel, allowing me to curl against his chest, and Caid spooned me. I was completely content between my wolf and my vamp. They were mine now and I was theirs.

"Good night, sweetness, I love you." Stel brushed his lips against my forehead.

"Sweet dreams, I love you, Kenzie." Caid kissed the back of my neck.

"I love you, Stellan. I love you Caid." I drifted into a deep, contented sleep.

CHAPTER 36

KENZIE

Sunlight streamed in from the windows. Groaning, I rolled over and buried my head under the pillow. Ugh, I wished it was still night. I was never a morning person. And this morning was not going to be the one that changed my mind.

The guys weren't in my bed, but their scents lingered. The memories of them marking me last night came flooding back and had me clenching my thighs together. I could already feel myself getting wet. My pussy was tender from being double dicked, but the more I thought about it the more I wanted a release. That was hands down the best sexual experience in my life. After spreading my legs apart, I reached down between my legs.

"Ahem!" Someone cleared their throat.

I snapped up to a seated position, gathering the sheets around me. Caid sat in a chair next to the bed, and Stel stood at the foot of the bed. Their heated gazes were focused on me.

"How long have you been sitting there? Creepers!" I threw pillows at both of them.

Stel swatted the pillow away, and Caid caught his and held it in his lap.

"If you're going to that, you at least have to give us a show," Caid said with a big grin.

"I don't know what you're talking about," I replied sheepishly, my face heating.

"Sure, you don't, sweetness," Stel grasped my foot that was tucked under the sheet and tugged me to him, and kissed me.

"Hey! I thought we had to go?! Not that I want to," Caid said, interrupting our kisses.

"He's right, sweetness, we need to go. The bath is almost ready, and we'll bring you something to eat." Stel moved away from me.

"Where and why?" I pouted my lips.

"Our father has asked to be introduced to you properly." Caid reached out for my hand. "And we need to get those sheets cleaned. We would've done it earlier but didn't want to wake you."

I held his hand and peered down at the sheets. The once soft fabric was stiff in places and covered in dried blood. It was a bit unsanitary, but the memories of last night came rushing back to the forefront of my mind again. So worth it. My face grew hot and my pussy ached.

Caid scooped me up into his arms, and carried me into the bathroom. He stood me up next to the tub, and left chaste kisses on my neck, and breasts then released me abruptly making me stagger.

"Love, we'll never get out of this room if I don't leave right now," He adjusted his hard cock that strained against his jeans, and then vamp speeds out of the bathroom.

Stellan stepped up to me and ran his tongue over the mark he'd left on my shoulder. A moan of pleasure escaped me, my knees buckled, and my pussy was slick with arousal. I moved Stellan's hand down to my core, encouraging him to finger me.

"Oh, fuck! Kenzie, that's so not fair. Your pussy is dripping."

Caid returned to the bathroom and said, "Not fair at all, love," he pressed against my back.

I hooked my arm around his neck, and bucked my hips to meet

Stellans finger. "Please, I need to come. Please." I pleaded with them both and guided Caid's hand to my core.

"I can't resist." Stel growled.

In one swift movement, Stel had me on all fours on the bathroom floor and dropped his sweats. He rubbed his hard cock over my clit, making me moan. Caid stepped out of his jeans and knelt in front of me. He wrapped my hair around his fist and slid his cock around my lips. I flicked my tongue over his head and opened wide. Both brothers slammed into me at the same time. It was heavenly being completely filled by my guys. Stel gripped my hips, thrusting deep into my aching cunt. I wrapped one arm around Caid's waist, for balance. With my other hand I sucked and stroked Caid's dick matching Stel's pace.

Caid made gentle strokes over the mark on my shoulder, Stel's mark. I moaned around his cock. My pussy squeezed Stel's length. Stel groaned and pushed into me deeper and faster. My body started to quiver I was on the edge ready shatter. Stel leaned over my body and licked the mark Caid left on my neck.

The euphoria of having both of my marks stimulated was like an automatic orgasm button. I lost complete control, and my orgasm exploded. Both men came with me, groaning. Caid shot ropes of cum down my throat, while Stel nearly bit me again while he released himself inside me.

The three of us slumped on the bathroom tiles. Caid leaned against the bathtub, my body slumped over his and Stel's body slumped over mine. I was a quivering mess, panting and smiling from ear to ear.

"Are you satisfied now, sweetness?" Stellan asked.

I nodded against Caid's chest and smiled. "For now."

"I fucking love you." He kissed both of my marks which shot sparks of arousal through my entire body, and then moved away from me. I whined a little.

"We really have to go, sweetness. You have ten minutes to get ready. I'll bring up your swamp drink." And then he was gone in a flash.

"He's right love." Caid said, as he helped me sit upright. He kissed my nose.

I pressed my body further into his, wanting more.

"Oh no you don't! You wily seductress!! Get your fine ass downstairs in ten minutes!" He swiftly moved out of my clutches, making me laugh.

"Wily seductress?! Who says that?"

"I do! And will call you that from now if you're not down in ten." He left the bathroom.

"I'll never be ready in ten minutes!"

"Good! You've got eight!"

I was suddenly freezing sitting on my bathroom floor all alone. I stood, took a quick pee and looked at my reflection. Well shit, the bite on my left shoulder from Stellan looked like a half-moon, tattoo. I stroked it gently and a shiver rippled through me.

"Kenzie! Stop that!" Stellan yelled from downstairs.

I giggled. Well, I guess this mark went both ways. Now I was curious, and looked over at my neck. The puncture wounds from Caid resembled stars. I ran a finger along the two marks and got the same tingling reaction. Fucking hell, I was horny again.

"Mackenzie Jameson, I will throw your ass in the shower if you don't stop doing that." Caid stood in the bathroom doorway.

Startled, I turned to face him. Wanting to push my luck a little further I gave him my best seductive look, and glided my hands up my breasts to my collar bone.

"Don't you dare!" He shouted before I reached my marks.

The shock and disbelief on his face were priceless. Laughing, I got in the tub and sank down into tepid bathwater.

He shook his head. "You're the worst!"

He came over to the tub, kissed my head and left my Green Goddess drink on the ledge. I was still laughing.

CHAPTER 37
KENZIE

It didn't seem appropriate to make the Alpha wait, so I took a quick whore bath. The only evidence of our night together were memories and my new mate marks. I was quite fond of my special tattoos. Were they permanent? Guess I should've asked before they marked me.

Using my air magic, I dried off, and made myself presentable to meet the Alpha, the one who had waved around the spine. That image was embedded in my head forever. After applying moisturizer, Stellan returned to my room.

"Dad is here, sweetness. Are you almost ready?"

"Oh! I didn't realize he was already here. I'm sorry. Yes, I'm ready." I dabbed on a little lip gloss.

"You look beautiful," he kissed on my cheek.

I felt all warm and fuzzy inside. There was no way for me to hide my elated smile.

In the short amount of time I had been given to prepare for "meeting the parents," I chose bell bottom jeans, a white floral blouse with peach flowers on it, and white wedge sandals. It was a casual girly outfit, something I'd wear to Sunday brunch. I couldn't look more human.

Upon leaving my room, butterflies swarmed my belly. Nervousness was not a familiar feeling for me, and I didn't like it. It was important for their father to like me, at least a little bit. Usually, I didn't give a rat's ass if anyone approved of me, but this was different and I couldn't really say why. When did I get so weird?

Stellan held my hand, reassuring me, as we descended to the living area. Caid greeted me at the bottom of the stairs, with a big smile. Their calm demeanor eased my nervousness.

The great Alpha of the Republic stood at the window, his back toward me. He slowly turned, and I got panicky. Just as I remembered, he looked like a typical college kid. If typical college kids ripped out their enemies' spines, that is. His approval meant everything to me. Maybe it was the Alpha thing that had me fidgeting before him. If I didn't know better, I'd bet the confidence got dicked out of me. Stel and Caid noticed my nervousness and took protective stances near me.

With all my training and experience as a merc, my emotions were always in check. At that moment, I felt like a child. It was a weird feeling, and I didn't like it. Taking a deep breath and slowly exhaling, I willed myself to calm the fuck down.

Of course, the Alpha noticed my attempt to calm myself. He relaxed his stance a bit and flashed me a warm smile.

Caid broke the silence and said, "Dad, this is Mackenzie."

Their dad was appraising me but not in an obtrusive way. With his heightened shifter senses, he probably had me all figured out in the span of twenty seconds. Thank the gods, he wasn't giving me a disapproving look.

"Hi! Nice to meet you." I extended my hand to shake his.

He clasped my hand and placed a kiss on the back. Stellan stiffened beside me, his "territorial-ness" seeping out. His father noticed it as well and raised his eyebrows.

I retracted my hand and stepped back between the brothers, leaning closer to Stellan because it felt right.

"It is nice to meet you as well, Mackenzie. My sons have told me so much about you. It seems we are in your debt."

"It's fine, sir. Considering my dad tried to take you out. I think we're even."

They all laughed, which eased the tension. I relaxed and was able to act like a normal person instead of a scared rabbit. We talked for a bit, well, it was more like me answering the Alpha's questions. I rolled with it; he was a concerned father after all. He just wanted to know who his boys were shacking up with.

I WONDERED if they'd told him about marking me and what that meant for them. Would it change their role in the pack? Are we like married or something? Those were questions I should've asked before last night. I knew being marked by them made me off limits to other shifters and vamps, and I was on board with that. But was there more I hadn't considered? I've known them for only about a week. Holy shit, what did I get myself into?

Too late to take it all back. Before I got myself overworked about the unknowns of being marked, I offered drinks and something to eat. I was confident I'd be able to scrounge up something in the kitchen. They were in the dining area visible from where I was cooking pork chops, mashed sweet potatoes, and preparing a salad. Thanks to modern-day technology, the food would take no longer than thirty minutes. As I worked in the kitchen, I participated in their conversation, but I was mainly fascinated by their interactions.

Their father was completely relaxed. He was one of those unassuming males, easy-going, and fun-loving, until he wasn't. He joked with his sons and matched their banter back and forth as they all took turns giving each other shit about various things. Both brothers were different around him, boyish almost, but no less fierce. Their deep level of respect and love was reflected in their body language and mannerisms. It made me wonder if they were like that around their mother as well.

I brought glasses and a pitcher of lemonade to the table. Stellan asked me to tell their father about my first impression of him. We'd had a conversation about this when I woke up, and he'd found it hilarious then and I could tell it was still giving him the giggles.

Caid and his father were looking at me, dying to hear what I had to say. I looked from Stellan to his dad, then to Caid.

"Well, sir, pardon my French, but you're scary as fuck."

They all burst out laughing.

I just shook my head. "I mean really, who tears out a guy's spine then just waves it around like it's the Superbowl Trophy!"

All three of them bowled over laughing. I didn't know why that was so funny. What he'd done was not fucking right, but hey, at least I wasn't on the opposite side of them, right?

After a fine hour of eating and laughing, the Alpha said, "I'd like to speak with Mackenzie alone for a moment. If that's okay with you?"

"Sure." I replied, but I was a little uneasy about it, his stern manner putting me on edge.

"Nope," Caid said.

"Dad, anything you say to her you can say in front of us." Stel stood and squared his shoulders.

Whoa! What just happened? I looked back and forth between them, searching for a clue. The brothers stared at their father, their gaze not relenting.

Joseph, as he insisted I call him, rolled his eyes and said, "They are protective of you, because of the marks. Even though they know I am not competition, the marks are new and they, like you, need time to nest. They should've told you this before completing the mark."

I didn't know what to say to that. It seemed all my unanswered questions were about to fall in my lap, and I may not like what I was about to find.

"Dad, we didn't mark her hastily. Yes, it's only been a few days, but you saw how we reacted when she was unconscious. She belongs with us." Stellan said.

"Son. I am not questioning your decision. What's done is done."

Both Caid and Stellan breathed out a sigh of relief.

"And I approve of this union. But..."

Of course, there was a "but". I held my breath. "...there is a lot of information you left out. You both know what I'm talking about." The Alpha crossed his arms over his chest.

Both brothers paced nervously. Ok, what were these fuckers hiding? To avoid their hyperaware senses, I kept my facial expression placid, my heart rate steady and prayed they were unable to smell my anxiety.

"That's a conversation between the three of us, Dad," Caid said softly.

Joseph, gave him a subtle nod. He was allowing his sons to have the conversation with me in private, a chat that should've taken place days ago.

Slowly, he turned to me and took my hand. "Mackenzie, you are delightful. I can see why both my sons are taken with you. For everything you have done for my pack, and for the love that you have shown my boys, you will always have full support from me and my pack. You will always be one of mine."

He said all this with such conviction, a wave of magic brushed against me. It was similar to what Stellan had done with me in the pool after I'd expended so much energy proving a point to Sandy. But this was different. There was a lot of power behind the Alpha's gesture combined with endearment, the kind of love I felt for and from my dad. A tear drop slid down my cheeks. Lord knows I tried to hold it in, but I couldn't. It wasn't sadness or fear that moved me, but joy. In that split second protection and support cocooned me. I knew right then this was what family felt like.

Wiping my tears, I gave him a small smile and said, "Thank you, Alpha."

CHAPTER 38

KENZIE

I said goodbye to the Alpha at the door. His fatherly actions toward me still resonated with me. The brothers cast hesitant stares in my direction. Caid finally stepped up to me first and kissed my cheek, promising to be right back.

Stellan shut the door behind Caid and his father and turned to me, "I love you, Kenzie. We'll be right back."

I nodded as he enveloped me in his arms assuring me, but of what, I wasn't sure. He released me and exited.

I was apprehensive about my situation with the brothers. There was a lot we needed to discuss. The marks they'd given me were significant and I was nervous about it but not angry. We needed to have a discussion soon. I accepted responsibility for my own ignorance. I wanted the mark, and didn't regret consenting to them. Fuck, I hoped my hasty decision didn't come back to blow up in my face.

While the guys were gone, I kept myself busy. I cleaned the kitchen, washed the sheets, cleaned the bathroom and made important business phone calls. I spoke at length with Tris and Dad.

Tris was rocking it at the office. I was so lucky to have him covering for me. I wasn't being fair to him. He never complained, he continued doing all the things that needed to be done. Tris had postponed my meetings till next week. I'd been slacking and that needed to end.

Dad was concerned about me. He was torn between giving me space to deal with the pack on my own and marching down here to get me away from them. I did my best to placate him by telling him I was fine, and the brothers were good to me. I added that I was still me. I didn't lie to him. I just left out the marking part. I needed more info on that before talking about it with anyone else. Dad told me that something had come up, and he had to leave tomorrow. He wanted to see me before he left. I had no idea what was going on with the guys, but I promised to meet him.

Two hours later, the house was cleaned, and I'd caught up with work, the guys still hadn't returned. I had nervous energy, and waiting around would drive me nuts. I scribbled a quick note to Caid and Stel and headed down to the hotel gym.

When I arrived, the gym was empty, which was nice. I needed to run a mile or two to clear my head. I stretched and did a quick weight circuit, then got on the treadmill. As I ran, thoughts whirled. The absence of the guys and the unknowns about being bonded to them were freaking me out. What had I done? What did this mean? What was I going to do now? Where were they? What did their father mean, when he'd mentioned there was a lot I should've been told? What did he really think of me? The questions kept bombarding my mind.

Forty-five minutes later I was running full out, sprinting as though zombies were chasing me. I was a sweaty, hot mess, but my nerves were under control, my thoughts a bit more focused. Little by little I slowed my pace until I'd come to a brisk walk.

Brody and Erik showed up. Both of them got on the treadmills on either side of me, and I slowed, walking at a leisurely pace.

"Hey!" I said to them. "Where've you two been?"

"We've been around. Didn't think you would notice," Erik smirked.

I think being a surly asshole was just part of his nature.

"Yeah, I've been in touch with the guys. They told me you were out and that you woke up yesterday. You look gorgeous, radiant." Brody swept his admiring gaze up and down my body.

"I hope you learned your lesson about putting off training. After that last stint you had with using your magic, you need it. When you're not busy running from the devil, of course," Erik said.

That last part made me laugh, so I ignored the dig about my magic. This guy had a sense of humor, who knew. Still, I wasn't ready to commit to training since there was much to do at my office, and I'd probably cancel on him, which meant he'd revert to being a dick again. So, I changed the subject.

"How long have you guys been here?" I asked them.

Gosh, if they'd been here the whole time watching me run for my life, I was going to die of embarrassment.

"Long enough to see you were working through some shit," Brody grinned.

Yep, they saw me running from the devil as Erik had so poignantly put it.

"That obvious, huh?"

"Let's just say you won that race. I'm surprised you didn't break the treadmill at that speed," Erik said.

That had me laughing so hard I had to stop.

"You giving up?" Brody asked me as I stepped off the treadmill, catching my breath and stretching my legs.

"I can help you stretch," he added with a wink.

Oh boy, I had too much going on in my head. I didn't need to add more to the mix by luring Brody and his big D into my bed. Caid and Stel were all encompassing in every way, but Brody was still on my mind. I missed him.

"Very funny." That was the best I reply I could come up with. Smooth, real smooth.

Brody got off the treadmill and said, "I'll walk with you to the elevators."

That wasn't an offer, it was a statement. He was walking with me no matter what I said. I kind of liked this domineering side of him.

I waved bye to Erik and left with Brody. He didn't say anything at first, but when we stopped at the elevators, neither of us pressed the button to call the elevator. Instead, he stepped up in front of me, his fingers on my chin. His dimples were on full display, and I couldn't resist touching them. He didn't stop me. His smile got wider and he finally said, "Kenzie baby, I'm glad you're ok. I was worried. We all were, Erik included."

"Sorry. And thank you for being concerned. Stel and Caid said you and Erik are still helping with this mage thing."

"No apologies needed. And yes, we're all working together." He hesitated pressing his lips together. "I know things are somewhat complicated for you with the guys heading home at some point. I'll be going back and forth between here and California. I hope we can spend more time together. For now, I can respect your space, but I will come calling soon."

His brown eyes were like a warm cup of hot chocolate, sweet and comforting. I lifted up on my tip-toes and placed a kiss on his lips, "Ok. I'll hold you to that."

He smiled, his eyes twinkling.

The elevator doors opened and I walked in. He remained in the corridor, still smiling.

When I got to my place, the guys were back, and they looked nervous.

"Hi!" I said.

"Love!" Caid wrapped me in his arms even though I was still sweaty. "You smell like Brody." He smiled.

"Hi, sweetness. Do you want me to run your bath?" Stellan pulled out of Caid's arms to embrace me.

"Um...yes and no. Yes, I ran into Brody at the gym, and we talked for a few minutes. And no, I'll just take a quick shower. Is everything ok? How's your dad?"

"How about we talk after your shower? We'll have a glass of wine waiting for you," Stellan said.

I stood on the first step of the stairway, bringing me almost to their eye level. I looked back and forth between the two brothers. They looked anxious. Stel scrubbed his hand over his face and Caid was wearing a frown that didn't belong on his handsome, smiley face.

"Actually," I climbed to the next step up, "I think it might be a whiskey night. Any chance of getting a bottle of the magically brewed stuff?"

"Of course! Outlaw Whiskey coming right up." Stellan pulled his phone from his back pocket to call someone.

"Anything for you, love," Caid said as I went up to my room.

CHAPTER 39

KENZIE

I closed my bedroom door and stripped out of my workout clothes. Something was not right. I could tell I was about to get bad news.

My phone beeped; it was a text from Dad.

> Dad: Mac, I have to leave town tonight. Sorry we didn't have time together. I'll be back soon.

> Me: Ok Dad. Hope to see you soon. Safe journey.

> Dad: Be safe. Text me when you're at home. I love you.

> Me: Love you too.

Typical Dad. He had always been on the road. I was disappointed more than usual though. Spending a few hours with the guys and their dad made me miss my own. We never had the type of relationship they have, which was unfortunate, but again, not new. I just wished one day my father would surprise me by sticking around.

With Dad leaving town and the guys about to deliver bad news, I did not want to face the world. To avoid the inevitable as long as I possibly could, I took my time to getting ready. I spent extra time in the shower and even more time, applying serums, creams, and curling my hair. I even put on makeup only to take it off because I had a feeling I'd be crying and didn't want raccoon eyes. To further delay things, I got it in my head that I should wear something appropriate for breaking up with someone. Two someone's in my case. I couldn't decide if I should wear something sexy as in "you're going to miss this" or cute as in "I'm emotionally vulnerable, please take it easy on me," or casual as in "I don't care."

After trying on a dozen outfits and making a mess of my closet, I chose PJ's. I put on satin shorts with a matching long-sleeved top. My unbound curled hair, was overkill now that I was dressed for bed, so I piled my locks on top of my head. It didn't help much. Shrugging, I made my way to the bedroom and paused, placing my forehead on the door. Fuck it, I may as well get this over with.

As soon as I opened the door, delicious food smells tickled my nose. Was that Thai food? It smelled like green curry and Pad Thai noodles. Suddenly ravenous, I raced down the stairs.

The guys were in the kitchen unpacking the Thai food, from my neighborhood restaurant. How did they find this place? I was about to ask when the doorbell rang.

"I'll get it!" I turned back out to answer the door.

"Hi Miss Kenzie!" Jason stood in the doorway holding a laptop. "May I come in?"

"Just Kenzie," I replied and motioned for him to come inside.

"Can't this wait?" Caid offered a glass of whiskey to me.

"Um...not really, Alpha said to tell you this in person. I'll be quick." Jason set his laptop on the table.

"It's fine, Jason. We're just about to eat," I told him.

Caid made a grumpy face, so I kissed him on the cheek. Stel was plating food and frowned at Jason. Geez, these two really knew how to make someone uncomfortable. He placed the plate of food down and motioned for me to sit. I kissed him on the cheek also, and then I realized, maybe they had pack business to discuss, and maybe I should leave, which would be fine with me.

"I'll just take my plate upstairs and give you guys some privacy to discuss whatever it is you need to talk about," I said before my ass hit the chair.

"NO!" Caid and Stellan said at the same time.

"Sit, sweetness, Jason will only be a minute." Stel said.

"I don't mind."

"Please stay, love," Caid motioned for me to sit and he sat next to me.

"Go on, Jason," Stel said abruptly. He looked over at me, then said. "Jason, would you like some food?"

Thank you, I mouthed, and he gave me small smile.

Jason plated up some Thai food and started speaking with his mouth full. This kid was growing on me. His youthful energy made me relax about the impending conversation I had to have with the brothers.

"So, Brody came back from California with more info about the lab Carlos was involved in. And well, it's a freakshow." Jason tapped away on his laptop. He pulled up a video then stopped it.

Brody hadn't mentioned a word to me of this to me, which was fine. The Republic was now his employer, not me.

"Maybe not that one," Jason muttered, tapping away on his keyboard again.

Caid, Stel, and I looked at each other, and then back at Jason.

"Is it gross?" I asked, because I was curious. I wasn't squeamish, but we were in the middle of eating delish Thai food, and anything gory was a hard pass.

"Um…no." Jason said with a squeak in his voice. Lie. "It's, how do I put this? It's unsettling" he looked at me.

"Maybe I should go," I said again.

"No, no, it's ok. I forwarded the legit sick shit to these two. And I will show you this one, which is a precursor to the other stuff you don't want to see while eating."

"Legit sick shit?" I frowned.

"Some people are fucked up, Kenzie." Jason said and stuffed some Thai food in his mouth.

"Preach." He wasn't wrong.

The precursor video was pretty sickening, which meant legit sick shit was seeing something you could never come back from. I was grateful for Jason's consideration at that moment.

The stars of the precursor were Carlos and the rogue mage and a human. They were running experiments, taking magical DNA, blood, stem cells, you name it, and injecting into the human subject along with some magical potions and dramatic spell casting. The human subject in the precursor video turned into a monstrous humanoid form for all of one minute and twenty-seven seconds, and then convulsed. Before he died, he was foaming at the mouth and bleeding out of his eyes, ears, and his nether regions which was obvious by the change of color in his trousers. The narrator of the video said it was a combination of a heart attack followed by a brain aneurysm. I didn't know those two things could happen at the same time.

I was speechless and sick to my stomach. Frowning, I pushed my plate away.

"Fuck," Caid peered over my shoulder to watch the video.

"Shit, we'll need to get out there," Stel said.

"Well, the team there is about to torch the place." Jason glanced up from his laptop.

"Fuck." Stellan said, and made a phone call.

The brothers took the laptop to look at Jason's info a bit more, and to begin the process of getting to the lab and seeing the facility themselves.

After a few moments, Jason and I continued eating, although the food didn't taste as good as it had before I'd seen the awful video. We didn't speak for a minute, then he looked up at me.

"Is everything ok?" he whispered.

I nodded and shrugged my shoulders "I think so."

"Seems really tense in here."

"Yeah, kind of. Guess there's a discussion we need to have."

"I hope it works, miss, I mean just Kenzie. I like you and they're nicer when you're around."

I giggled and whispered back, "I like you too, Jason."

"What are you two whispering about?" Stel had come up behind me.

"Nothing!" Jason and I said, both giggling.

I was sure they'd heard every word. It was just fun to have Jason to kid around with.

After eating, Jason stuck around for another hour. He took over cleaning the kitchen, allowing me to relax and drink my whiskey. He made me laugh with hysterics about his first date.

As he prepared to leave, I stood and gave him a hug. "Jason, I'm going to adopt you as my little brother."

"Really?! I don't have a sister."

"Well, you do now!"

He hugged me back and said, "Thanks, Sis."

CHAPTER 40

KENZIE

"All right, spit it out!" I said to the guys as soon as we were alone.

I was feeling tipsy and brazen, thanks to all the whiskey.

Although Jason's playful banter had lightened the mood, it was time to get down to business.

Caid spit out his whiskey and handed it to me, "You're welcome to this but I'm happy to just refill yours," he said, trying to be funny. Not so much.

"I know you two have something to say, so just rip off the Band-Aid and get it over with!" I glared at the brothers.

Silence.

"Well?" I tapped my foot on the floor, which was kind of ridiculous since I was wearing fuzzy slippers.

"Ok, please calm down, love. Sit, please," Caid said.

Clutching my whiskey with one hand, I glared at them. "This seems like a conversation that calls for standing."

"Sweetness, please," Stellan reached to grab my hand but I slapped his away. "Please don't be angry."

"You're freaking me out! What the actual fuck, guys?! What's going on? What did your dad mean by 'there are things we should've discussed'? What do these marks really mean?"

"Okay, breathe, this is a lot. We'll just start with the marks," Stellan said.

"Yes, that's simple. Like we said, it marks you as ours. If another shifter or vamp ever gets close to you, they will sense our mark. Our smell mixes with yours, making you off-limits. They won't be attracted to you." Caid blurted as though there was nothing to be concerned about.

I already knew this part, so I stood there my whiskey glass clutched in my hand.

"We'll be possessive of one another. There will be a constant need of wanting to be near one another. We will be able to find you and feel your emotions. The intense part of all of this, is that when we are not near, we will feel a deep sense of emptiness, almost like there's a void. And I mark a mate once. Shifters in general mark only once. We are bonded until death." Stel added, his expression solemn.

I pondered this, as I sipped my whiskey. This was stuff we'd talked about before. What am I missing? I reviewed what they'd just told me. Finding me, feeling my emotions, not being able to have sex with other shifters or vamps, were all okay with me. Then it hit me.

"Wait! What?!" I pinched the bridge of my nose. "What do you mean 'we' will feel empty? What is this void business? And you only mark once? That can't be a bad thing, but 'bonded until death'? What exactly does that mean? Are we married?!" I shrieked.

"Calm down, love," Caid rubbed my back.

"Don't try to pacify me, Caid." I jerked away from him.

Stellan put his hand on my shoulder. "Okay, okay, yes, I mark once. Wolves find one mate in their lives. It's a combining of souls, two becoming one. Like we talked about after that first night, it's something we feel and are sure of, and it can't be stopped. I felt it the moment I laid eyes on you. Even if you had refused my mark, I'd be following you around for the rest of my life. My wolf will not allow me to be away from you, well, not for very long anyway. And yes, you may feel the same. I guess in human terms, it's kind of like we're married."

"Fuck my life, what did we do? I 'may' feel the same way? What's going to happen when you go back to Texas?" I focused on Caid. "And you, you can mark more than once? Have you done it before?"

"Vamps bite. We sire children this way. We talked about that. You won't change. We didn't do that. And no, I haven't done it before, but if I wanted to, I could mark someone else. But, I won't though because I love you."

I pressed one hand on my aching temple. "What does 'kind of like we're married' mean?!"

"Marriage is not the right term. It's not legally binding, or anything like that. But like marriage, we are committed to you, and you to us," Stel explained as though the situation was simple and common.

"Committed? You just saw me have sex with Brody a couple nights ago. How does that factor into being committed to either of you?" I was exasperated.

"Brody is different. He's not an issue. I explained this to you. We, and Brody, accept this arrangement." Stel said.

"Wait?! You already discussed this marking thing with him and what it meant? Before talking to me?" I wanted to stab someone.

"Yes, it's fine, love. Calm down, please," Caid said in a somewhat soothing voice.

"No! No calming down. The three of you have been planning my life without me and you want me to calm down. Don't you think I should've been part of this conversation?! Considering it's my life as well." Uncomfortable heat spread through my body, and I squeezed my whiskey glass.

I was pissed and they both knew it. I didn't even know where to begin.

"Also, you may find it difficult to be away from us, and it will be difficult for us to be away from you," Stellan muttered.

"Cut the shit and stop sugar coating this. What does that mean?" I demanded.

"Like heartbreak. The worst heart break ever," Caid whispered.

I was in utter shock. If I understood them correctly, I'd be heart-breakingly sad without them, which was not going to work. I lived here, and they lived thousands of miles away. And I was married to them both? I couldn't have their children. They knew that about me. There are things that I probably should know about them.

So many other questions swirled in my mind, and I was overwhelmed. I didn't want to be without them, but I didn't know how we'd be together forever while living apart. Was I supposed to leave my life here behind?

No doubt, the sex was incredible. There was more between the three of us. I couldn't deny that, I felt deeply for them, and my actions made that clear. I had gotten in the middle of a shifter war for them. I gave them free roam in my home. To say I missed them when they were gone was an understatement. And aside from Brody, I had no intention of being with anyone else. I loved them more than I ever loved my ex. And this mark, this love, was infinitely more intense than anything I'd ever felt.

I gulped my whiskey, feeling it burn from my throat down to my belly. The guys remained silent, staring at me expectantly. I wanted to say something but I couldn't find the words. Suddenly, I was exhausted, and all I wanted at that moment was my bed.

"I'm really tired," I said softly and headed toward the stairs.

"Should we go?" Caid said behind me.

"No!" I blurted. "Please stay, I just, um, I just want to sleep. I don't want to talk, but I don't want you to go."

I was mad as hell at them, but I wanted them to stay, even though I knew they were leaving soon for Texas.

"Let's go to bed, sweetness," Stellan took my empty glass from my hand, set in on the table and led me upstairs.

Caid followed closely behind.

We got comfortable in bed. I was lying on Stellan's chest

listening to the reassuring sound of his heartbeat. Caid's chest was pressed against my back, his warm breath brushed across my shoulder.

"I want you both to know I'm overwhelmed and anxious about what this all means when you leave. I feel like we should've talked about this before. But . . . if I'm being totally honest, I don't regret it."

"We'll figure this out," Caid kissed my shoulders.

"Kenzie, there's more," Stellan turned his head away from me.

I shook my head. "No, no more. Not right now. I'm emotionally drained."

"I love you," they both said to me.

"I love you both too."

Sleep eluded me at first. My mind was all over the place. This "marriage" happened way too fast. A big part of me wanted this to be real. I wanted to be loved by these two men for the rest of my life. Did I dare dream and allow myself to fall for these two? Who was I kidding? I've already fallen. I didn't regret it, not one bit. I knew with every fiber of my being that I was in love with them both. Was I nervous about the future? Absolutely.

There was more. Stellan had admitted that much. Whatever it was, it would be worse.

If there was anything I was confident about, it was my resiliency to bounce back from adversity. And more so, Caid and Stellan loved me. I felt their emotions in me now, swirling through my blood like a love song. Gods damn it, I couldn't stay mad at my guys. They were strong, I was strong, and together we'd get through this.

I turned over only to hit my face against Caid's shoulder. He kissed me on my forehead, whispering "I love you."

Stellan snuggled against me, kissing my shoulder and draping an arm around my belly. I fell asleep with a contented smile. Maybe this would work out somehow. It had to, or I was fucked.

THE END

AUTHOR'S NOTE

Thank you for choosing Kenzie's story! I hope you enjoyed it. Please leave a review as I'd greatly appreciate your feedback. As a new author I am whole heartedly interested in what my readers have to say. Your feedback helps me hone my craft and publish books you'll enjoy reading. Connect with me on my website at: genaviecastle.com

ALSO BY GENAVIE CASTLE

The Kenzie Chronicles - Series Complete

Fae Magic, Book One

Fae Blood, Book Two

Fae Bonds, Book Three

Fae Chaos, Book Four

Banished, An Elemental Kingdom Novel

Pure Blood Duet - Series complete

Chained

Unchained

The Sentinels Series

Nightmare Girl, Book One

Brother's Sins, Book Two

Family Rules, Book Three

Midway Mystics Collection

The Seduction of Duality, A Dr. Jekyll & Mr. Hyde Retelling

Book Two - Available 2026